Celtic Curse

Wendy Dingwall

Praise for Hera's Revenge:
An Yvonne Suarez Travel Mystery

"The author's love of Greece and her insights into a tour group's dynamics make this light romantic suspense debut a welcome distraction for an armchair traveler. A series to watch."

—Library Journal

"For a debut novel I will say that it is excellent work. I loved the mix of Mythology, Greece, and Mystery. I think the best thing was how the mystery sort of crept up on you as though you were actually watching it all unfold."

—Rita Reviews, Holiday Travel Guide

"The premise for this mystery series is a refreshing addition to the mystery genre. ... Yvonne Suarez is an intriguing character ... The mystery is one readers will be challenged to solve, filled with twists and turns and plenty of red herrings.

—**Christy Tillery French**, reviewer for Midwest Book Reviews and author of *The Bodyguard* series.

"Embark on a good mystery and explore Greece via author Wendy Dingwall's tale where lives and lands crisscross."

—**Maggie Bishop**, author of, *One Shot Too Many*, her latest Appalachian mystery.

"... a well-written, impressive debut novel. Travel, adventure and romance—what more could a reader want?"

—**Betty Dravis**, Award winning journalist and author of *1106 Grand Boulevard* and other beloved novels.

Books in the Yvonne Suarez Travel Mysteries:
Hera's Revenge (2011)

Short Stories
It Was Only Right (High Country Headwaters, 2012)
Off Beat (High Country Headwaters, 2012)

Scott

Celtic Curse

An Yvonne Suarez Travel Mystery

Wendy Dingwall

*Enjoy Scotland
Wendy Dingwall*

 Canterbury House Publishing

www.canterburyhousepublishing.com
Vilas, North Carolina

Canterbury House Publishing, Ltd.
www.canterburyhousepublishing.com

Copyright © 2013 Wendy Dingwall
All rights reserved under International and Pan-American
Copyright Conventions.

Book Design by Tracy Arendt

AUTHOR'S NOTE:
This is a work of fiction. Names characters, places and incidents are either the product of the author's imagination or are used fictitiously, and any resemblance to actual persons living or dead, business establishments, events, or locales is entirely coincidental.

Library of Congress Cataloging-in-Publication Data

Dingwall, Wendy.
  Celtic curse / by Wendy Dingwalll. -- First edition.
  pages cm. -- (An Yvonne Suarez Travel Mystery)
  ISBN 978-0-9829054-9-4 (alk. paper)
  1. Travel agents--Fiction. 2. Disappeared persons--Fiction. 3.
Scotland--Fiction. I. Title.

  PS3604.I475C45 2013
  813'.6--dc23

     2013004641

First Edition: May 2013

For information about permission to reproduce selections from this book write to:
  Permissions
  Canterbury House Publishing, Ltd.
  225 Ira Harmon Rd.
  Vilas, NC 28692

DEDICATION

I dedicate this novel to my husband Walter who is of Scottish descent. He has shown me the beauty of Scotland, introduced me to the loving and loyal natures of the Scots and has encouraged me to write.

CAST OF CHARACTERS:

Yvonne Suarez	Travel Agent, mom and sleuth, searching the best destinations for her clients or the clues to solve their mysteries.
David Ludlow	Software designer, friend and lover, he stands by Yvonne, ready to fight for her safety and self-esteem.
Fiona Batson	Housekeeper, referred by Janice Armstrong, dreams of finding her missing brother with Yvonne's help.
Duncan Ross	Fiona Batson's older brother, last seen at the Peebles Woolen Mill in Peebles, Scotland in 1965 at the age of 18.
Cameron Douglas	Fiona Batson's cousin, strongly motivated to host and help Fiona search for clues to the whereabouts of his missing cousin, Duncan.
Kendra Douglas	Devoted wife to Cameron, mother, retired English teacher, youth advocate volunteer, rose gardener, and helpful hostess.
Keith Turner	Woolen mill foreman, Darleen Turner's husband, boyhood friend of missing Duncan Ross.
Darleen Turner	Married to Keith Turner, daughter of retired woolen mill owner, once in love with Duncan Ross.
Craig MacIntyre	Retired woolen mill owner, father of Darleen and husband of Margaret. Spends his retirement reading and collecting Scottish legends and lore.
Margaret MacIntyre	Wife of Craig, mother of Darleen. Preparing woolen mill for tourists during the Beltane Festival.
Inspector Gordon	Police Inspector, Peebles Police Station.
Ullrick Ferguson	Laborer at Peebles Woolen Mill, son of retired foreman, Randy.
Randy Ferguson	Retired foreman from Peebles Woolen Mill.

MINOR CHARACTERS:

Rhona Munro	Police Constable, daughter of Cameron's friend retired Assistant Chief Constable, Innes Munro.
Innes Munro	Retired Assistant Chief Constable, Rhona Munro's father and Cameron Douglas' friend.
William Fraser	Tour Guide, Edinburgh.
Mrs. Brodie	Tour Guide, Edinburgh Castle.
Alistair Connery	Peebles news agent.
Linda McLaren	Peebles travel agent.
Nigel Sutherland	Wealthy owner of the Sutherland Guest House in Old Town section of Peebles, Glenna's husband.
Glenna Sutherland	Wife of Nigel.

RECURRING CHARACTERS:

Christy Gianetti	Yvonne's seven-year-old daughter.
Eduardo Suarez	Yvonne's Cuban-American father.
Nancy Suarez	Yvonne's English-American mother.
Gino Gianetti	Yvonne's cold and calculating ex-husband.

Cailleach

(There were two slender spears of battle

Upon the other side of Carlin,

Her face was blue black, of the luster of coal,

And her bone tufted tooth was like rusted bone.

In her head was one deep pool-like eye

Swifter than a star in winter.

Upon her head gnarled brushwood

Like the clawed old wood of the aspen root.)

"Scottish lore has Cailleach (pronounced kālʲəx) to be the daughter of Grainne, or the Winter Sun. She is affectionately known as 'Grandmother of the Clanns' and 'the Ancestress of the Caledonii Tribe', sometimes referred to as Scotia. The Neolithic goddess Cailleach, also known as 'the blue hag', the 'Bear goddess', 'Boar goddess', and other similar names, invoked worshipers from the British Isles early after the recession of the glaciers. Celtic peoples honored her and blended her varying aspects, creating images invoking both love and terror."

—From Campbell: The Yellow Muilearteach,
in Popular Tales of the West Highlands Vol. 3.

Chapter 1
MACINTYRE WOOLEN MILL
PEEBLES, SCOTLAND
MAY 2004

"Cameron says that Fiona Ross ... Her name's Fiona Batson now, is comin home to Peebles. He says she wants to find out what happened to Duncan. Can ye believe it—after all these years? I've a bad feelin aboot this, Keith." Darleen Turner crossed her arms over her chest and held herself, looking him directly in the eye. "Why can't folk let sleepin dogs lie?"

"What's it to ye? He's been gone for decades now. Ye can't still be missin 'im. Maybe ye wish it'd been me that disappeared." Keith grabbed a rake and pushed it into the steaming vat to agitate the wool that needed washing.

Darleen noticed the extra force he used. She focused on his thin and sinewy muscles, remembering how they'd bulged large and fit when she'd first married him. It was, after all, his strong caring arms that brought her back from her depression.

"If his own mother and cousin, Cameron, couldn't find him, what makes ye think she'll have any luck?" Keith gave the wool another jab. "Please, don't say it's yer second-sight tellin ye this." He lifted the rake out of the large wash tub and threw it against the wall.

Darleen felt her jaw tighten. "Fine then, I can't believe ye'd be spoutin that same old tune after nearly forty years of faithful marriage." She retreated to her office. Orders needed processing but she couldn't concentrate. Her mind wandered to earlier, innocent times. "It's no use thinkin aboot it now." She spoke out loud convincing herself to focus on work.

Chapter 2
FORT LAUDERDALE, FLORIDA
MARCH 2004

*T*he stout Mrs. Batson sat ram-rod straight, as if willing herself to be tall. Her eyes sparkled with excitement while Yvonne explained the situation. "So, Debra, uh ... Ms. Pinkerton, the owner of the agency, says I may plan a familiarization-trip to Scotland. We call them fam-trips. This will allow me to book hotels and bed and breakfasts at special travel agent rates—some nights may even be given to us for free."

"Please, call me Fiona." Mrs. Batson clasped her hands, tightly weaving her fingers together and set them on the edge of Yvonne's desk. "I can't believe you're doing this for me? Janice said you were a lifesaver, but I never believed you'd help in such a way." Fiona unclasped her hands and reached into the baggy brown purse on her lap, coming out with crumpled tissue. She dabbed at the tears welling up in her eyes.

Yvonne flashed on Janice Armstrong and their trip to Greece and the Greek Isles the previous year. After all the trouble Janice endured on the trip, helping her housekeeper get to Scotland so she could search for her long lost brother would give Yvonne the opportunity to make amends. Not that Janice would have looked at it that way. As far as Janice was concerned, Yvonne was her hero. When Janice first asked Yvonne to help Fiona, Yvonne had resisted the idea. Then, she thought about all the wonderful stories she'd heard about 'Bonnie Scotland' and decided it would be a terrific opportunity to learn first-hand about the place that she'd booked

12

so often for others. Next time she'd be able to give first-hand recommendations.

Yvonne had a secret she dared not admit, not even to herself. This would be a chance to help solve another mystery. She enjoyed sleuthing. It wasn't much different from researching destinations and fitting the right place to the right person. Only she'd be fitting the guilty person to the crime he or she'd committed.

Fiona shifted in her chair, bringing Yvonne back to the moment. "You'll need to pay the cost of your air fare and meals, but we'll take care of transportation and tours within Scotland." Yvonne flipped up to a fresh page on her letter-sized tablet and picked up her pen. "I'll need to get specific details about your search for your brother in order to plan our trip around the investigation of his whereabouts."

Yvonne watched Fiona look around the agency and sensed she was nervous, or maybe she felt exposed in the open atmosphere. Large picture windows facing Ocean Boulevard drew the sunlight in. Normally this would cheer folks planning fun vacations, but sometimes trips were scheduled for funerals or other unpleasant reasons. Yvonne wondered if the cheerful atmosphere would be inappropriate for what Fiona needed to disclose. "There's a nice little café around the corner in this plaza—a few minutes-walk—away from noise and other distractions. Let's have lunch while we're at it."

"Oh my, you've been too kind already, I couldn't impose on your lunch time."

"Nonsense, it's a good excuse to have a break. Normally, I'd work right through lunch. I'll just forward my phone to another agent, and we can go." Yvonne dialed in the code needed to forward the phone to a back-line agent and straightened her desk. She grabbed her notepad, pencil and purse, then ushered Fiona out the door.

Located on the Galt Ocean Mile on A1A in Fort Lauderdale, the one-story Galt Shopping Plaza runs east and west with four quaint walk-only blocks, each separated by courtyards, with shops offering everything from clothing boutiques and jewelry stores to upscale gift stores and art galleries. At the head of one of these blocks, The Pinkerton Travel Agency faces A1A directly. The other side of A1A is populated with high rise condominiums inhabited by well-to-do professionals and wealthy retirees. Le Café faces the courtyard center where an olive tree gives shade to the sidewalk by the entrance. Inside, the large windows are set off with white lace curtains. Tables for two line the front so patrons can watch passersby while they eat. The creamy white walls are adorned with Parisian-style impressionist paintings, and the solid oak tables, covered with white tablecloths, hold a small vase of pink or purple carnations stuffed into fragrant parsley and assorted herbs.

Yvonne led Fiona toward a quiet back corner opposite the entrance to the kitchen. The faint smell of garlic and dried herbs lingered over their table like a comfortable memory.

"Mm—it smells delicious in here," said Fiona.

They waited about five minutes before a busy waitress noticed them. Apparently miffed that they sat away from her regular station, she threw two menus on the table with a noticeable thump. She kept a dour look when she took their drink orders; water for Yvonne and cola for Fiona. Yvonne took this behavior in stride, familiar with the haughty attitude of some wait persons in upscale Fort Lauderdale. Fiona didn't appear to notice the attitude at all. When the waitress returned they each ordered the lunch special of *Tuna Salad Nicoise*.

Clearing a spot to write, Yvonne lifted her pad and pen onto the table. "Tell me about your brother." Yvonne left her pen sitting on the table, thinking it best that she concentrate on what Fiona had to say.

Fiona smiled as she conjured up memories of her brother. "He was a handsome lad, strong, too ... and a comic. His pranks got him into trouble with the old folks, but the young folk all loved him." Fiona waited while the waitress put drinks on the table. "Once, a couple of years before he went missing—he would have been sixteen and I was fourteen—well, it was perfectly fine for him to tease his little sister, but when my cousin, Cameron, picked on me, Duncan decked

him. Don't you know? Cameron was always kind to me after that."
She chuckled. "You'll meet Cameron when we get to Peebles."

Yvonne smiled at Fiona. "I can see why you'd miss him so much.
When exactly did he go missing?"

"Oh my, he's been missing for ages. Lately ... I ... I've been dream-
ing about him." Fiona watched Yvonne make a note on her pad. "A
voice in my head keeps telling me that I need to return to Edinburgh
to find out what happened to him. Not knowing what happened to
Duncan is what killed my mum. She died of a broken heart. Eventually after losing his son and wife, and after I'd grown up and moved
away, Dad's delayed grief sent him to an early grave. So can't you see?
It's up to me to figure out what happened and bring peace to my family." Fiona waited silently while the waitress served their salads. She
took a tiny bite of tuna and sighed with satisfaction.

"If you'll pardon my saying so, it seems rather odd that your father
would leave your mom and brother behind and move so far away."

Fiona set her fork down and took a minute to think. "The morning we were to move to America, Duncan borrowed his best friend's
bike, his own having been sold a few days before. He pedaled over
to Peebles Woolen Mill where he'd been working after school. He
was to pick up his last week's wages and return home immediately.
Duncan had been working at the Mill for over a year doing odd jobs
so he could save money to help with finances once we got to Chicago.
Dad had warned us it could take awhile to get work, and we needed
to survive until he secured a good job. He didn't want to be a burden
to his brother who was sponsoring our stay in America." Fiona took
a breath. "Duncan never returned, and Mother refused to leave without him, fearing he'd been hurt.

"Dad thought Duncan had changed his mind and run off with
Darleen, the daughter of the owner of the Woolen Mill. He thought
she'd convinced Duncan to stay behind and marry her. Dad refused
to cancel the plans to move that he'd worked so hard to arrange.

"I begged my father to return to Scotland after it became apparent
that Duncan had truly disappeared. You see, no one ever heard from

my brother again, and it was obvious that Darleen hadn't run away with him. But, by then we couldn't afford to return, though Dad had found work as an electrician. He hoped that Duncan would eventually turn up, and in the meantime, he saved money for airplane tickets so Mum and Duncan could someday join us in Chicago."

"How did your Dad take it when your Mum died?"

"Not well. He blamed himself for not going back to Scotland to find my brother, and at the very least, for not bringing Mum to live with us in America—even though she'd refused to leave without Duncan."

Fiona took a sip of her coke. "Dad took his angry feelings out on me. From then on, I couldn't make a move without his approval. He'd lost his son and his wife, and 'by God' he would make sure he didn't lose me." She smiled sadly. "He never allowed me to date or attend after-school activities with friends. He insisted I always come home right after school. For me, it was just school work, house cleaning and taking care of Dad. I didn't gain any freedom until I graduated from high school." Fiona took another sip of her cola and sighed. "I worked up the nerve and told him it was time I got a job. He said, no, that I could continue to keep house and take care of him, that he would continue to support me. We argued for weeks. Finally, he gave in when I said I'd leave him for good.

"I went to work in the Sears Tower as a secretary to a merchandising executive. Then, just after I turned 20, I met Michael Batson and fell head over heels in love, but that story's for another day." Fiona smiled at the thought.

"Did your Mom try to find out what happened to your brother?"

"Of course she did, but she found nothing. At first she wanted to join us but was heart-sick when Duncan never turned up. To this day, I think she died of a broken heart."

"How do you expect us to find Duncan if your mom couldn't, and why look for him now?" Yvonne looked directly into Fiona's determined blue eyes.

"I just know that I have to try. I've carried the guilt around for so long. I should have convinced my father to return to Peebles to find out what happened to my brother, but the truth is, I was excited about being in America. It was all glamorous to me back then. Lately, though, I dream about Duncan. In the dreams he's lost, and he's calling out to me to find him. I'm feeling guilty all the time, wishing I'd done more. Besides, I have relatives there, an uncle on my mother's side and some cousins. I'm hoping they can help." Fiona's eyes narrowed. "You aren't changing your mind, are you?" She dabbed her mouth and wiped her hands with her pink cloth napkin, then placed it on the table next to her empty plate, all the while staring me in the eye.

"No, but what if we don't find him? What if I'm no help at all?" With my fork, I pushed around the remaining limp lettuce on my plate.

"Are you afraid? Janice said you were so brave and just the person to help me with this."

"I'm *afraid* Janice may be exaggerating my abilities. I'm a travel agent after all, not a detective." I signaled to the waitress to bring our bill.

"Well if Janice thinks you're capable, that's good enough for me." Fiona picked up her purse from the floor with a flourish and placed it in her lap.

Later, on her drive home from the agency, Yvonne's mind drifted to the day's lunch meeting. ... Am I up to the task of helping Fiona? There are so many unknowns. It all happened so long ago. I've never planned a fam-trip before. It's a great opportunity, and the experience will be good for me. It'll be tricky though, trying to familiarize myself with Scotland while helping investigate Duncan's disappearance.

Yvonne turned on her left blinker and moved into the center lane on Federal Highway to avoid the stop-and-go of cars that were making turns. She caught a red-light at 26th street, meaning she'd catch them all until she turned into Christy's after-school care center beyond the tunnel on the south side of Broward Boulevard. This would allow her more time to think. In the next instant, a twinge of guilt plagued her, knowing Christy anxiously waited to be picked up.

Yvonne took a deep breath like she'd practiced in yoga classes. The minute she felt anxious for any reason, she'd breathe and refocus her thoughts. This doesn't mean she wouldn't face reality, but she'd face it calmly.

Her thoughts returned to Fiona and their upcoming trip. She questioned herself. What if Duncan's disappearance was the result of foul play? Could it be dangerous? Can I risk it? I was lucky last year that I came home in one piece. Getting involved with the Armstrongs' marital problems, the murder investigation, and the art thefts in Greece—what a disaster. *Dé gracias a Dios!* If it hadn't been for David I don't know what I'd have done. He was one of the few good things that came from that trip. She smiled, flashing on David's lingering kiss at the end of their recent date. "Focus now. Don't go there." The sound of her own voice brought her back to the present.

Yvonne wondered, what about Janice? She's a friend, and I want to help *her* friend, but I'll have to leave Christy for an extended period, again. She's getting older now. She'll miss me less ... I think. I can plan the trip for June, during her court-appointed month with her Dad. That will eliminate the need to pay a baby-sitter. Damn. I wanted to be here for her during her stay with Gino. She's never stayed with him longer than a weekend before. On the other hand, if I hover, I'll make matters worse. Christy doesn't understand why we split. She'll be confused. I know Gino, he'll spoil her one minute and abandon her emotionally the next if she doesn't fall in line with his control issues. Mom and Dad are coming for dinner tonight. Maybe they'll know what to do.

Yvonne envisioned how the evening would go: Dad, being a man and of Cuban descent, will have his hot-blooded reaction to the problem. Act first. Think later. Mom, on the other hand—the typical English cool cucumber—will remain calm. In the end they'll balance each other. Although they rarely see eye to eye on how to solve a problem, they've learned to meet in the middle. And so, in the end I'll have the right solution to my dilemma about leaving Christy with Gino while I'm in Scotland.

Satisfied for the moment that she had rationalized the situation, Yvonne reflected on her own shortcomings. ... It's too bad I inherited Dad's impetuous nature. But with yoga and meditation, I'm getting better at it staying calm in chaotic situations.

Yvonne jumped at the sound of the horn beep coming from a black Camaro close on her bumper. The light changed. She stepped on the gas while glancing in the side-view mirror and switched lanes, escaping the tail-gating teenager and his rocking car. She drove along Federal Highway and merged with Sunrise Boulevard until it split again turning in a southerly direction. A few minutes later, after passing the heart of downtown with its ever changing skyline, a few blocks south of Broward Boulevard, she arrived on time to pick up Christy from the Mother-Goose After School Care Center.

Yvonne took thawed ground chuck from the microwave and began mincing onion. "Okay, Christy, it's time for your magic touch." She directed Christy to wash her hands, then allowed her to pour in the garlic salt and seasonings. Together they smooshed the ground beef concoction with their fingers to form patties. "Christy, go wash your hands again, then brush your hair. Nana and Poppy will be here soon."

"Okay, Mommy." Christy ran to the bathroom holding her greasy hands in the air like a surgeon until she reached the bathroom sink.

Yvonne poured half a package of frozen French fries into the deep fryer. Next she doctored the canned baked beans with some dark molasses and a little mustard. She gave her colorful, lettuce and tomato salad, a quick toss just as the doorbell rang. "Come on in. I'm in the kitchen."

Christy raced from her room, hair brush in hand. "Nana, will you brush my hair? Poppy, we're having burgers, and I helped make them!"

"*Mi chica dulce.* Give, Nana and Poppy a hug first. Then we talk about burgers and hair brushing." Eduardo Suarez scooped up his granddaughter, hairbrush and all, and gave her a kiss on the cheek followed by a hug. When Christy squealed from his tight squeeze, he handed her to his wife.

Nancy Suarez carried Christy to her room where she brushed her hair and clipped in her barrettes. It brought back memories of Yvonne at that age, but the pleasure of brushing Christy's hair, and watching as the barrettes held her long golden tresses away from her delicate face, gave her more pleasure than she'd ever expected.

After dinner, Eduardo and Nancy waited on the back patio, sipping burgundy, while Yvonne readied Christy for bed. "I wonder what she wants to talk about. She says it's important." Nancy frowned, her worry apparent to Eduardo.

"It's that *Bastardo*, ex-husband. He's always a problem. I can't believe we thought he'd make a good husband to our daughter. I should have known. I could have stopped it."

"Darling, don't go jumping to conclusions. It may have nothing to do with Gino. You must stop blaming yourself for something you couldn't have known. No one knew. Yvonne kept it a secret. If anyone should have known, it should have been me. I'm her mother." Nancy took a sip of wine. They'd had this same conversation a hundred times since learning about the abuse Gino Gianetti had inflicted upon their daughter, and it never helped to salve their consciences.

Yvonne joined her parents with her own glass of wine and explained her dilemma about leaving Christy with Gino for the court-ordered month during the summer. If it had not been for Gino's slick lawyer, she would never have allowed him to keep Christy for this long. But, since she had no choice, she'd take whatever precautions necessary.

Eduardo was uncharacteristically silent as his daughter explained the reason behind her trip to Scotland. Yvonne was sure that he would try and talk her out of this sleuthing junket, so she was surprised when he waited until she was finished before he said, "This Fiona, you say she has had dreams about her brother?"

"Now, Papa—" This was exactly what Yvonne had been afraid of.

"No, no querida mia, you misunderstand me." He reached over and took her hand, smiling gently. "Some things are stronger than we can know. I just want you to be careful."

Nancy nodded, "Your father and I both come from superstitious islands, sweetheart. You must do what you can to help this woman. There is a reason she came to you. Don't worry about Christy."

Astounded, Yvonne stared at her parents. She had been right to talk to them first.

The grownups decided they would arm Christy with Nana and Poppy's phone number. The grandparents would check on her periodically, and Eduardo assured his daughter that Gino would give them no problem with their continued presence in Christy's life during the month in question. Yvonne's Dad had made sure that Gino kept clear of her since the divorce and that he followed the rules of the court regarding his time spent with Christy. Yvonne often wondered at her dad's ability to keep Gino at bay. When they first divorced, Gino had stalked Yvonne, making her a nervous wreck. Then the stalking stopped abruptly. She wondered why but was afraid to ask. Over time her fear of Gino lessened. Was that a good thing? Did her Father have something on Gino? Goosebumps ran up both arms as she thought about it.

Chapter 3
FORT LAUDERDALE, FLORIDA
SATURDAY, MAY 29TH

"Christy, thank David for taking us to dinner and the *Scooby-Doo2* movie." Yvonne smiled at David.

"Thank you, David. Mommy, can David come in, and we can play a game? It's Saturday, and you know I get to stay up late on Saturday nights." Christy tugged on David's hand pulling him inside.

David gave Yvonne a questioning look. "It's up to your mother."

"Okay, but a time limit of one hour on whatever game we play, it's already past your bedtime." Yvonne looked at David and shrugged. Then looked at Christy and said, "Run up and get ready for bed first—brush your teeth too."

Christy raced upstairs to her bedroom, pulled out her Princess Jasmine nightgown, hurriedly discarded her clothes, and put the gown on, glad that she had taken her bath before going out. Next she went into the bathroom to brush her teeth, counting the brush strokes five times on each tooth like mom had shown her. She brushed just as fast as her small hand would move.

Yvonne heated coffee, and made a glass of chocolate milk for Christy. "David, I'm going to miss you. I wish you were going with me. I'm worried that I may have taken on more than I can handle with this whole trip."

"What do you mean? I thought you were going to familiarize yourself with the Scottish tourist destinations. It sounds like fun to me. Wish I could go." David seated himself at the kitchen table and set up Christy's favorite game, *Sorry!* "Is there anything I can help with while you're gone?"

Yvonne opened a bag of corn chips. "No thanks. Mom is going to come over and water the plants, and she and Dad are going to check up on Christy for me while she's with Gino."

As always, David rankled at the sound of Yvonne's ex-husband's name. He often fantasized finding himself with an opportunity to knock him into oblivion. "Tell me what you haven't told me about your trip."

Yvonne heard Christy's bare feet slapping lightly as she descended the wood stairs. "I'll explain later after I put Christy to bed."

Christy started yawning halfway through the game. She gave no argument when told it was bedtime. Yvonne carried her up to her room, tucked her in, and as she drifted off to sleep, kissed her goodnight and whispered, "*Te quiero a mi novia.*" Yvonne had loved it when, as a child, her father spoke to her in Spanish. The words meant, "I love you my sweetheart." Yvonne wanted Christy to hear the soft melody of those loving words she imagined had been passed down from her Grandfather's ancestors. She hoped that Christy would feel protected and special, the way she had felt growing up.

When Yvonne returned to the kitchen, she found David packing up the rest of the game pieces. "Let's have a glass of wine. Any more coffee and I won't sleep for a week. We can take it out to the back patio. Who knows, we may catch a cool breeze." She tucked the game board away in a cabinet devoted to Christy's stuff and grabbed two wine glasses from the small bar that divided her kitchen and dining area from the living room. She poured the Merlot and handed a glass to David.

They sat side by side, holding hands, in a worn metal swing that came with her purchase of the townhouse. The back and forth squeak of the swing blended with the sound of crickets and undistinguishable voices carried on the wind from across the nearby Intracoastal Waterway. A faint smell of ocean breezes, mixed with the scent of gardenias from her next-door neighbor's backyard, calmed her.

Yvonne hated to interrupt the peaceful mood. "Remember, I told you that Janice Armstrong referred a travel client to me?"

"Yes, you're to help her connect with relatives in Scotland if I recall." David released her hand and put his arm around her shoulder, pulling her close.

She leaned into him. "There's more to it than that. Fiona wants me to help her find her brother who went missing forty years ago. And, now I'm wondering if I haven't made a mistake by agreeing to it." She snuggled up and laid her head on his shoulder.

"Why does she want to look for him now after so many years?"

"She says she's been having dreams about him, and something is nagging at her to do this. I know, she sounds a bit dotty, I believe she's been troubled by this her whole life, and I wanted to help her get closure." Yvonne sat up, reached for her glass of wine, took a sip, hoping for false courage. "Now I'm worried there may have been foul play with his disappearance, and maybe I shouldn't have gotten involved. It will be just the two of us traveling, and I won't have you there to help me if there's trouble."

Yvonne set her glass back on the patio side-table. "I'm probably just worrying for nothing. I mean, after all, they must have had the authorities and relatives looking back then. If they didn't figure out what happened to him, I'm pretty sure there's no way that I will find him. Then of course, I'll be letting Fiona down. You see, I've set myself up so I can't win."

David sat upright, and stopped the swing. "You haven't made her any promises, have you?"

"No, but ... "

"Then you can't expect her to hold you responsible for the outcome. I'm sure she'll be grateful that you're there for moral support. Your main objective should be doing your job and familiarizing yourself with your tourist attractions. I want you to promise me that if anything gets weird or the least bit scary, you'll leave it alone, and you'll call and discuss it with me. I may not be with you, but I'd like to help, and I definitely don't want you putting yourself in any danger."

"It all sounds so silly now that I've told it to you. I'm sure there will be no danger at all. Besides, when I told my parents they seemed to think that the whole thing is somehow predestined. "

"I'm going to miss you, Yvonne, but you are strong and smart. You'll do a fine job and be home before we know it." David stood up, turned and offered her his hand. When she took hold he pulled her into his arms. He kissed her first on the lips then brushed his lips along her cheek until they reached her ear. "Are we going to have any alone time before you leave?"

His breath on her ear gave her goose bumps. "How about to-morrow—noon—I'll get a babysitter." She pushed him away and smiled seductively. "You'd better leave now or ..."

"Uh huh." David gave her a peck on the cheek and left.

Chapter 4
FORT LAUDERDALE
MONDAY, JUNE 1ST

"**M**ommy, don't worry. Daddy will be nice to me while you're gone." Christy, still under four feet nine inches in height, spoke from her booster seat in the back of the dark blue Toyota Camry.

Yvonne's eyes welled with tears as she glanced at Christy in the rear view mirror. "I know Sweetie. Mommy's not worried." I'm lying, she thought. I always swore I'd never lie to my daughter, but I can't allow her to be upset, not now when she needs to be happy and feeling safe about staying with her father. It wouldn't be fair of me to burden her with my own doubts and insecurities.

On their way to drop off Christy at her Dad's two-bedroom apartment near trendy Las Olas Boulevard, Yvonne chastised herself for the close call of upsetting her daughter. What are the chances Gino will lose his temper and take it out on her while I'm gone? He's never done so before, but. ... good grief ... the judge and psychologists all said he'd worked hard during his anger management therapy and deserved a chance to prove himself. I'm sure she'll be fine. Especially if I'm not around, he'll be happy to have her all to himself, and he does have that happy, charming side to his personality when things are going his way.

Yvonne drove through the entrance to the Spanish style apartment complex landscaped with varieties of lush palms and olive trees. She wound her way to Gino's building. He was waiting for them by his designated guest parking spot.

As soon as Yvonne parked, Gino nodded to her and opened Christy's door. Christy unhooked her seat belt and climbed out chattering. "Daddy did you get to take the whole month off, like you said?"

"Hi, Squirt. Sure, I got the time, just like I told you. How about a hug?" Gino squatted down and accepted her enthusiastic hug. "I've missed you sooo much," he said.

Yvonne opened the trunk and pulled out Christy's pink *Barbie* suitcase, a red canvas backpack stuffed with books, her favorite DVD's, pencils and crayons. Then she grabbed Christy's pillow and favorite worn pink blanket. Christy had carried the blanket around since she was old enough to walk. It had seen better days, and Yvonne had tried giving her new larger blankets to fit her growing body, but Christy always grabbed this one when she wanted something to snuggle. A security blanket, to be sure.

Christy let go of Gino and took her suitcase from Yvonne. "Daddy, will you carry my back pack and stuff?"

Gino reached to take the items from Yvonne. He smiled, looking her directly in the eyes, with the seductive look that had always caused her stomach to flip-flop.

Yvonne looked away and focused on Christy. "Be a good girl for Daddy. I'm going to miss you, *mi Chica Dulce.*" She fought back tears. It would do no good to upset Christy. She must be strong. Let Christy feel confident all was well. Yvonne kissed her on the cheek, gave her a firm hug, and released her.

"I see you still confuse her, switching from English to Spanish." His cold stare was back.

Gino's barb reminded her of old times. "All the parenting books say raising a child to be bilingual is a good thing. Telling her she's my sweet girl in Spanish is a term of endearment. I see no harm in it." Once again he had her on the defensive.

"Christy, the front door is open. Go ahead and put your suitcase in your bedroom," said Gino.

"Christy has my mobile number and my parents' number in case she wants to leave early. They're in her backpack."

"That won't happen. I'm entitled to a month with her, and that's what I'll have."

"Well, if you need a baby-sitter or a break, they're available." Yvonne forced herself to smile, wanting to leave on a positive note for Christy's sake.

"Don't worry, Yvonne, we're going to have a great time. And, if I need a babysitter, I've got family, too."

"Of course." Yvonne pictured the stern face of Gino's elderly mother. "I'll be off then."

"I'm surprised you would choose to be so far away from her. What if there was an accident and she needed her mother? It would take you a whole day to get here." Gino's eyebrows were scrunched in the critical way she'd always hated. Then he gave her a smug smile.

She recognized the smile as the one he indulged in when having the last word on any given subject. Usually the subject involved finding fault with her. "I'm counting on *you* to see that she is safe and happy." She kept a smile on her face, hiding the twinge of guilt she felt at his remark.

Chapter 5
EDINBURGH, SCOTLAND
TUESDAY, JUNE 2ND

"**I couldn't help but notice** that your ring finger is naked. How come a pretty girl like you is still single?" Fiona replaced the flight magazine she'd been reading to the pouch in front of her. She attempted to find an accommodating position in the cramped quarters. The eight-hour non-stop flight to Edinburgh would challenge their comfort zone, but she was energized from the excitement of travel.

"I'm divorced—little more than two years." Yvonne set her Insight Travel Guide on the pull-down tray in front of her and focused on Fiona as details of the trip and her guide duties ran through her mind.

"Sorry, I didn't mean to pry. Do you have children?"

Yvonne stifled a smile, "Yes, a daughter, Christy. She's seven years old."

"How nice—quite a responsibility—raising a child by yourself. Then again, you are here, so perhaps you are not raising her alone?"

"I have custody of Christy, but she has visitation rights with her Dad. He has her for one month in the summer, giving me the opportunity to make this trip."

"It's good for your daughter that you have good relations with her father." Fiona opened a small bottle of wine remaining from her dinner tray and poured it into a clear plastic cup, then took a sip.

Yvonne kept silent on the subject of her relationship with Gino.

"Janice told me all about your adventure in Greece last summer. She says you saved her life. Imagine, she thought her own husband was trying to kill her, and him, mixed up with those criminals. Who would have believed it? Janice is such a refined lady—so delicate. She was lucky you were there and brave enough to help her."

"Well, I don't know if I would go quite that far."

"Nonsense, don't be so modest."

Yvonne laughed out loud. "Fiona, I think we are going to become fast friends."

The plane landed on time at seven-forty-five the following morning. They arrived jet-lagged but enthused to be on the ground.

From the airport, it took about twenty minutes by cab to arrive at the Bonham hotel, three blocks from Princes Street and a half mile to Edinburgh Castle. Yvonne marveled at the extensive use of stone masonry in the ancient buildings and the cleanliness of the city, much smaller than she'd imagined, considering Edinburgh was the capital city and home of the Scottish Parliament.

A Victorian townhouse, the Bonham hotel elicited Yvonne's approval the minute she stepped inside, styled with bright colors and modern art. "I prearranged with hotel management to store our luggage until our rooms are ready for check-in at two," she explained to Fiona. "I hope you don't mind coming along on the walking tour of Old Town. It will allow me to familiarize myself with the local history and experience the tour company's service. The tour will take about two and a half hours. Then we can have a leisurely lunch before checking into our hotel room."

They turned in their luggage to the concierge and refreshed themselves in the public washroom, then walked the short distance to Princes Street.

Fiona took a deep breath of fresh air while turning around for a panoramic view. "Things haven't changed much in thirty-nine years. Still impressive as I remember, the old Castle is. The Scots are good for taking care of their historic buildings."

"Thanks for putting up with the tour. You probably know all this stuff already." Yvonne handed Fiona her tour ticket.

"Don't remember much actually. It will be good to remind myself where I came from. See things from the eyes of a tourist." Fiona shifted her ticket to her left hand and patted Yvonne on the shoulder. "It's okay, dear. We'll have plenty of time to do our investigating once we get to Peebles. I've waited this long, I can wait another day."

"Will you be okay with the walking?"

"Lord, yes. Don't you know—we Scots have strong legs—made for walking. Just ask any Highlander."

They joined the group at the Esplanade near the castle entrance. The guide caught their attention right away, holding a small sign that read "Edinburgh Discovery Tours." William Fraser was dressed in the traditional Scottish formal wear: jacket, dress kilt and sporran. They looked at him and then at each other, and grinned. "Now I see the advantages of the kilt. Better to show off those masculine legs," Yvonne whispered to Fiona.

William Fraser had pitch-black hair and fair skin. His piercing blue eyes twinkled so with glee that Yvonne had to stifle the urge to giggle like a school girl.

"Welcome, lads and lassies. Ye'll be having a merry time for sure on our walkin tour. First, I'll take yer tickets and then we'll be on our way to discover Edinburgh." William's deep melodic brogue easily held everyone's attention.

Fiona watched Yvonne's reaction to William. "Scottish men are known for their handsome good looks and their formidable physiques. But, be careful, Yvonne, they are also known to be rascals."

"Just make sure we each get a picture with him before the tour is over." Yvonne patted her shoulder bag, making sure she had her camera.

Eight couples, including Yvonne and Fiona made up the tour group. William explained about the Royal Edinburgh Military

Tattoo held each August since 1950. "The Esplanade has been enlarged over the years and can now seat as many as seventy-seven hundred spectators for each performance. Originally a military regiment's corps of drums, or drums and pipes, were played to tavern owners at the end of the evening's recreation. 'Doe den tap toe,' or 'tap toe' (pronounced 'tap too'), later became 'tattoo', literally meaning turn off the taps. The tattoo was played to turn off the taps of the ale kegs, so the soldiers would retire to their beds at a reasonable hour. Later in the eighteenth century it became a ceremonial last call of duty for the day and a form of entertainment. In modern times pipe bands from around the world gather and perform to sold-out audiences of over two hundred thousand people a year." Yvonne imagined the melancholy sound of bagpipes she'd heard played during police funerals. She tried to imagine how it would sound magnified by hundreds. She hoped to hear happier tunes piped during her visit.

Strolling through the Esplanade, they were given a brief history of the wars of independence. Then William led them up Castle Hill to the top end of the Royal Mile where processions took place during times when the castle was a royal residence and the old Scottish Parliament met. Situated at the top he showed them the Cannonball House, which looks down on the castle. "There are two conflicting stories of how a cannonball came to be embedded within the motley assortment of stones in the fifteenth century tenement house," William's softly rolling brogue and the ancient buildings transported Yvonne centuries back in time. "The most popular story described how the castle guard fired on the Jacobites during their rebellion in 1630 and hit the house by mistake." Yvonne took the small camera from her tote bag and snapped a picture of the building, focusing on the marred spot in the stones where the cannonball was embedded.

Continuing down the hill, William pointed out homes of Scottish significance. One that caused particular interest was that of the mother of Mary Queen of Scots. Everyone had read books or heard the stories about Queen Mary and were thrilled to be standing where such a famous historical figure had once lived.

Looking around at the remaining old homes, Yvonne observed a man standing apart from the group. She noticed that when they stopped, he stopped, when they proceeded, he proceeded.

"Fiona, don't look now, but I think we're being followed." Fiona turned and looked behind her.

The man stepped behind a few of the sightseers in the back of the group.

"You weren't supposed to look."

"Sorry dear, just a reflex action." Fiona focused on Yvonne. "What did he look like? Can you describe him?"

The group moved again. William led them toward the Lawn Market. They continued walking with the group, and Yvonne leaned sideways and whispered to Fiona, "He looked like a regular person. Stocky, short sleeve shirt, slacks, thinning hair—I think. I didn't get a close look before he stepped out of sight. I'll be aware if we see him again, and I'll take a better look then."

"Next," William said, "We'll make our way to the Heart of Midlothian. Literally—there is a heart-shaped design in the cobblestones near St Giles Cathedral. It marks the entrance to the Tolbooth, set up in 1561, as the name implies, to collect tolls. After 1640 it was used as a prison. There was a scaffold for hanging criminals, rebels and traitors. The heads of the more famous victims would be displayed on spikes in the face of the building." William waited while the comments about the gruesome history died down. "The Tolbooth was demolished in 1817, but the Heart remains. As a sign of disrespect to the town council, it became common for passers-by to spit on the cobblestone design. While this is not encouraged these days, it is wise to give the emblem a wide berth when walkin past—just in case!"

Everyone looked at the Heart from several feet away. Their mood shifted to awe for the magnificent St. Giles Cathedral, the historic City Church, known as the High Kirk of Edinburgh. "It is the Mother Church of Presbyterianism and contains the chapel of the Order of the Thistle, Scotland's chivalric company of knights headed by the Queen. Ye'll note the 15th century gothic style. Then, direct yer eyes to the most notable external feature, the crown spire on the tower." William pointed to the towering steeple in the center of the building.

"Ye should arrange a tour of the interior church. Inside is a wonderful bronze relief, a memorial to the Scottish writer, Robert Louis Stevenson. Renowned American sculptor, Augustus St. Gaudens, a great admirer of Stevenson, donated the relief in 1904 to honor Stevenson who had died in Samoa in 1894."

Yvonne whispered to Fiona, "I hope we'll have a chance to tour Edinburgh Castle and the Cathedral before we leave Scotland."

Fiona, feigning agreement, smiled at Yvonne. Impatient to be on her way to Peebles, she wouldn't dream of rushing her new friend and helpmate to satisfy her own desires.

William continued his narrative, "Another feature of interest within the cathedral is the Great West Window, installed in 1985. It's the work of the Icelandic stained-glass artist Leifur Breidfjörd. The window celebrates our prized poet, Robert Burns, and the themes in his poetry in a semi-abstract style. The lowest section is mainly green, representing the natural world that Burns portrayed so vividly. The middle section contains many human figures as it celebrates human unity, regardless of race, color or creed. The topmost tracery contains a glorious sunburst of love, blossoming 'like a red, red rose'. I highly recommend a visit. I promise ye won't be disappointed."

Yvonne had to admit, between his brogue and charming script, William was doing a great job enticing them to purchase other tours.

"Next we'll walk to the entrance of the Princess Street Gardens where we'll find the Scott Monument honoring, Sir Walter Scott, the father of historical fiction. Ye will note the monument is housed in an unusual Victorian gothic structure that resembles a gazebo with steeples. Travel writer, Bill Bryson has described it as a *gothic* rocket ship." William gave the sight-seers the opportunity to take pictures in front of the monument. There were individual shots, a group shot of all taken by William, and several pictures snapped individually posing with their brawny tour guide.

"Another time if ye wish to tour the Princess Gardens, ye'll see the beautiful Floral Clock, the Ross bandstand where concerts are held, and the lovely Ross Fountain often used in the foreground for pictures of Edinburgh Castle."

The tour ended at the World's End Pub. Built within the area of a great stone wall, it was once considered to be the end of the world to long ago Scots. It reeked of age and atmosphere. Dark wood paneled walls and heavy walnut tables gave it a cave-like feel. The walls were plastered with photos and memorabilia of famous people who had frequented the pub over many centuries.

Yvonne indulged in McEwans Scottish ale of medium gold color and Shepherd's Pie, comfort food at its best. She looked forward to getting a cab back to the hotel as soon as they finished lunch. The beer, food and jet lag were all making her sleepy.

Fiona ordered McEwans dark ale, to go along with her bangers and mash, the British name for sausages and mashed potatoes. Mmm ... "I have missed good bangers. You can't get ones like this in the States."

Yvonne felt, rather than heard, a presence behind her. She looked up from her plate and saw Fiona's eyes widen in surprise.

"Cameron, is that you?" Fiona looked over Yvonne's shoulder with anticipation.

"I wondered if ye'd recognize yer old cousin after all these years." A stocky man with a slight resemblance to Fiona stepped around to greet her.

"He's the one—the man who was following us on the tour."

Fiona got up from her seat and hugged her cousin.

The man directed his comments to Yvonne. "Sorry to trouble ye, lass. I didn't want to interfere with yer sight-seein. I followed ye from the airport, and meant to call on Fiona at the hotel, but then ye stayed only a few minutes and left."

"Please, have a seat, Mister ... .?"

"Douglas, Cameron to ye, Lass. Fiona is my first cousin on my mother's side." Cameron pulled a chair from a nearby table and sat between them. "Duncan and I were best friends—before he went missin. Keith Turner was our best too. We were known as the Three Musketeers in those days."

"Would you like to join us for lunch?" Yvonne caught the eye of their young waiter and signaled him to come over.

"Nothing to eat thanks, but I'd not refuse a whisky." Cameron nodded to the waiter. "Bar brand is fine lad." The waiter returned to the bar to fetch his drink.

Cameron turned his attention to his cousin. "Fiona, it's wonderful to have ye home. What took ye so long?"

"Aw ... you know how it is. I always meant to come but with the kids and the family. I never had the chance. Now that I'm on my own, I have time on my hands."

"Ye say ye've come to find Duncan after all these years. How is that possible? Yer mam and I, we searched high and low. There was no trace of him anywhere. It was like he up and fell off the face o' the earth." Cameron looked down at the table, averting his eyes from Fiona's probing gaze.

"Well, I may not find him, but I intend to find out what happened to him, and if I don't—at least I tried. In the meantime, I can get reacquainted with my family and old friends." Fiona smiled at Cameron.

"Speakin of old friends, Darleen Turner called. Ye know how news travels fast in Peebles. She was sniffing around, trying to find out why ye were coming home after all this time. Wanted to know why ye'd want to open up 'old wounds.' Her words, not mine." Cameron took hold of Fiona's hand. "Ye should tread carefully with her. I don't think she ever got over Duncan, even if she did marry Keith. He was always second best to Duncan, and to make matters worse, theirs is a childless marriage. Other than her father's business, I dinna ken what holds them together."

Seeing Fiona squirm, Yvonne thought it time to end the conversation. "Cameron, we're checking into the hotel soon. We'd like to travel to Peebles tomorrow. Perhaps we can meet then, and you can tell us about Duncan's disappearance and who you talked to at that time. It would give us an idea of where to start."

"My, my, lassie, a travel agent who investigates missing persons, I'd say that's an unusual combination of talents." Cameron gave Yvonne a hard stare.

Hmm, a bit touchy isn't he, wondered Yvonne. She took a sip of her ale, covering her unease. She knew she was jet-lagged but was this just sarcasm or was he threatening her? "I've agreed to help Fiona—for moral support. I don't consider myself an investigator. At the same time, I don't see what harm there is in asking a few questions about her brother's disappearance if it helps put her mind at ease."

Yvonne gave him a broad smile. "I'm looking forward to learning all I can about Edinburgh and seeing as much of Scotland as possible in the small amount of time allotted for our trip." She reviewed the lunch bill briefly, added a tip, retrieved her credit card from her wallet and placed it along with the bill on the money plate for the waiter. Then, Yvonne made arrangements with Cameron to meet the next afternoon at his home in Peebles.

"Ye'll be stayin with me and Kendra—no arguments, we insist." Cameron gave Fiona a hug and a nod to Yvonne, bidding them goodbye.

The two weary travelers took a taxi to the Bonham, checked in at 2:15 and settled into their shared room. Yvonne left Fiona napping while she kept her appointment with the hotel manager for a hotel inspection. The mixture of modern décor into 1880's Victorian luxury impressed Yvonne. Though the wall colors and art accessories were bold, the use of velvets and suede in the furniture and draperies gave her a sumptuous and comfortable feeling. She was impressed with the large luxurious conference room. A small boutique hotel, it would be perfect for her corporate customers. Both suites were occupied, so she couldn't view them, but was thoroughly impressed with the superior bedrooms, which were roomy and offered several amenities including terry cloth robes. The cozy dining room, elegantly appointed with art work on dark paneled wood walls, held contemporary dining furniture set in a classic white linen and crystal style. According to the manager, the restaurant was one of ten in Edinburgh rewarded with two Rosettes.

Returning to their room, Yvonne determined not to let Fiona's cousin unnerve her, fell on her bed and slept deeply for an hour. They arrived in the dining room for "high tea" at five. Already in full swing, patrons were enjoying a choice of either Darjeeling or Earl Grey. Traditional tea sandwiches included a variety of breads spread with butter and filled with watercress, cucumber, tuna fish, or pimento cheese. There were scones, macaroons and Scottish short bread for those with a sweet tooth. "These scones remind me of my mother." Fiona added a large dollop of clotted cream and strawberry jam to her scone. "Only we always had them dry and crumbly."

Yvonne mused, someday I'd like to bring Christy here. Everyone's so polite and refined. Thoughts of her mother came to mind. Wouldn't it be nice to find a tea room like this in Fort Lauderdale? There are so many transplanted Brits in the area, there's bound to be one somewhere. David would love it—then again—maybe not, there's still so much I don't know about him. Her expression changed to one of melancholy. She hated to admit it, but she missed sharing all this with him. In spite of the danger, he'd kept things fun and upbeat when we were in Greece.

"Are you homesick for your daughter, Yvonne? I'm sure little Christy misses you, too."

Yvonne smiled at Fiona, squashing a twinge of guilt as she realized how easily her feelings of missing Christy had moved on to David.

After tea, they walked along Haymarket Street, passing hotels, restaurants and pubs. Haymarket has easy access to Princes Street, motorways to other parts of Scotland, and the Haymarket Railway Station. It's the country's major station and jumping off point for all Highland trains, offering one-hour commuter service to Glasgow.

Invigorated, Yvonne enjoyed the fresh air and vibrant atmosphere of mixing with the local business people and tourists from around the world. She loved the stone and brick architecture, mostly from the Victorian era, and imagined herself walking on the same streets as Sir Walter Scott. Using her yoga techniques, she breathed in prana, taking energy, or life force, from the ancient city. She felt grounded and strong and independent. She remembered feeling weak and inadequate only a year ago. Smiling to herself, she knew she would never be a victim again. In fact, she thought, a little sleuthing on the side could become her specialty. Travel agent-sleuth, she liked the sound of it. Now, I'm being silly, she thought, but ... one never knows.

When they returned to their hotel room, Yvonne double-checked their itinerary for the next day. She had hired a driver to take them to Peebles, not wishing to drive on the left side of the road. She glanced at her phone sitting on the night stand next to her bed. Her eyes shifted to the clock. It was six-fifteen now, that meant it would be one-fifteen in the afternoon in Fort Lauderdale. This might be a good time to call Christy, she thought. She placed the call, but there was no answer. She left a message saying that she'd call back later. "I wonder what they're up to," she whispered.

Fiona had browsed through the hotel magazine and tuned in BBC T.V. then drifted into another nap, snoring loud enough to keep Yvonne awake and focused on her mystery novel.

At seven-thirty Yvonne roused Fiona and they dressed casually for dinner. Instead of eating in the hotel dining room, they walked to a popular bar-bistro, Whigham's Wine Cellar, known for its seafood, vegetarian fare, and selection of forty wines by the glass.

It had been highly recommended by the hotel concierge. The restaurant was an eclectic mix of old candle-lit vaults and an airy modern dining area. "It's crowded with local diners. This means good food and reasonable prices," commented Yvonne. After they were seated, they shared the recommended favorite, a Seafood Platter offering a mélange of langoustine, oysters, clams, tiger prawns, shrimp, mussels, smoked mackerel and trout. On the side they shared a roast beef salad made with the local favorite, Silverside Sirloin from Buccleuch Castle. For dessert they indulged in traditional sticky toffee pudding. "I wonder if the food will be this delicious everywhere in Scotland? You always hear British food is boring." Yvonne finished the last of her wine.

Fiona had ordered coffee and sipped it. "The English and Scottish had a reputation for serving bland food, but they've learned a lot from the French and Eastern Europeans since World War II. The better restaurants serve continental cuisines, but I'd be willing to bet that the average Scotsman still eats plain meat and potatoes. Wait till you eat your first meat pie. It's nothing more than ground beef in a pie pastry—very bland and dry. Some Scots flavor it with Worcestershire sauce."

They walked back to the hotel. "Let's make a pact," said Fiona.

"About what?"

"Tomorrow we don't eat so much otherwise you'll have to get a wheel barrow to tote me around the rest of the trip."

"Agreed. Except ... I feel like a kid in a candy store with all this great food, and I don't have to cook. I'm not used to being waited on. I could get used to it." Yvonne and Fiona laughed as they entered the Bonham.

Back in their room, Yvonne called the night clerk and requested a wake-up call for seven.

When they were each settled into their own twin bed, Fiona yawned. "I'll say goodnight then." She turned off her bedside light and pulled her covers up to her chin and closed her eyes.

"Will it bother you if I read for awhile?" asked Yvonne.

"Not at all, dear. I'll be out like a light in no time."

Yvonne plumped her pillows and sat up in bed, opening her cozy British mystery. She laughed to herself. M.C. Beaton's, Hamish Macbeth mystery series about a country Sheriff in the Highlands of Scotland relaxed her.

It wasn't long before Yvonne heard Fiona snoring softly. Her own eye lids grew heavy. She set her book aside, turned off her light and snuggled under the goose-down covers. She wasn't sure if it was the rich meal, the mystery novel, or Fiona's cousin showing up unannounced, but several hours passed before she slept.

Chapter 6
PEEBLES, SCOTLAND
WEDNESDAY, JUNE 3RD

From the back seat of the hired car, through the lens of her camera, Yvonne gazed beyond the large expanse of green lawn, with a single road leading to the front entrance of Dalkeith Palace. She had directed the driver to stop for a moment, allowing her to snap a photo. Though, on their way to meet with Cameron and his wife, she wanted to make the most of her fam-trip. Even on the short drive to Peebles, the long Scottish history revealed itself in the architecture and well-worn, yet manicured, landscape. She'd read that from the time Dalkeith was built in the twelfth century it had a long exciting history. She recalled that in 1642 it was sold to Francis Scott the 2nd Earl of Buccleuch*. The Buccleuch family gained and lost ownership several times over centuries. The family's residence in the Palace ended in 1914. Since then it has been used for public and private businesses. In 1985 it was leased to the University of Wisconsin for a study abroad program. Yvonne thought it interesting that currently, sixty to eighty students lived in the Palace taking classes from U.S. and U.K. faculty members.

Fiona, lost in thought, stared out the car window at the rural scenery, hardly taking notice of the ancient landscape. By her estimates, they'd arrive early for the one o'clock meeting at her cousin Cameron's home.

*Buccleuch pronounced: BuckClue

The timer on Yvonne's cell phone buzzed, reminding her to call Christy. Gino answered her call on the second ring and handed the phone to his daughter without comment.

"Hello *mi chica dulce*, did you have a nice day yesterday?"

"Yes, Mommy. We went to the beach with Daddy's friend, Angela, and after the beach we ate Bar-B-Q."

Yvonne kept quiet, listening while Christy took a breath. She wondered, who the blazes was Angela? *Una mujer con mala fama?* She hoped not.

"Mommy, my face and hands got all sticky with the ribs, but Daddy said it was okay cause they tasted 'sooo good.'"

Yvonne smiled. She missed Christy's little idiosyncrasies that were so endearing like her fussiness over getting dirty. "I'm glad you're having a nice time. What are your plans for today?"

Yvonne heard Gino's muffled voice in the background.

"Daddy says I have to hang up 'cause it's time for breakfast. Sorry, Mommy. Will you call me again tomorrow?"

"What? We've hardly had a chance to talk."

"I know, Mommy."

"Be a good girl for Daddy. I'll call you again soon. I love you *mi chica dulce.*"

"I love you too, Mom—" The phone went dead abruptly.

"*Ay Dios mio!* Why does he have to be so mean?" Yvonne felt her jaws tighten. She knew better than to think he'd take his anger out on Christy. Chances were he'd be doing the opposite, being sweet and playing nice while belittling her for abandoning Christy for the sake of her job. I mustn't let him get inside my head.

Fiona asked, "Is something wrong? Is Christy all right?"

"Yes. She's fine. It's my ex, he's—I don't know why I let him bother me so. You'd think I'd know better by now."

"There, there, dear, everything will be okay. You're right not to let him upset you. There's nothing you can do from here, anyway."

Yvonne looked squarely at Fiona. She realized what she said was true, but it didn't make her feel better. Instead she felt less in control.

Along the way, the rural setting of Edinburgh Road had changed to residential with homes set along the street at a discreet distance. "Oh look. Here we are," said Fiona. The car lurched to a stop in front of the Douglas' home.

A traditional thatch-roofed English home surrounded by a bevy of blooms greeted them. Kendra, Cameron's wife, gardened in the English tradition. Ivy climbed the outer walls of the house. Artfully-placed trellises with abundant cherry-pink country roses scented the air along the stone walkway. Fiona hurried up the path carrying her luggage. Yvonne pulled her luggage with wheels along the bumpy walkway. Half-way, she paused, lifted her chin, straightened her spine and inhaled the pungent fragrance of the roses for a momentary feeling of calm, then proceeded to the Douglas' front door. The smell of roses brought a flash of happiness, an image of her mother pruning and picking roses in their backyard garden. Rose bushes with little or no scent were never allowed in her mother's garden, no matter how pretty they might be.

Yvonne couldn't help but smile. *This is the part of my being I've least identified with. I've always felt I take after Dad, only. But, now, being here, I see, I am linked to my mother's family history too. Someday, I'll have to learn more about Mom ... and her family ...*

While they welcomed Fiona, Kendra watched Yvonne approach. She noticed her demeanor change from stiff reserve to relaxed and friendly. After hugs and introductions, Cameron and Kendra treated Yvonne and Fiona to a lunch of poached Salmon direct from the river Tweed, with tatties and neeps, a combination of mashed potatoes and turnips, and peas with mushrooms.

After lunch they settled in the living room. Kendra served Pimms, a Sprite drink with gin, and slices of lemon, lime and orange. Cameron quizzed Fiona about her children and life in the states. They spent time catching up with family on both sides of the ocean and reminisced about their childhood.

Cameron's reminisces gravitated to his boyhood days and paling around with Duncan. "Remember the time Fiona, when Duncan climbed onto that old highland cow at the Henderson farm? He couldn't have been more than thirteen at the time. Keith and I were too scared to try it, but, Duncan, he was fearless, or crazy, I'm not sure which." Cameron laughed. "It took him about ten minutes to get up onto the cow and only aboot two seconds to get thrown off. He landed on his tail bone and couldn't sit down for a week." Cameron's eyes moistened. The reminder of having lost his best friend, saddened him.

"I do remember," said Fiona quietly.

During the momentary lull in the conversation, Yvonne took the opportunity to get to know Kendra. "Are you from Peebles?"

"No. I grew up in Glasgow. After graduating from Glasgow University with a degree in English, I moved to Peebles accepting a placement as English Honors teacher at Peebles High School. I'm retired now but volunteer some and garden some, of course." Kendra took a sip of her Pimms.

"What kind of volunteering do you do?"

"Mostly reading to the blind, and I mentor through referrals from Peebles High School, students at risk of leaving school early."

Yvonne studied Kendra. She appeared quiet and self-assured, not prone to tooting her own horn. Her sweet fair face and slight build caused Yvonne to wonder how she'd handle belligerent teens. "Mentoring sounds very rewarding. Do you have much success?"

"I'd say nine out of ten students will remain in school after our program."

"You have an actual program?"

"Yes. It's an eight-week project that helps them build self-esteem and hopefully motivates them to stay in school and become productive citizens in society."

"That's terrific. It sounds like you have many of the same problems here in Scotland that we have with our youths in the States." Yvonne liked Kendra—respected her matter-of-fact attitude toward her accomplishments.

"I suppose children are the same everywhere. Nature versus nurture and all that. There will always be children discarded emotionally or physically in most societies. Whatever the reasons, be it the result of divorce, drug addiction, or worse, abuse." Kendra looked over at Cameron. "In Britain, it often falls on the teachers to fix the kids who are broken. When we can't, then it's a step closer to a criminal life ending in a prison sentence."

Yvonne sensed her sadness and thought it best to change the subject. She thought this might be the best time to bring up the all-important reason for their visit. "Cameron, you were going to tell Fiona and me about the inquiries into Duncan's disappearance. Were the police involved?"

Cameron sat in his dark blue, over-stuffed chair. He tried to sit up straighter, but the chair wouldn't cooperate. He remained sunken into the comfortable impression made from many years of use. He relaxed and let the chair have its way. "Aye. The copper's name was ... Officer Gowrie, if I'm not mistaken. I heard he passed away some ten, maybe fifteen years ago. Heart attack—I think."

"That's too bad. Would there be records of the investigation?" asked Fiona.

"It was almost forty years ago. Not sure how well they kept records back then."

Fiona turned to Yvonne. "He went missing in 1965. Computers were the old fashioned kind that took up lots of space, but seems they'd have kept records in some form or other." She hesitated a moment. "I have letters my mother sent to father saying they'd questioned family, friends, neighbors and workers at the woolen mill. No one claimed to have seen him."

Yvonne took out her notebook and her pen. "What do you suggest, Cameron? Should we start by talking to the woolen mill people? Do you know if he made it there to pick up his check, or did he disappear before that? I'm not clear on the sequence of events."

"He did pick up his—"

Fiona cut off Cameron. "Craig MacIntyre was the last to see him. Craig owned the woolen mill, and he personally handed out the paychecks. He told the police that Duncan picked up his check and bicycled back in the direction he came from, excited to be leaving for America."

Yvonne looked at the two cousins for a moment and made up her mind to follow up on the paycheck question later. "I think we should start at the Peebles police station, review the records—see if anything or anyone looks suspicious. That way when we make our inquiries, we'll have as much background as possible of previous statements. There might be a clue somewhere if someone's story changes after all these years."

"Very clever, Yvonne—Janice was right—she said you'd know just what to do. To the Peebles Police Station then." Fiona stood up from the multi-color floral divan she'd been sitting on.

"You'll need a car." Cameron pulled himself out of his cushy chair and walked to a key rack hanging next to the front door.

"I don't think I'd better drive. Perhaps we should call a cab." Yvonne rose from her seat.

"Tell ye what. I'll drive ye," said Cameron. "I've nothin better to do since retirin. Kendra complains about my bein underfoot half the time, anyway."

"Nonsense, darling, I love having ye around the house, especially now that ye've got the hang of dishwashing ye're ever so helpful." Kendra's eyes twinkled.

Yvonne wondered if she'd ever have a comfortable lasting relationship like theirs. An image of David sneaking up behind her when she washed dishes at home, placing his hands on her shoulders and kissing her neck popped into her mind.

"The truth of the matter is I haven't been much help wi' his disappearance. Not now and not in the past. I know ye'r countin on me, and I'd like to make it up to ye ... and to Duncan."

"We'll take you up on your offer," said Fiona. "Let's go."

Yvonne capped her pen and gathered her belongings together. Perhaps it was just the jet-lag, she scolded herself. There was no sign of sarcasm in Fiona's cousin, today.

From Cameron's house in northern Peebles on Edinburgh Road, the drive took about four minutes to arrive at the police station on Rosetta Road. A thirtyish fair-skinned woman with ruddy, red cheeks and orange hair peeking out from under her black derby hat adorned with the distinctive black-and-white checked band of the UK police, greeted the threesome with a smile of perfectly straight teeth. Her mandatory crisp white shirt and black trousers commanded the respect due a police constable. "May I help ye?" A name plate pinned to her shirt pocket gave her name as Constable Munro.

"Rhona, Och my Jings! Look at ye, all grown up. How's yer father? Ah haven't seen him in a good while." Cameron's eyes lit up at the sight of Rhona Munro, daughter of his old friend, retired Assistant Chief Constable Innes Munro.

"My father is sonsie, Mr. Douglas. I'll tell him ye were asking aboot him. Now, what brings ye here to the police station?"

Cameron introduced Fiona and Yvonne to Constable Munro. "We'd like to see the old records about my cousin's missin-persons case from 1965. The case was never solved, ye see."

"It's my brother, Duncan Ross. He went missing, and we want to check the files before we start our own investigation." Fiona looked at Yvonne for reassurance then set her purse on the counter waiting for Constable Munro to reply.

The constable looked at the threesome, perplexed. "I've not had a question of this sort before. Generally speaking, ye should apply to the Force Information Unit at Police Headquarters in Edinburgh. They will let ye know if ye are allowed to access the information."

"But—that will take too long. I'm only here in Scotland for a short while. Tell her, Yvonne." Fiona stepped away from the counter and waved Yvonne forward to stand between herself and the constable.

Cameron nodded at Yvonne, encouraging her to jump into the conversation.

Yvonne, used to negotiating special rates and amenities with travel vendors, smiled sweetly. "Constable Munro, my friend, Mrs. Batson has traveled all the way from Ft. Lauderdale, Florida to discover what happened to her brother. His disappearance was reported and investigated in Peebles. Why make her go to Edinburgh? Surely you can access the information here—more quickly. Keep in mind, the case of his disappearance has never been solved. So perhaps the information is still open in your files. Won't you have a look for us?"

Constable Munro looked to her father's friend for support. Her perfect smile barely reached her cerulean blue eyes. "Surely, ye'll understand, I must get permission from Police Inspector Gordon. He's not here now so ye'll have to check back later."

"Do ye need to be botherin yer police inspector aboot this? Your da and I have been friends for a long time. That must count for somthin."

"I wish it did, Mr. Douglas, but I have my livelihood to think aboot. Inspector Gordon is nae understandin when it comes to breakin rules."

"Alright Constable, we'll come back later."

On their way back to Cameron's house, Fiona complained, "Well now ... that was a waste of time."

"Not necessarily. Constable Munro never denied having access to the records, so we know it's probable that they're still in storage at the station. I think if we keep at it, she'll eventually come around and help us out," said Yvonne.

Cameron made a quick u-turn throwing the ladies off balance for a few seconds.

"What the devil? Where are we going?" asked Fiona.

"It's aboot time I visited with an old friend." After a few turns, Cameron pulled up in front of a modern apartment house. "Follow me, ladies."

Yvonne and Fiona followed Cameron to a first floor apartment. Cameron knocked at number 3 Kingsmeadow Road. The door opened after a minute and a hefty man with fading orange hair answered. "Well, look who's here. If it's nae my auld mukker, Cameron."

"Innes, ye auld scoundrel, how are ye?"

"Come in, come in—bring these pretty lassies with ye."

Fiona and Yvonne followed Cameron through a short narrow hallway into Innes' living room.

Innes hurried and moved the newspaper debris from his well-worn couch to a side-board cabinet on an adjacent wall. "Please be seated, and I'll git ye some tea right away."

Cameron gave Yvonne and Fiona a stern look indicating they were not to disagree. "Cheers, we'd love some."

Yvonne studied the room while waiting for Innes to return from the kitchen. It lacked a feminine touch. The well-built, old furniture held clutter of dusty knick-knacks, family photos and dated books and magazines—all strewn around with no rhyme or reason. She assumed these were remnants of his life before losing his wife. Yvonne surmised that Innes' wife had died and not divorced him.

Innes entered carrying a tray with a teapot, four cups and saucers and a pitcher of milk. He set the tray on the coffee table, pushing clutter aside with the tray itself. He took a seat in a straight back chair at one end of the table and poured the tea into cups for his guests. "Now, who are these bonnie lassies and what brings ye to my humble home?"

"Before we get into that, tell me how ye've been." Cameron accepted a cup of tea and declined the milk.

Innes continued pouring tea for Fiona and Yvonne while answering Cameron. "I've nae complaints. I've my daughter to cheer me. She visits often. I only wish she'd marry and gimme me some grandkids."

Fiona added milk to her tea, Yvonne did not.

Cameron smiled warmly at Innes. "Speakin of Rhona, we saw her at the police station. She's gae professional and bonny too—a real chip off the auld block."

Innes grinned. "That she is, and, what were ye doin at the police station?"

"First, let me introduce my cousin, Fiona and her friend and travel agent, Yvonne."

"Very nice to make yer acquaintance, I'm sure." He smiled and nodded at them.

"Thank you for the tea. It's delicious. Do you mind if I ask what kind it is? I've never had any quite like it." Yvonne set her cup in the saucer.

"It's called Scots Teatime. The Scots are famous for blending braw teas. This is a blend of mellow teas from India, Ceylon and Kenya. Ye may have heard of our most famous Scot who traveled to Ceylon and worked with James Taylor to grow the Tea industry in the late 1800's—Thomas Lipton." Innes poured more tea into Yvonne's cup. "For ower a hundred years the best tea merchants in bonnie Scotland is Brodie's. Ye'll see their teas sold in all the tourist shops."

"Very Interesting, I'm sure." Cameron smiled at Innes, steering the conversation to the reason for their visit. "Ye may remember my cousin, Fiona." Cameron nodded at her. "Her brother, Duncan, went missing back in 1965. Officer Gowrie was the lead detective on the case, but it seems ye were just fresh with the police department aboot then. We wondered if ye might remember anything of importance that might help us to find out what happened to him."

"Well, let me think for a minute, twas a long time ago and there were nae solid leads as I recall." Innes rubbed his chin with his hand. "I do remember that Gowrie suspected Duncan's chum, Keith Turner. It was well known that Keith had eyes for Duncan's girl, Darleen, but they never proved he acted on his feelings until long after Duncan was gone. They questioned Darleen's father, Craig MacIntyre, too. He never approved of his daughter's feelings for Duncan—thought she was too good for the lad, but they found no evidence of foul play. After awhile it was decided Duncan had probably run off to Australia or some such place to make his own mark in the world, and the case was dropped."

"It seems to me if Craig MacIntyre told Fiona's mother that he gave Duncan his paycheck and saw that he was on his way home, excited about going to America, Duncan wouldn't have gone elsewhere. The facts don't add up." Yvonne spoke her thoughts out loud.

"I believe the same," said Fiona.

"Well, the long and short o' it is; they did not have evidence of foul play, so they had to come up with a theory," Innes replied sharply, defensive of his comrades.

Cameron noisily cleared his throat. "Rhona is a fine smart lassie. ye must be proud of her!"

"Sure, I'm proud. ... So, ye'r serious then, aboot looking into the lad's disappearance ... again?" Innes directed the question to Cameron.

"Yes. Fiona has flown all the way from North America to find out what happened to her brother, so we must do our best to help. I should have done more myself back then. But, I was young. I missed him desperately and was ready to believe anythin—rather than think he might have died ..."

Chapter 7
PEEBLES WOOLEN MILL
THURSDAY, JUNE 4TH

"Cameron Douglas called at eight this mornin. He wants to bring Fiona and this travel agent o' hers by to discuss aboot the day Duncan disappeared." Darleen stared straight ahead at the company's outdated computer screen and avoided looking toward Keith.

"And what did ye say?" Keith stood in the doorway of her office and clenched his fists.

Darleen looked at Keith. "I said I thought it'd be a waste o' time, but to come at ten. The sooner we get it ower with, the better. Like I told ye—I've a bad feelin aboot this." Darleen turned back to her computer, dismissing Keith.

"'Tis time to see to the sheep shearing." Keith turned and stomped out of the building, heading for the shearing pens.

Yvonne watched from the back seat of Cameron's compact Ford as he drove them on a tour of Peebles. She stared with delight at the park land running adjacent to the river and the pleasant riverside walkways. Surrounded by scenic hills dotted with evergreen forests, she saw castles and manor houses peeking out from their secluded landscapes. Peebles lay in the Tweed Valley, quaintly occupying both banks of the River Tweed. "What a beautiful town you live in, Cameron. Thanks so much for giving me a personal tour. I'd love to find time later to shop on High Street—have tea and scones and stroll along the river."

"I think that can be arranged. Kendra will want to join ye lassies for that excursion."

Fiona sat up front next to Cameron. "I can't believe how busy traffic is. When I was last in Peebles, it was a quiet town."

"Ye may not remember, Fiona, in the summertime twas aye busy. That's the way with toons like ours that have rollin hills for golfin, hikin, and mountain bikin, and rivers for fishin. We are a 'destination.'" Cameron drove along High Street giving his guests the opportunity to admire the Victorian architecture of the shops. He cruised along Eastgate then pulled onto Innerleithen Road turning right. "Twill be just a few minutes and we'll arrive at the Peebles Woolen Mill."

"What is the Woolen Mill like? Is it a big place?" asked Yvonne.

"The Turners, Keith and Darleen, run tours two times a week throughout the summertime. Unlike the Edinburgh Woolen Mills that are mainly shops to sell woolen goods to tourists and are now manufactured with modern equipment and technology in China, Peebles Woolen Mill is aye using the auld fashioned methods. They have several acres of land and employ aboot twenty-five folk. Keith runs the operations, and Darleen keeps the books and manages the woolen shop employees."

About ten minutes from Peebles, adjacent to Innerleithen Road, a modest wood-carved sign for Peebles Woolen Mill stood next to the driveway leading to an enormous Georgian stone manor house. With an understated symmetrical elegance, the peaked roof sported two chimneys, one on either side of the peak, and three dormer windows along the front of the roof. A grouping of three thatch-roofed outbuildings sat off to the right of the house with a cobblestone driveway leading directly to them. Yvonne felt a sense of whimsy when she looked at them, as if in a fairy-tale she might see the seven dwarfs come marching out any moment. Another sign pointed to the Woolen Mill entry and gift shop building. The property was surrounded by acres of hilly farmland. Large trees were interspersed between the various buildings and gave off a shady and welcoming ambience. At a distance, dozens of sheep and highland cows could be seen in the fenced areas of the farm.

"My goodness ... I had no idea it would be so grand," Yvonne pointed at the stately house.

"Tis the family home. Craig and Margaret MacIntyre are in their seventies now. They live in the main house along with Darleen and Keith. Craig is aye Laird of the manor so to speak.

Cameron led Fiona and Yvonne along the cobblestone path to the first thatch-roofed outbuilding. A neatly clipped evergreen box hedge bordered the front of the building on either side of the entrance door. An artistic hand painted sign read, Woolens Gift Shop. A bell tinkled when Cameron opened the door for the ladies. He followed them inside and looked around for a sales-clerk.

A woman of medium height and stocky build approached them. "May I help ye?"

"We have an appointment with Darleen Turner," said Cameron.

"Mrs. Turner's office is ower there." She pointed to the rear of the shop.

Cameron hesitated. "Perhaps I should see if she's ready for us. Take a look around th' shop while I check with Darleen." He left them staring after him.

"I guess we'll look around." Fiona fidgeted with her purse.

Yvonne took her time browsing the various tables and racks of woolen goods. She was amazed to see scarves of every tartan plaid imaginable. The tags on the scarves gave the names of the clans they represented. Familiar names like, Stewart, MacDonald, and Campbell caught her interest. She remembered some of the clan war stories and their colorful histories that she'd read in her research prior to planning the trip. The shop also offered wool knit sweaters, many sporting the purple thistle, Scotland's national flower. Capes and kilts, stockings, caps, and stuffed Nessie toys fashioned in the image of the loch ness monster filled the shelves.

Fiona followed along behind Yvonne, half-heartedly browsing through the store.

Yvonne smiled at Fiona. "What a delight, I'll need to buy some souvenirs before we leave." Yvonne put down a plush toy and wished Christy was with her. "Someday, I'll return and see Scotland through Christy's eyes. It's times like these, I miss her most." She imagined presenting the little green Nessie toy with the red and blue plaid scarf tied around its neck to Christy when she returned home. She rubbed her hand along a soft cashmere scarf the color of Scottish Heather, something her mother might appreciate.

Yvonne turned to ask Fiona about the pattern and noticed that Fiona stared off into the distance, her purse squeezed tightly in both hands. "What's wrong, Fiona?"

"Sorry to spoil your fun, Yvonne, but, now that I'm here, I'm worried that it has all been a waste of time."

"No need to apologize, Fiona. You're nervous, that's understandable. I agree with you. Your dreams are a sign, and it's important to find out what happened to your brother. I don't want you to regret later, not trying."

"I know you're right, but—"

"Don't worry, I'll help you get through this." Yvonne looked up and saw Cameron motioning to them from an open door at the back of the store.

"Look—Cameron's waving to us. We should go." Yvonne gave Fiona a quick hug, and they walked to Darleen's office together.

Darleen stepped around from behind her desk to welcome Fiona and Yvonne. She smiled tentatively and offered her hand to shake. "Fiona. How nice to see ye, and this must be yer friend, Yvonne is it? Please, have a seat." Darleen returned to her desk chair. Fiona and Yvonne took a seat in front of her desk and Cameron stood behind them.

"Can I offer ye some coffee?"

"No thank you. We won't take up much of your time." Fiona fidgeted, sitting up straight on the edge of her chair.

"Cameron tells me that yer're here to ask aboot Duncan's disappearance. I'm surprised, after all these years ..." Darleen frowned, her forehead scrunched together between her faded green eyes.

Yvonne judged Darleen to be in her mid-fifties, slim and attractive for her age. She had ash-blonde hair, jumbled with a mass of curls that seemed to have a mind of their own, yet her attire was the opposite, crisp and professional. Yvonne supposed that Darleen's lavender wool skirt and blazer came from her own shop.

Sensing Fiona's nervousness, Yvonne answered for her, "Fiona hasn't had the means to come back to Scotland—until now. It's important that she get some closure about what happened to her brother."

Fiona leaned toward Darleen's desk. "I'm sorry. I know it's been a long while, but would you mind telling me about the last time you saw Duncan?"

"Not sure I remember much aboot it, but I'll try." Darleen sat looking at the trio for several seconds. Sadness in her eyes belied the smile on her lips. "Twas the mornin Duncan was to leave for America. He came to pick up his last paycheck from my father. We had awready said our goodbyes the night before. He found me rinsing the wool and said he couldn't bear to leave me. He said he'd send for me when he'd made his mark and we'd be married. I tellt him I'd be patient and wait—I'd come to him as soon as he was ready." Darleen blushed. "We kissed one last time ... and ... I never saw him again." A hint of moisture showed in her eyes.

"Do you know where he went after leaving you that morning?" Yvonne glanced at Fiona and then focused on Darleen, watching her closely as the woman bit her lip as if deciding how much to say.

"He went to find my father. Father would've been right here in this office. Back then he kept the books and managed the business. But I'm sure he's tellt all he kens. He gave Duncan his check and wished him well on his way.

Cameron asked, "Can ye tell us who else worked that morning?"

"'Twas a long time ago. Not sure I remember now." Darleen's voice rose to a higher pitch. "All these questions were asked and answered. Why put us through this again?"

"We're sorry. We don't mean to upset you, Darleen. But a person doesn't just up and disappear for no reason. Someone knows what happened to him." Yvonne leaned forward and lowered her voice. "There would be time cards or records of who worked that day, wouldn't there?"

"Not anymore. They would've been thrown out a long time ago. We're only required to keep records for five years."

"After Duncan's disappearance and the police investigation—surely your father would remember who'd worked that day. We should speak to him." Yvonne looked at Fiona and turned to see if Cameron was in agreement.

"Father's not been himself lately. His memory's not what it used to be. Do ye need to disturb him?" Darleen wrung her hands.

"We just want to ask him a few questions. We'll be as gentle and quick as possible. Don't you want to know what happened, too?" Yvonne looked Darleen in the eye.

Darleen blinked once and held Yvonne's gaze. "After all these years, I don't think it matters anymore."

Darleen switched her focus. "Sorry, Fiona, but I grieved for Duncan for years. Och, how I loved him, but our parents were against us from the start. My father insisted I was too good for him and then Duncan's father wanted to take him away from me to America. For years I wondered how come life is so cruel? I blamed the Cailleach's Curse. Chust like that auld gypsy tellt me at the carnival, all those years ago. Ye remember, Fiona, the time we went to the Carnival and had our fortunes tellt. I've always been unlucky. First, no Duncan, then, no children. I'd put it all behind me.

"Poor Keith had to put up with my grieving ower Duncan, and then finding I was barren and couldn't have bairns. We finally settled into our marriage and accepted our life and now ye're here to bring it all back to us."

Fiona could hear Cameron shifting his feet behind her and spoke quickly, sensing that he was about to escort them out, "I see how distraught you are, but don't you see; none of us will ever rest easy until we know what happened. It's time we found the truth of what happened to Duncan."

"Hmpf ... " Cameron cleared his throat, having enough of all this female emotion. "I think it's time we let Darleen go back to her work. I'm worried we've overstayed our welcome. Maybe, we can learn more from her father."

Fiona turned to look at Cameron, shrugged her shoulders, tucked her purse under her left arm then pushed herself up placing her right hand on Darleen's desk. "Thank you Darleen for talkin to us."

Yvonne stood. "It was nice to meet you, Darleen. Your shop is wonderful. I would love to come back after speaking with your father, and purchase some items to take back as gifts for my family."

"We'd thank ye for yer patronage." Darleen dismissed Yvonne with a nod and turned to look at her computer screen.

Margaret MacIntyre answered the knock at the front door, having been alerted by a call from Darleen, and ushered them inside with a friendly smile.ushered them inside with a friendly smile.

They entered a wood paneled foyer with a ten-foot ceiling. Yvonne spied the hilt of a two-handed Claymore, also known as a Broadsword, inserted into a stand that looked similar to those used for umbrellas beside the door. A shiver ran up her spine as she thought about the damage it could do. She'd read that in Medieval times they were used for clan warfare and border fights with the English. She wondered if Craig MacIntyre was making a statement by having it handy as guests entered the house.

Her attention returned to Margaret MacIntyre—a delicate beauty—for a woman in her mid-seventies. Her thick silver-gray hair, cut medium length, perfectly framed her brilliant blue eyes, and flawless ivory skin. She dressed in a woolen suit similar to the one Darleen wore, except that it was light blue and had a silver pin in the shape of a Scottish thistle pinned to the lapel. When she spoke her voice was soft and lilting. "My husband is in the library, he would love the company. Please follow me."

The threesome followed her to a doorway that opened on the left side of the foyer.

Margaret peeked into the room. "Sorry to interrupt Darlin but ye have company."

They entered into a spacious darkened room. Two walls, lined ceiling-to-floor with mahogany bookshelves held an abundant array of antique books. On the fourth wall, gold and green-colored tapestries were cracked open about six inches allowing a bit of sunlight through what appeared to be a large picture window.

Near the window an over-sized desk strewn with papers and miscellaneous office items glowed with jewel-toned colors reflected from an expensive Tiffany lamp. Yvonne stifled a laugh when she noticed an old-fashioned black telephone that required dialing rather than button-pushing, just like the one her own father's desk.

Yvonne's gaze went to the sitting area with a large marble-topped coffee table centered between a worn couch and two comfortable arm chairs.

Craig MacIntyre gently placed his open book, pages down, spine up on the coffee table, he stood with ease considering his intimidating height and girth.

Cameron stepped forward, speaking loudly, "Mr. MacIntyre, ye may not remember me. I was a boyhood friend of yer son-in-law, Keith. Duncan Ross was my cousin and this is his younger sister, Fiona and her friend and travel agent, Yvonne Suarez." Cameron reached out his hand in greeting.

MacIntyre's eyes narrowed. He put up his hand to stop Cameron. "To what do I owe this visit?"

"Darlin, I'll have Heather bring us some tea." Margaret turned to Cameron. "Or, maybe ye'd prefer coffee?"

"Tea would be lovely." Cameron answered for the three of them.

Mrs. MacIntyre left the room, leaving her husband to fend for himself.

"Sit yerselves down then." MacIntyre growled.

Yvonne drew closer to one of the bookshelves squinting at the faded spines.

"Aah, Miss Suarez, ye take note of my library." He brightened at her interest. "Here, let me show ye." Ignoring Cameron and Fiona, he guided Yvonne to the far wall. "Scottish mythology and legends are my favorite treasures." He smiled broadly at Yvonne. She took in his twinkling eyes and slightly yellowed but straight teeth, his upper lip sported a salt and pepper mustache. She thought he must've been a heart-breaker in his day, he was quite handsome and fit, for his age.

The books all had mystical leanings. He had a set of four books called *Popular Tales of the West Highlands* by J.F. Campbell published in 1880. He pulled book one out for her to thumb through and she glanced at stories of folklore beginning with Celtic Mythology. Another by Campbell, the Celtic Dragon Myth told of Giants and Mermaids and Sidhe. There were two volumes of Carmina Gadelina by Alexander Carmichael which offered blessings, prayers and charms in Gaelic from the Western Highlands and several other books about fairies and folk-tales, clairvoyance and prophecies.

"What an interesting collection. Tell me, Mister MacIntyre, do you believe that some people can tell the future or have the second-sight?"

"Hm ... absolutely, I do. There are too many instances to scoff at."

"I'm inclined to agree with you."

"Here," He handed her a book called *The Folklore of the Scottish High-lands* by Anne Ross. "Take this book with ye, to read at yer leisure."

"Thank you. I'll return it to you before I leave."

"Are ye of Spanish descent?"

"Yes, why do you ask?"

"Do yer ancestors not believe in spirits?"

"That's an interesting question. I've never given it much thought. Being Catholic, we're discouraged to believe in such things."

"I see." MacIntyre nodded as if she'd given him the answer he sought. "Shall we join yer friends?" He led the way to the sitting area and waited for Yvonne to sit before taking his former seat.

"Now, to my original question—what brings ye to my home?"

Before anyone could speak, a buxom young woman, dressed in a white short-sleeved blouse tucked into a black skirt and wearing sturdy black shoes, carried in an ornate silver tray laden with teapot, and the accompaniments. She sat it on the coffee table and left. "Heather will return in a minute or two with some shortbread," commented Margaret.

After an awkward silence, Heather returned with a tray of cookies.

"Mister and Missus McIntyre, you have a lovely home." Fiona took a deep breath. "Thank you for taking time to speak with us." Fiona looked at Yvonne, her eyes pleading, indicating she should start the questioning.

Yvonne addressed her questions to MacIntyre. "What can you tell us about the last time you saw Duncan Ross, Fiona's older brother? You may recall—he worked for you and has not been seen since he left with his paycheck in 1965."

"I tellt the police everythin that happened that day. ... I paid him his wages, and he left."

"Can you tell us who else worked that day?"

"No. The police have the list. Ye'll need to ask them."

"You must remember something or someone," said Yvonne.

MacIntyre's eyes rolled upward a moment. "Aye, there was Darleen o'course and my Foreman Randy Ferguson, but that's all I can mind. Twere a busy time fer us."

Cameron picked up a shortbread cookie and took a bite. Crumbs spilled down his chin onto his shirt and pants. He reached for a napkin spilling crumbs onto the floor. He did his best to gather the remaining crumbs into the napkin. His movements interrupted the intense conversation. "Delicious shortbread Missus MacIntyre."

"Please, call me Margaret."

Yvonne reached for a cookie. "What about Darleen's husband, Keith. Was he working that day?"

"I dinnae ken—he may have come later." MacIntyre turned to his wife. "Margaret do ye mind Keith on that fateful day?"

"No, tis all a jumble in my mind." Margaret smiled sweetly at her husband.

Yvonne sighed, this felt much too civilized. So far, they were getting nowhere in this investigation. This whole family seemed to be stonewalling. They needed to go elsewhere.

Yvonne addressed another question to MacIntyre. "You mentioned your foreman. May we talk to him? Perhaps he'll remember something."

"No, Randy retired some years ago. Keith, my son-in-law, is the foreman now."

"Does Randy live nearby?"

"Och, aye, but I doubt he'll be much help."

Margaret reached for the plate of shortbread and held it up in front of Yvonne. "Please, take take another one, and ye, too, Fiona. We wouldn't want them to go to waste now would we?"

"Heavens, these are wonderful, Margaret." Fiona brushed some crumbs from her bosom.

Yvonne glanced at Cameron before saying politely, "We really mustn't take up so much of your time, Mister and Missus MacIntyre."

"Thanks for inviting us to take tea, Margaret. It was grand." Cameron rose from his seat.

"To be sure," said Fiona

"Your shortbread is delicious, Mrs. MacIntyre. Thanks so much for sharing them with us." Yvonne turned to face their host. "Sorry to have turned up unannounced Mr. MacIntyre. We thank you for taking the time to answer our questions ... and the loan of the book. I'll be sure to return it before I leave Peebles."

"Och, weel, not sure we were much help? But, we surely wish ye luck in yer quest to find Duncan. We often wondered why he'd run aff the way he did."

After leaving the house, Yvonne headed in the direction of the gift shop. "I'd like to pick up a few souvenirs from the Woolen Shop if you don't mind."

Cameron turned toward Fiona taking hold of her arm. "Not at all. Fiona and I will stroll around back. Mayhaps have a chat with my old pal, Keith." They walked off toward the rear of the outbuildings.

Yvonne returned to the gift shop. She purchased the "Nessie" toy for Christy, a lavender sweater for her Mom and a Black Watch tartan scarf for her Dad. Several customers milled around the shop looking for handmade wools. Yvonne waited in line to make her purchases.

There was no sign of Darleen. She wondered if she should wait a day or two before returning to question Keith. She'd want to question Darleen again, but first she needed to see the police report.

She found Fiona and Cameron chatting with a thin rugged looking man standing out in front of a large barn. She could hear sheep bleating in the background.

Cameron made introductions. "Aah, Keith, this is the young lassie we mentioned. Yvonne, this is Keith, Darleen's good man."

Yvonne extended her hand.

Keith ignored Yvonne's outstretched hand. "How d'ye do?" He took an exaggerated breath which puffed up his chest. "I cannae understand how come yer're wasting yer time lookin for Duncan. He'd o' showed up by now if he'd o' been able too." Keith turned his attention to include Fiona and Cameron. "We were good mukkers."

Yvonne smiled at Keith. "I hear they referred to you, Cameron, and Duncan, as The Three Musketeers. Don't you want to know what happened to him?" She glanced at Cameron to see if he supported her pushing the issue. Cameron nodded.

"For a long time I did. But, we finally had to put it behind us. Twas destroying our lives and we chust don't want to dredge it all up again."

"We understand, but it would help us greatly if you'd tell us what you remember about that day?"

Keith gave Yvonne a disgusted look and threw down the work gloves he'd been holding in his hands. "I guess yer're not goin to be satisfied until I talk to ye."

Cameron picked up Keith's gloves and handed them back to him. "I know ye're upset and justly so, but Fiona's come clear across the Atlantic to put this to right, and I ... feel guilty that I let down our best friend."

"Och, weel, I wouldn't want ye to feel guilty, now would I?" Keith tucked his glove in the back pocket of his dungarees. "Fine. I'd arrived to work that day, after Duncan had come and gone. I don't know any more than ye do. I know he'd been wantin to take Darleen away with him, and she was sobbin and upset that he was leavin her behind. I did my best to calm her, but she was distraught for a verra long time."

"When did you find out that he hadn't left for America after all?"

"The next day when Missus Ross came lookin for him. She was beside herself that he hadn't come home in time to fly away." Keith hesitated a moment. "After that the poliss came and questioned everybody at the mill."

"Was anyone angry or upset at Duncan?"

"No, everybody liked him. Well ... except ... Randy's son, Ullrick. He was a bully and jealous of Duncan, I think, because he had Darleen's favor."

"Do you think he may have had something to do with Duncan's disappearance?" Yvonne crossed her arms holding them across her middle.

"Like I tellt ye, I didn't arrive tae work till after Duncan left."

Yvonne uncrossed her arms and turned to Fiona. "Are there any other questions you'd like to ask Keith?"

"I don't know. Cameron? Can you think of any?" Fiona looked hopefully at Cameron.

"No. Sorry, I can't think o' anymore."

Cameron turned to Keith. "We'll be off then. Mayhaps we kin meet at the Bridge pub for a pint ... soon ... talk aboot the ol' days?"

"Mayhaps, if I have the time." Keith nodded good day to them and strode back to the shearing barn.

The silence in the car on the drive back to Cameron's house, spoke volumes. Fiona stared out the window with moist eyes. She sniffled, trying to hold back tears. When she spoke, her voice cracked. "We haven't learned a thing...what can we do now?"

"Cameron, what do you know about this retired foreman, Randy?" asked Yvonne.

"I remember him. He was tough to work for. Ruled with an iron fist. We mostly stayed out o' his way when we worked. I heard his son was sore disappointed when Keith was made foreman. Randy had trained Ullrick to take ower."

"Does his son still work for the MacIntyres?"

"Could be, why does it matter?"

"It probably doesn't, just curious. I think we should talk to Randy. Do you know his last name?"

"Yeah, it's Ferguson, we called him 'Froggie Fergie'—not to his face o'course."

Fiona turned in her seat to face Yvonne in the back. "Do you really think it will do any good to talk to him?"

Hoping to instill confidence in Fiona, Yvonne looked her directly in the eye. "It can't hurt. You never know, he might have the missing piece to the puzzle. The other thing I was thinking—we should check the Peebles newspaper archives—see if there were any articles written about Duncan's disappearance, the smallest detail could give us a lead to pursue."

"Thanks, Yvonne, for not letting me give up." Fiona sniffled again as she faced forward in her seat.

Cameron parked the car on the street in front of the house then grabbed hold of Fiona's hand in a comforting manner. "I'm sorry, Fiona that I weren't much help to ye and yer family in the past, but I'm here for ye now."

"Thank you, Cameron." Fiona sniffled.

"Och, weel. I guess we have our work cut out for us tomorrow." He rushed out and ran around to open their doors, giving a hand to help Fiona exit the car. "Lassies, shall we see what Kendra has fixed for supper?"

Chapter 8

*C*ameron declined to join the ladies on their tour of High Street and said he'd made other plans. "The bike'll be fine for me. Kendra will drive ye to town."

Kendra suggested they start their mini tour of High Street at the Tweeddale Museum and Art Gallery so that Yvonne would learn about local artisans and the cultural history of the area.

Standing in the art gallery, Yvonne found herself staring intensely at an oil painting of the nearby Stobo Castle, getting lost in her thoughts about all the different hats she wore and how she'd gotten better at keeping them all separate. Her ability to focus on a specific task had improved. She thought about what she wanted to accomplish on this trip—gather facts that would solve the disappearance of Duncan and gather facts that would give her an edge in selling Scotland. Donning her mom hat, she wondered what she could take home to Christy that would make up for leaving her with Gino. Then there was David, she'd need to spend more time with him when she returned home. Was she spreading herself too thin?

Fiona watched Yvonne study the picture. "I hear it's a very lovely health spa these days."

"What? Oh ... guess I was a bit distracted. Yes ... this ancient version of the castle is—well, it's hauntingly beautiful. But ... I must admit, my mind's been wandering and I've been thinking about your brother, too. We should visit the local newspaper as soon as we finish here. I think it's important that we see what, if any, news occurred around the time of Duncan's disappearance."

Fiona cocked her head sideways. "What makes you think that's so important?"

"I'm not sure. It's just a gut feeling—maybe there's more to the story than we could imagine."

"I see. I ... just don't want to hurt Kendra's feelings. She's very proud of Peebles and its history."

"Of course ... and, I wish to learn as much as possible about the area too."

Yvonne gave a slight nod to Fiona indicating that Kendra had come up behind her.

"Yvonne, look here." Kendra pointed to a wall plaque situated above a case filled with history papers. "Ye should read this."

Yvonne retrieved a small notebook and pen from her purse. Her interest picked up instantly thanks to Kendra's enthusiasm for her towns history and she read the plaque aloud. "The name, Peebles, derived from the Cumbric name Pebyll, an early form of Welsh, means a place where tents are pitched." Yvonne imagined Gaelic tribes settling temporarily along the River Tweed, fishing and hunting, then moving north or south along the river as the fresh game diminished. Yvonne jotted down a few notes to remind herself later what she learned.

Kendra pointed out that Peebles' origins as a market town and later the center of the woolen mill industry came as a result of communities springing up around the River Tweed, a necessary source of water.

Kendra led Yvonne and Fiona around the museum pointing out items of interest. Yvonne continued taking notes. While admiring a portrait of Scotland's King David I, pictured with a crown fitted tightly around his forehead, setting off his square face, brooding eyes and long mustache, Kendra told them that in 1152, during the

King's reign, Peebles became a Royal Burgh and for many centuries was visited by Royal Monarchies.

Kendra further explained, "It remained untouched by border skirmishes and internal political wars prevalent in other border towns until the late 1500s to mid-1600s when the English invaded the area, using it as neutral ground to bring other border towns under control."

Kendra took a breath and continued, "By the early 1700s, Peebles had entered its darkest period. Poverty and hunger became the norm. It wasn't until the Industrial Revolution slowly made its way into the culture that Peebles once again progressed to become the third largest town in the Scottish Borders.

"How in the world do you remember all of that?" Yvonne had stopped taking notes.

"It's easy because I've recited it so often. Ye see, I bring my at-risk students here to help them gain a sense of their history and heritage. So often they are drifting and don't feel a part of our culture."

The more Yvonne got to know Kendra, the more she was impressed by her intelligence and her dedication to the kids in her care.

At the end of Kendra's tour she brought their attention to the plasterwork friezes commissioned by renowned publisher, William Chambers who, in 1859, founded the Chambers Institution where the art and history museum was located today.

Yvonne, anxious to move on with the investigation, but careful to appreciate Kendra's efforts, said, "Thanks for guiding us through the museum, Kendra. It's so much nicer to hear the history from a local resident." Yvonne gave her a friendly hug.

"I'm ready for a sit-down," said Fiona

Yvonne and Kendra laughed at Fiona's abrupt comment. "Let's go to the News Agents office next. I'm sure they'll have an empty chair." Kendra held the exit door open for them.

A few minutes' walk later, they entered 72 High Street, the Peebleshire News Agents. The front office held two desks. One was empty. A name plate on the occupied desk indicated the editor's name, Alastair Connery.

Yvonne's heart sank. A small operation, she wondered if they had the facilities to keep newspapers from the sixties.

Alastair looked up from his desk. "May I help you?" He spoke with a perfect English accent.

Yvonne gave him a broad smile. "Are you by chance the owner as well as editor?"

"Heavens no. We are just a small cog in a large wheel. UK Media owns us. Why do you ask?"

"I wanted to be sure I was speaking to whomever's in charge. We are investigating a missing-person case from many years ago, and wondered if we could search through your news archives from that period. Would they be available here?"

Alastair glanced at Fiona and Kendra, standing next to Yvonne.

"Forgive me," said Yvonne, "My name is Yvonne Suarez, this is Fiona Batson—"

"And, this is Kendra Douglas," finished Alastair. "It's nice to see you again. How's Cameron? I haven't seen him for several months."

"Same as ever. Since he's retired he's been keeping busy with his fishing and hiking. Lately, he's thinking of taking up bee keeping. He does love his honey." Kendra laughed and rolled her eyes.

"I gather these ladies are friends of yours." His blond-gray eyebrows lifted, emphasizing the creases in his wide forehead.

"Alistair, this is Fiona, Cameron's cousin from across the pond. She was raised here in Peebles. Her brother, Duncan, went missing in the mid-sixties before her departure to North America, and she has returned to try to make sense of it. Yvonne, her travel agent and friend, has accompanied her to help search for the truth of what happened."

"Nice to meet you." He nodded at them. "It happens that we do keep our archives in the storage room through that door." He pointed to a door at the rear of the office. "Articles prior to the 1980's were once stored on microfilm, but we have since had them scanned into digital format. They are now computerized and consistently backed up with the latest methods." He stated this proudly.

"That's wonderful," said Yvonne, impressed.

"Yes. Yes." Glad that Yvonne knew about computers, Fiona bobbed her head up and down.

Yvonne asked, "Would you allow us to search articles around July 1965?"

"Give me a few minutes to boot up the computer and pull up the appropriate files, then I'll lead you back." He directed them to wait in chairs lining the wall near the front entrance.

Yvonne watched out the large window at the cars cruising by and pedestrians walking past. She was jarred from her feeling of being in another world, when her cell phone played its ring-tone. The caller ID said, "David." Her heart skipped a beat. "Hi! David, how are you?"

"I'm missing you, Yvonne..."

She could hear the sadness in his tone, and it thrilled her. "I miss you too."

"Are you having a good time? Are you learning anything about your friend's brother?"

"Yes to the first question, and not much to the second. We're at the local newspaper office waiting to read some news articles around the time of his disappearance."

"Sounds very professional. You sure are getting the knack of being a detective."

Yvonne blushed. "Now, you're just teasing me." She stifled a laugh.

"I assume you're not alone."

"I'm here with Fiona and her cousin-in-law, Kendra. We had a nice morning visiting the local museum. I wish you were here to share this with me, Peebles is beautiful. The whole country, from what I've seen so far, is like being in Renoir painting with brilliant green landscapes, glistening waters of the river Tweed, blue skies and castles. And, I absolutely loved Edinburgh and plan to go back for a tour of the castle."

"I hope to see it with you someday when you're not working. ... Call me when you're alone so we can talk privately." His voice took on a seductive tone.

Yvonne tried her best not to blush again. "Okay, David. I'll call you later."

"Love you, sweetheart."

She felt his warm smile zing through the cellular universe. "Me too." She clicked her phone closed.

Alistair brought in two straight-back chairs from the waiting area for Fiona and Kendra. Yvonne took the chair facing the computer screen. She flipped through articles from the week before Duncan's disappearance. A headline, dated two days before the Ross family were scheduled to leave for Chicago, caught her attention: *Peebles Woolen Mill Suspected of Dumping Chemical Waste.*

Reading through the article, she noted that the Woolen Mill was one of several under investigation of dumping chemicals into waterways with runoff leading to the River Tweed. She scanned for further articles but found none until she spotted a small byline about the disappearance of Duncan Ross. It was written about a week after his disappearance, citing similar facts to those Yvonne had already heard. It asked anyone who might have information about Duncan's whereabouts to come forward and call the local police station.

Yvonne continued looking at articles for several weeks after his disappearance and found no more about Duncan or the Woolen Mill. "I guess our next step is to revisit the police station—see if anyone—came forward with information." She turned to look at Fiona.

Fiona sat up straight, reminding Yvonne of the first day she'd seen her in the travel agency, except this time she had tears in her eyes. "Don't be discouraged, Fiona. After all, we learned something new today. We need to find out whatever became of the investigation into the Woolen Mill. Duncan may have known something that would put him in harm's way."

"Then again, maybe it doesn't have anything to do with him." Fiona dabbed at her tears with a tissue.

"If not, we'll learn that too."

Kendra helped Fiona up from the chair. "Let's finish our stroll along High Street and have afternoon tea at the Tontine Hotel. Ye'll love it, I promise."

Yvonne closed the file on the screen and they returned to the front office.

"We're finished, Mr. Connery. Thanks so much for your help." Yvonne extended her hand to Alastair.

"Please call me, Alastair. I hope you were able to find something helpful." He shook Yvonne's hand as he stood up to see them out. "I hope you'll remember to let me know if a story breaks surrounding your brother's disappearance, Fiona."

Flustered and confused as to how to respond, Fiona nodded her agreement.

The walk around High Street and the grand Georgian architecture of the Tontine hotel revived the ladies. Yvonne took a cursory look around at the stately surroundings. She made a few familiarization notes in her small journal, for future recommendation purposes.

The dark rose-colored walls of the dining room with crisp white ornate moldings around the doorways and windows had a soothing effect on Yvonne. "This is so elegant." She scanned the room, noting the beautiful brass and crystal chandeliers. They were welcomed by the Maitre d' who seated them near a window with a view of the Tweed Green and the river. The tables were dressed with white tablecloths, white china with gold embellishments and crystal water glasses. A crystal vase of fresh yellow flowers graced the center of the table.

"Welcome to Tontine Tea. Would ye ladies like to include a glass of champagne with yer tea today?" His serious no-nonsense demeanor went perfectly with his tall, slim, dark-haired good looks. Dressed in formal attire, he reminded Yvonne of the butler cliché in a murder mystery.

"That sounds lovely." Kendra spoke directly to the Maitre d', and then turned to her tablemates. "Fiona, Yvonne, this will be my treat."

"No, we couldn't." Yvonne spoke to the Maitre d', "Please, give the bill to me."

"Sorry, Madam, I must give the bill to the first person who asked for it. It's our policy."

"Good, that solves that problem." Kendra laughed. "God bless the policy."

"I will inform yer waiter to pour the champagne and serve tea. Thank ye once again for patronizing the Tontine." He smiled and walked hurriedly toward a row of waiting waiters. A few moments later champagne was being poured and tea sandwiches being served by an attentive waiter.

After enjoying the watercress and pimento tea sandwiches, scones with clotted cream, and petit fours, it was unanimously decided that they should return to Kendra's home and take a rest.

Later that evening, Kendra served a light supper and the foursome spent time rehashing what they had learned at the news agency and planning their next interviews.

The night came to an end when Cameron bid the ladies goodnight.

The small bedrooms that Yvonne and Fiona occupied belonged to their hosts' now grown son, Cameron Junior—Cammie for short and daughter Marni.

Marni's room, with faded, predominantly pink floral wall covering, felt warm and comfortable. Any girlish mementoes belonging to Marni had apparently been stored away. The room was furnished with a small bedside table holding a lamp, a dresser, a wardrobe, and a combination dressing table that doubled as a desk and a small chair.

Yvonne slipped off her shoes and made herself comfortable sitting up against the headboard, legs comfortably stretched out on the bed. "Let's see, it's eleven here—five hours ahead of Fort Lauderdale so it will be six there—David might be home from the office."

Yvonne grinned. I feel like a schoolgirl, she thought. can't believe how much I miss him. She picked up her cell phone from the night-table and pushed the key programmed with David's number.

He answered on the first ring. "Hello Darling. God, how I've missed you."

"I hope I didn't interrupt your dinner. Were you eating?"

"Of course not, I was waiting for your call." David lowered his voice. "I couldn't wait to let you know how I'm going to ravish you the next time I see you."

"Oh really? And how is that?" Yvonne blushed.

"Well first, I'm going to start by gently taking your luscious hair in my hands, breathing in your sexy scent, and bringing your face close to mine until our sweet lips meet. Then I'm going to kiss you like you've never been kissed before. ... Next, I'm going to brush you with soft sweet kisses ... slowly, all the way from your ears to your toes—"

"Please—stop. You're not even here, and I can't take it. I won't be able to concentrate on the investigation tomorrow if I'm thinking about our next time together. *Ay Dios mio!* You make me all sweaty and hot." Yvonne fanned herself with her hand.

"Do I now?" David laughed in a low sexy voice. "Okay, Sweetheart, tell me what's been going on."

Yvonne laughed at the corny tough-guy accent he'd switched too. "You always put me in a good mood, David. I love that about you ..."

"I hope that's not the only thing you love about me." David switched back to his sexy voice.

"*Ay, Ay, Ay!* ... Okay, David ... today we may have made a little progress. We found an article around the time of Duncan's disappearance that indicated Peebles Woolen Mill and some other businesses were being investigated for polluting the River Tweed. I found it strange, though, that there was only one article in a six-week period. I didn't read further out as time wouldn't allow, but it seemed like they may have dropped the investigation. I'm not sure why. I do plan to find out tomorrow when we talk again to the Peebles police." Still feeling a warm glow from David's talk of what he planned to do to her, Yvonne took a deep breath and waited for his response.

He was silent for a few seconds. "It sounds like you think Duncan might have stumbled onto something that may have put him in danger."

"It's a long shot, I know, but it was the first thing that popped into my mind. I'm learning to listen to my instincts. I think it's important if I'm gonna be any good at investigating this for Fiona. I've used these same instincts when researching hotels and tour operators. I've learned to read between the lines when something doesn't sound right in the descriptions. It's not so different, really."

"If your instincts are correct, this might become dangerous. ... Yvonne, maybe I should take some time off and join you. It might help to have a man along. Females traveling alone could be viewed as vulnerable, especially by criminals who are backed into a corner."

The concern in his voice didn't escape her. "That won't be necessary, David. We've had Cameron along on most of our queries, I'm sure we could get help if needed. ... I do appreciate the offer though. I don't want you to feel you need to rescue me all the time. I can handle myself."

"If you're sure—but promise me you'll ask for help if you need me. After all, a man who loves his woman should be available to help and protect her. I know it's not an easy concept for you, but think about it. I'd be devastated if something happened to you, and I wasn't there to help. Imagine how your daughter and parents would feel if they lost you ..."

"That's not fair. Now you're playing on my maternal guilt and emotions. That's the same thing Gino always did—still does—in fact. Listen, David, this is something I have to do, and I prefer to do it by myself. I thought you understood that I need to be strong and independent again. I need to do this for Christy's sake. She needs to grow up and learn she shouldn't take bullying from men or anyone. She needs to learn that she can ask for help when necessary, but she can make those decisions on her own."

"Okay. I give up. Have it your way. Just know that I'm here when and if you do need me." David took another second to think. "You must be tired. I should let you go."

"I am tired, but please don't be mad at me. ... I do wish you were here but only to share the good stuff. Maybe someday we can take a trip together just for fun."

David sighed. "Together, just for fun. I'll hold that thought. Goodnight then. I love you."

"Buenas noches, mi amor." Yvonne closed her phone and replaced it on her night-table. Too wound up to sleep, she pulled a thin yoga mat from her suitcase and spread it on the floor. Standing at one end of the mat in mountain pose, she took several deep breaths. Then she bent her knees, lowering herself into her favorite relaxing, child pose. She stayed there for ten long breaths, then sat up and assumed a cross-legged meditation pose, breathing in positive energy and exhaling negative energy and saying affirmations, "Christy will feel my love flowing to her from Scotland. We will discover what happened to Duncan. Our trip will be safe and successful." She repeated these affirmations five times, said, "Namaste," and climbed into bed sleeping soundly through the night.

Chapter 9
PEEBLES POLICE STATION
SATURDAY, JUNE 6TH

Cameron drove Yvonne and Fiona to Peebles Police station at ten the next morning. Once again, Rhona Munro greeted them, this time with a bright smile. "Good maarnin. I've spoken to Inspector Gordon, and he has agreed to speak with ye. He will have the files concerning the Duncan Ross missing person's case available to refer to in answerin yer questions. I'll check with him to see if he has time to see ye now."

Rhona dialed the inspector's extension. "Sir, I have Fiona Ross and her cousin and her travel agent here to see ye. ... Yes sir, I'll send them right back."

She directed them down a long hallway to the last door on the right. Cameron held the door open while the ladies entered.

Seated behind a large desk was a thick-set man with a broad face and large dark eyes. Inspector Gordon rose and directed the ladies to seats in front of the desk and a third chair against the wall for Cameron. Yvonne studied the inspector's face. His broad nose looked like it had been on the losing end of several fist-fights. She wondered who'd have the nerve to tackle with him.

"Are ye Fiona Ross?"

"Yes, it's Fiona Batson now." Uncomfortable and afraid that she'd have to justify once again why it had taken her so long to return to find Duncan, Fiona glanced nervously at Yvonne.

"I understand ye're here to find out what happened to yer brother all those years ago. The case is still open since we have never found a trace of him. O'course the longer a case is open the colder it becomes."

Fiona steered the focus elsewhere. "This is my cousin, Cameron." She turned and gestured at Cameron, then to Yvonne. "And, this is my friend and travel agent, Yvonne Suarez. She would like to ask you some questions about my brother's case."

"Is that right?" Inspector Gordon turned his attention to Yvonne.

She felt his penetrating stare bore right through her. "Y-yes, sir." Yvonne took a breath to gain composure. She wasn't about to let his overbearing presence intimidate her. "We read an article written around the time of Duncan's disappearance at the Peebles News Agents yesterday, and it raised some questions."

"Raised some questions, did it?" The habit of repeating questions back to interviewers was his well-practiced way of clarifying what others really meant and ferreting out fakers and liars.

Yvonne held his gaze. "The article about his disappearance asked for anyone who might have information to come forward and notify the police. We wondered if you received any tips at all." Yvonne glanced at Fiona who once again fiercely clutched her handbag.

Inspector Gordon opened the case folder and quickly scanned through many pages. "I see that we received several tips of sightings of a young boy on his bike, heading in various directions. We followed up each lead, but nothing came of them." He continued reading. "Hmm."

"What?" All three spoke simultaneously.

"We received an anonymous phone call from someone claiming to know where his body was buried, but he hung up before we could put a trace on the address. To my knowledge, he never called back."

"Does it say who took the call?"

"I don't see what difference it makes now." Inspector Gordon's eyes narrowed to tiny slits. "He looked back at the note in the folder. "It was young PC Innes Munro, a newly hired constable at the time. He didn't have the experience to keep folks yammerin on the tele yet—went on to become one of our best Chief Constables, though."

"Thank you, Inspector. Was there anything else that might help us find a clue to what happened to Duncan? Did the police have any theories?"

"Only that he may have gone off on an adventure to Australia. His friends said he'd always been keen on the idea. Darleen MacIntyre and his mum, Mairi, thought otherwise.

"Sadly, there was no trace o' him or his bike anywhere. Our theory was that had he come to foul play—we would o' at least found his bike somewhere unless he'd left the area."

Fiona sniffled, holding back tears.

Yvonne glanced sympathetically at Fiona then back at the inspector. "What friends thought he'd gone to Australia?"

The inspector checked the file again. "Says here, we got the same story from Keith Turner and Ullrick Ferguson." He checked further. "Cameron here told us that he'd been unhappy about leaving Darleen, but he planned to make his way in America and come back for her."

"That is true. We yammered aboot it chust the day before," Cameron added.

Yvonne shifted, sitting up straighter on her chair then leaned toward the inspector. "We noticed that around the time Duncan disappeared there was an investigation of the Peebles Woolen Mill and other companies. They were suspected of dumping chemical detergents into waterways that led to the River Tweed. Did anything ever come of that investigation?"

"Grrr. What does that have to do with this case?" Inspector Gordon laid the file down and put fisted hands heavily on the desk.

"We're not sure it has anything to do with it, but it struck me as odd that this happened around the same time, and I wondered if Duncan may have seen or heard something that put him in jeopardy."

Inspector Gordon's eyes widened in surprise. He took a quick look through the file. "I wonder why no one else thought of that?"

Yvonne sat back to an upright position. "Maybe they were too close to see the whole picture. I'm sure with everyone so upset and busy trying to find Duncan, the other activities may have faded into the background."

"I've often wished we had a full-time constable to work cold-cases for that reason. I've heard that objectivity and newer technologies often solve the old crimes." He looked at each of them in turn. "I'm afraid I must ask ye to leave now, but I will look into the other investigation and let ye know if something connects the two." He stood up from the desk.

Cameron reached to shake hands with the inspector before leaving. "Thanks for yer time, Inspector."

Yvonne and Fiona thanked him as well.

On their way out they saw a man, hands pulled behind his back and handcuffed. They watched the police constable push him hard toward a room that had Booking on the door, muttering, "What kind of monster murders his own pa?"

The prisoner cried. "I didn't do it. Ye can't think I'd do such a thing."

"Good, God!" Cameron grabbed a nearby chair to steady himself.

"What is it? Are you alright?" Yvonne went to Cameron and nudged him to take a seat.

Fiona rallied around his other side.

Cameron lowered his wobbly legs and sat. "That was Ullrick Ferguson, Randy's son."

"Oh no ... Does that mean ... ?" The gravity of what he'd said sent shivers up Yvonne's spine. "W-we were going to question Randy Ferguson, today."

Cameron's upper lip grew moist, the blood drained from his face. "I have not mentioned it yet ... but ... I went round to see

Randy yesterday. I thought it best not to subject ye lassies to his temper."

"*Ay Dios mio*. ... W-what did he say?"

"He said he knew nothin aboot nothin. He said we should stop poking around into what happened, or there could be consequences. I felt certain, because he threatened us, that he was hidin somethin—that he *knew* somethin." Cameron took a deep breath. "I left before we came to blows. Maybe I should tell Inspector Gordon what I know."

"No!" Fiona whispered her next thoughts, "What if they think you had something to do with it? You might have been the last person to see him alive."

"That's exactly why I must tell him."

"Did anyone see you there? If not, what good will it do to get involved? After all they've already caught the son."

"Yes, but what if he didn't do it, like he said?" Cameron turned and took hold of Fiona's hand. "Don't worry, lassie, it will be all right. I'm not going to stand by and do nothing ... like I did when Duncan went missing."

"For what it's worth, I agree with Cameron. If he doesn't tell them, and they find out later that he was there, it will throw suspicion on him. It's best to get it over with now while we're here." Yvonne glanced over at Rhona to see if she could overhear their conversation. She appeared to be engrossed in paperwork. "I'll go ask if we can see the inspector again. I'll ask her to let him know it's urgent." She walked over to speak with Rhona and waited while she relayed the message to Inspector Gordon.

"Ye can go on back. Ye know the way." Rhona turned back to her paperwork.

Cameron explained to Inspector Gordon why he'd gone to speak with Randy. And, how he'd been shocked when he'd seen how poorly Randy had aged, and even though he seemed frail by comparison to the burly foreman from Cameron's youth, he talked as mean as ever. Cameron assured the inspector that Randy had been alive when he left him around 11:30 the previous morning. "Ye ought to know, Inspector, that he was rantin and ravin about how somethin bad might happen if we didn't stop askin questions. I chust thought he'd cool down and I'd stop by again another day. I was angry but—"

"Are ye sure ye didn't get so angry ye'd picked up a nearby hammer and beat him with it?" Inspector Gordon's deep voice boomed throughout the room as he looked Cameron in the eye.

"Yes, I'm sure. If I'd o' kilt him, would I be here tellin ye I was there? No one saw me there, and I saw no one." Cameron stood up and stared back at the inspector. "We'll leave ye to yer investigatin now. It seems ye already caught the culprit as they've arrested his son, Ullrick. Everyone knows there was bad blood between those two." Cameron turned to leave, and Yvonne and Fiona followed.

Cameron stopped at Forsyths Butchers and Bakers to purchase a traditional beef and onion pie to take home for lunch so Kendra could join them while they discussed what they should do next.

Seated at the kitchen table, they ate pie accompanied by a salad and light ale and mulled over what had happened that morning.

"I wonder why Ullrick would kill his own father?" Kendra looked toward Cameron for an answer.

Cameron shook his head. "I have no idea. It does not make any sense."

"If what Inspector Gordon hinted at is true, Randy Ferguson's been beaten to death with his own hammer. How gruesome." Yvonne shivered.

Kendra took a drink of her ale. "An unusual occurrence in our town."

Fiona shrugged her shoulders, as if shaking off the horrible crime. "Who should we question next?" She smashed the last of her pie with her fork and mixed it with the gravy.

"What aboot goin back to Keith? Ah'd like to know why he thought Duncan had gone to Australia. Somethin don't feel right aboot that." Cameron chomped on a bite of pie.

"It's too bad we can't talk to Ullrick too...I wonder?" Yvonne's eyes shot upward as she thought it out.

"I doubt they'd let us in to see him. Nae, let's get to Keith and maybe Darlene again." Cameron finished off his last bit of ale.

Yvonne reminded herself that she'd be touring Edinburgh Castle tomorrow. "Let's go this afternoon." She finished her meat pie and ale and placed her napkin on the table.

They found Keith in one of the outbuildings washing white wool the old-fashioned way by hand in a large tub with soapy detergent and a rake. They had not expected a crowd but learned it was visitor's day. They listened to him sing a stanza from an old worksong to the visitors:

If it wasna for the weavers, what would ye do?
Ye wouldna hae yer cloth that's made o woo.
Ye wouldna hae yer cloak neither black nor blue
If it wasna for the wark o the weavers!

Keith then explained the washing process. "Thae wool hae been previously encased in nylon nettin an soaked in covered containers for two weeks in rain water to loosen the dirt an kill the insects. Afterward it's moved to this washin tub, and then on to th' rinsin tubs." He took a breath. "In thae olden days weavers didna wash the wool but only used the dye and urine to color and wash at th' same time."

"I would imagine the wool would have been smelly and scratchy then." Yvonne whispered to Fiona.

Fiona nodded her agreement.

They watched and waited until the wool was passed along to another tub where a different worker raked it through a rinse cycle. The wool passed along two more rinse cycles.

The crowd followed along to the drying room, but Yvonne, Fiona and Cameron stayed behind to speak with Keith.

It had been decided that Cameron should ask the questions. "Keith, we have a few more questions to ask ye aboot Duncan."

"Och! What is it now? Don't ye have nothin better to do than interrupt my wark day?"

"The chief inspector told us that ye told them ye thought Duncan had lit off to Australia. Where'd ye get that idea? He never said anythin like that to me."

"Well, he said so to me." Keith placed his rake against a nearby wall and pulled a plug in the tub to allow the dirty water to drain.

"When did he tellt ye that? Twas the same story Ullrick tellt the police constables. Duncan wouldn't have confided in Ullrick. Ye ken they didn't abide each other."

"I dinna ken. Maybe he overheard Duncan tellin me."

The smell of the dirty wool water caused Yvonne to sneeze.

"God bless ye," said Keith. "Ye should move outta here. It's nae good to breath this air too long if ye have sensitive noses."

Cameron returned to his questioning. "Exactly what did Duncan tell ye? Did he say he wished to go someday, or he were goin for sure."

Keith walked them back outside through the front entrance. "Och, he said he wished to gae there someday. Ah tellt the constables that."

"What else did ye tellt the constables?"

"There was nothin else to tell, I didna see Duncan that day. The constables didna take our word for it, they searched all thae buildings and the land lookin for Duncan and his bike. They even brought hounds, but got no scent of him on the MacIntyre land."

"Thank ye, Keith, for speakin with us. We'll not trouble ye any further."

They left him looking after them.

"We should speak to Darleen again," said Yvonne.

"What good will it do?" Fiona's temper flared. "We're getting nowhere."

"I know it seems that way," soothed Yvonne. "But, each time we talk to someone we learn a little more. Now we know that the police actually investigated and looked for Duncan on the property."

"What good does it do us to know that?" Fiona stopped where she was and waited for Yvonne to answer.

"Well, now we know that he may have been elsewhere when he went missing, or ... someone went to a lot of trouble to hide his body and bike."

Fiona was stricken when Yvonne said this. "That means you think he's dead for sure?"

"I'm sorry, Fiona, but, don't you think after all these years, if he were alive, he would have contacted you or even Darleen? From everything I've heard, he really loved her."

Fiona hung her head. "I know. I've just not wanted to face it." Fiona lifted her head and punched the air. "This doesn't change my mind. I want to know what happened to my brother, by God."

"I truly believe that if we keep pushing—keep asking questions— we'll get to the truth." Yvonne gave Fiona a confident smile.

Cameron brought them back to the task at hand. "Shall we speak with Darleen now, Lassies?"

Yvonne and Fiona agreed it would be best to get the interview over with.

The gift shop was crowded with tourists. They weaved their way through to the back office door, and Yvonne knocked on it. A few moments later it opened, and Darleen stared with mouth open. "Back again, are ye?"

"May we come in? We have few more questions to ask you about Duncan." Yvonne gave Darleen a friendly smile, hoping she'd get a better response.

"Okay, but be quick. I have wark to do."

The three walked in. Darleen left them standing without offering chairs. "What do ye want to know this time?"

"Had Duncan ever spoken to you about wanting to go to Australia?" asked Yvonne.

"No, but I heard he said so to Keith."

"Did you believe it?"

"That's an odd thin to ask." Darleen gave Yvonne a shocked look.

"Didn't you think it was odd that he told Keith about it and not you?"

Darleen frowned and pursed her lips together, thinking. "Well, yes, maybe I did, a little bit."

"We learned from your dad that Randy Ferguson was here that day. Do you know if his son, Ullrick, was here too?" Yvonne watched her stiffen up at this question.

"I don't remember. What would that have to do with anythin?"

"Have you heard about Ullrick being arrested for killing his father?" Yvonne shot this question at Darleen fast to see her reaction.

Darleen looked like she'd been slapped in the face. "N-No. ... It's awful. I can't believe he'd do such a thin. Ullrick has a temper, but he always respected his father, or maybe twas he feared him. I always felt that he was under the Cailleach's curse too. Nothin ever seemed to go right for him."

"What is this K-kay-lex curse you speak of?" Yvonne's curiosity piqued, maybe she should read the book she borrowed from Darleen's father tonight.

"Cailleach's an old Celtic Goddess—old as time itself. She takes on many forms—that of an old crone, a winter goddess, a protector of harvests. To have the Cailleach's curse is to have bad luck all yer life. Somehow ye have angered Cailleach, and she can be verra vengeful. She has cursed me my whole life—losin things I love most and cursing me with the second-sight, so I always get bad feelins and see bad thins before they happen." Darleen shook her head in sorrow.

Thinking of taking advantage of her second-sight, if indeed she really had such a thing, Yvonne asked, "Do you think it unusual that Randy Ferguson's murder happened now, when we are investigating Duncan's disappearance? What do your senses tell you about that?"

"I've had a bad feelin ever since I heard Fiona was returnin to Peebles. But I've had no clear visions. Sometimes when I'm too close to a situation, I don't see visions clearly."

Yvonne felt that Darleen responded honestly. She heard Fiona sigh, standing next to her.

"Darlene, we've heard that Duncan didn't get along with Ullrick. Can you think of any reason why he might have wanted Duncan out of the way?"

Darlene thought for a minute. "N-no, only that ... he may have been jealous of him. I think he may have had a crush on me."

"It seems you had a lot of admirers back then." Yvonne spoke softly.

"Och, ye ken, I was the boss's daughter." Darleen shrugged. "I didn't take it seriously, then or now."

That night, instead of pulling out *The Folklore of the Scottish Highlands* as she intended, Yvonne lay in bed looking up at the ceiling thinking about how Christy would love this little room. She wondered, was is it too late to call her? Gino will probably tell me she's already in bed. Oh, what the heck, at least I can leave a message for her. She pushed Gino's programmed number and hit the send button of her cell phone.

"Hello." Gino's curt answer didn't surprise Yvonne.

"Hi, Gino. I'd like to speak with Christy. I'll only take a minute. I just want to tell her goodnight." Yvonne spoke in a pleasant but firm voice, not wanting to sound desperate, knowing he'd take full advantage to make her feel worse.

"Hold on. Christy, it's your mom. Be quick, it's past your bedtime."

"Yes, Daddy." Yvonne overheard her say. "Hi Mommy. I miss you." Christy sniffled.

"Are you all right, Sweetheart? Is something wrong?"

"No, Mommy."

"I miss you, too. It won't be long now. I should be home in less than a week."

"Good, Mommy. Are you having fun?"

"Yes. One day I'm going to bring you to Scotland. You'll love it. There are lots of castles here. It will be like visiting in a fairytale."

Christy giggled.

"Time to hang up," said Gino.

Yvonne heard him in the background. "I love you, *mi Chica Dulce*. Sweet dreams..."

"I love you, too, Mommy." The phone clicked off.

Yvonne smiled and felt blessed to have such a beautiful daughter in her life. Torn between staying to solve the mystery and wanting to get home to Christy, Yvonne shoved her guilty feelings to the back of her mind.

Glancing around the room, her eyes came to rest on the bedside table where *The Folklore of the Scottish Highlands* caught her interest. She picked it up, moved to a chair by the window, and began reading. Tales of second-sight, prophetic seers, witches casting evil eyes, fairies, and ghosts, and myths about scary creatures like the Banshee had all been handed down through the ages by word of mouth or ballads. According to the book, these beliefs were held mostly by the Gaelic society of the Scottish Highlands and never spoken of in front of outsiders.

Yvonne woke with a start when the book dropped out of her hands. She dragged herself to bed, climbed under the covers and fell immediately to sleep.

She ran frantically through a stark windy meadow, a dismal cloudy sky pressed down on her from above. Jagged blue-gray mountains towered in the distance. She needed to get to the other side of those mountains to find something important. But, what? She couldn't remember. She ran, tripping on uneven ground, rocks and twigs, her eyes fixed upward toward her goal. Suddenly she fell headlong into a dank hole. She pushed herself up with her hands against the earth—she felt hard cylindrical rocks. She spit rotten earth from her mouth and looked at the ground beneath her. A dirty skull with large eye sockets stared back at her, the hard cylinders under her hands—the arm bones of a skeleton.

Yvonne's screaming woke the household. Fiona was the first to reach her, followed by Cameron and Kendra.

Chapter 10
EDINBURGH CASTLE
SUNDAY, JUNE 7TH

"Good mornin, Yvonne." Kendra had stepped into the kitchen from the back door with a gloved hand surrounding a bouquet of thorny pink and red roses.

"Good morning, Kendra." Yvonne, seated at the kitchen table, took a sip of coffee and waited while Kendra clipped the rose stems under running water and placed them in a round crystal vase.

Kendra placed the rose arrangement in the center of the kitchen table and smiled at Yvonne. "Now we can have a civilized breakfast. What can I make for ye? Eggs? Bangers? Oatmeal perhaps?"

Yvonne laughed. "You're going to spoil me. I'm not used to being waited on. Shall we wait and see what the others want to eat? Besides, I want to apologize to everyone for waking them in the middle of the night. I feel so foolish, screaming over a nightmare, of all things."

"Don't be silly. Ye're in strange surroundings away from home and family and helping Fiona find out what happened to her brother. It's no wonder ye had a nightmare." Kendra patted Yvonne's arm. "Cameron is gone out already, and I'm afraid I must leave soon. We're meeting with our Beltane Festival Committees. Cameron is on the Concert committee, and I am on the Fancy Dress Parade Committee. Ye and Fiona will have the day to yerselves, though I will eat breakfast with ye." Kendra poured herself a cup of coffee, sat down at the table across from Yvonne, took a deep breath, and inhaled the scent of the fresh cut roses.

"Do you have any boxed cereal or bread for toast? Either would be fine with me. I'm sure Fiona won't mind doing the same. In the meantime, do you have a few minutes to tell me about the Beltane Festival?"

Kendra leaned back comfortably in her chair. "The Beltane Festival is our biggest celebration each year. It's an old Gaelic tradition celebrated for thousands of years to welcome summer. This year it begins Sunday, June 20th, and ends the following Saturday. The weeklong festivities culminate in the crowning of the Beltane Queen and watching her procession march through town." Kendra got up and grabbed a two-sided flyer from a stack of papers sitting on a sideboard near the kitchen entryway. She handed it to Yvonne. "Here's the schedule of events."

Yvonne read through the flyer. "Gee, I wish we were going to be here for this. It sounds wonderful."

"Ye're welcome here anytime. Feel free to come back for it if ye wish."

Fiona strode into the kitchen, smelling of fresh soap from a shower, casually dressed for the day. "Good morning. Mmm...that coffee sure smells good."

"Help yerself, Fiona. The cups are in that cabinet above the toaster." Kendra got up from the table. "Now, I'm in the mood for eggs and bangers. Will ye ladies join me?"

"What can we do to help," asked Yvonne.

"Not a thing. Just keep me company while I cook." Kendra repeated her plan to work with the Fancy Dress Committee to Fiona while removing food from the fridge.

Yvonne glanced casually at the festival flyer, avoiding a direct look at Fiona. "I ... thought I might tour Edinburgh Castle today. Would ye like to go with me, Fiona?"

"Are you sure? Shouldn't we keep investigating?"

"A change of focus will allow me to clear my head, so I can get a fresh perspective on all we've learned so far. I need to familiarize myself with the Castle at some point, anyway." Yvonne watched Fiona's reaction.

"I guess I can understand that..." Fiona looked at Kendra.

Kendra's eyes narrowed, then widened. "I have an idea, why don't ye come with me today, Fiona. Our daughter Marni will be at the committee meeting. It will be a chance for ye to get to know her. I intend to invite Marni and her family and Cammie for dinner tonight— thought ye'd like to get to know yer extended cousins."

"Sure. I'd enjoy meeting Marni and helping with Beltane. It's been many years since I've had that pleasure. The last time I attended a festival, all the girls in our class dressed in white, and we marched with the Beltane Queen in the Coronation Parade." Fiona grinned.

Yvonne tried to imagine the matronly Fiona as a young girl.

Kendra changed her focus to Yvonne. "Ye should call my friend, Linda McLaren. She's a travel counselor and would be happy to book a tour to Edinburgh Castle for ye. Ye'll be back in time for dinner. It shouldn't take more than a few hours to tour the castle." Kendra smiled at Yvonne and Fiona, satisfied the day's planned activities had worked out to everyone's liking.

Kendra finished cooking the eggs and bangers while toasting the bread. "Yvonne, I'll drop ye at the Peebles Travel agency on my way to our meeting."

Yvonne and Fiona helped out by setting the table.

Linda McLaren, pleasant and efficient, booked Yvonne on a mid-morning Castle tour departing at 9:30. The tour bus would arrive at the Castle entrance by 10:00 and the tour would last four hours. She'd be back in plenty of time to dine with the Douglas family.

Yvonne made friends with a woman seated next to her on the bus. The woman called Olivia, in her mid-forties, had been born in Peebles but had grown up in Australia. She had always wanted to make a return visit to Scotland to learn about her family and ancestors. She'd confided that she couldn't come to Scotland without visiting the ever popular Edinburgh Castle.

When the small Peebles group arrived at the Castle car park, departing the bus they were greeted by Bagpipers playing *Scotland the Brave* from the Gatehouse Terrace. The bus driver escorted the tourists to the ticket office where he gave the manifest to the clerk. The clerk called the next available tour guide to come forward to escort them on their tour. She introduced herself as Mrs. Brodie.

Yvonne took her notebook and pen from her purse. She took a deep breath, breathing in fresh seventy degree air and thought to herself, just think, no clients to coddle, no one to look after, and no one to please but myself for four whole hours. Can't remember how long it's been since I've been totally on my own. A wide smile formed on her face. Her eyes twinkled with excitement.

Entering the castle, they made their way along cobblestone walkways that linked huge stone buildings, surrounded by castle walls, all winding around within a circle atop the hill.

They first stopped to view the One O'Clock Gun fired every day since 1861 except on Sundays, Good Friday and Christmas. Yvonne, thankful it was Sunday, didn't mind not having to delay her touring to listen to the pomp and circumstance of the noisy gun being fired.

"The firing of the gun is a tradition remaining from the days when it was a time signal for ships in the Firth of Forth and the port of Leith," The full-figured Mrs. Brodie said while leading them toward the National War Museum.

Yvonne, walking next to Mrs. Brodie, couldn't help but notice the snug fitting uniform and the way the pockets on her chest popped out, drawing attention to her top-heavy build. She had a momentary vision of what would happen if Mrs. Brodie tripped or stumbled. '*Ay Dios mio*. What a horror!'

Mrs. Brodie continued her spiel, "We will take a quick tour of some of the highlights of the Museum. There are several museums within Edinburgh Castle, and ye may wish to come back on a self-guided tour when ye can spend more time on yer own."

Yvonne switched her focus to the people walking with headsets on their ears, presumably listening to audio tour information.

Inside the War Museum, Yvonne thought of David as the tour guide pointed out personal mementoes, photographs and military objects revealing the history of Scots at war over a four-hundred-year time span. She inhaled the wonderful smell of oldness that reeked within the museum and wondered what David would think.

Exiting the museum, the guide mentioned, "This building was originally an ordnance storehouse, built in 1755." From there she moved them swiftly to the Regimental Museum of the Royal Scots Dragoon Guard, an important collection illustrating the history of Scotland's only cavalry regiment and its English and Scottish antecedents dating back to 1678. At the smaller Royal Scots Regimental Museum, the guide waited outside while the group browsed for ten minutes at their leisure, looking at the various medals and traditional red-coat uniforms of the world-famous regiment.

At noon they listened to a Bagpiper play an array of war tunes like *The Foggy Dew* and *Follow My Highland Soldier.* Then, they stopped in the Queen Anne café for a half-hour lunch break. From there the tour proceeded to the Scottish National War Memorial so they could view the honor rolls, listing names of those who'd died in the First and Second World Wars. Next, they viewed the Stone of Destiny used in coronations for centuries. The enigmatic Stone was taken from Scotland to England by Edward I in 1296 and finally returned to Scotland in 1996.

Yvonne entered The Royal Palace, the home of Scotland's Royalty for centuries, the place where Mary Queen of Scots gave birth to James VI in 1566. Hearing once again of Mary Queen of Scots, Yvonne gulped and placed her hand protectively on her neck.

Moving on, she stared in awe at the ornate furniture and the large framed portraits of past kings and queens, as well as the tapestries that adorned the walls. Yvonne was most impressed with the Royal Dining Room covered in various shades of green, with gorgeous intricate moldings, columns, window frames, and draperies. The chandeliers, the long eighteen-person mahogany table and chairs, the china, crystal and silver candle sconces were all most elegant. She imagined eating in style, rubbing elbows with royalty.

At two o'clock they listened to a short play; Mary Queen of Scots, recently returned from France, discussed plans with Lord Erskine about her plans for ruling Scotland. Watching Scottish history realistically portrayed piqued Yvonne's interest in her own English and Spanish ancestors. She wondered about David's ancestors. She could easily imagine him wearing a kilt. This thought made her giggle.

It hardly seemed that four hours had gone by when the small group returned to the bus. Yvonne had thoroughly enjoyed her day away from Peebles. She studied the copious notes that she had written while on the tour, cementing them in her brain for future use. She'd refer to them again the next time she had a client wanting to book a trip to Scotland. She tucked her notebook in her large purse along with a book she had picked up in the gift shop to read to Christy.

It was a sweet story about a Skye terrier named Greyfriars Bobby who became famous in the 1800s for sleeping every night for fourteen years on the grave of his master who had died of tuberculosis. During the day Bobby made friends of children from a local orphanage, and the local restaurant owners who fed him scraps of food, but every night, no matter how cold or rainy, he'd return to sleep on his master's grave. In 1867 he was at risk of being destroyed because he didn't have an owner, so the Lord Provost of Edinburgh, who also happened to be the director of the Scottish Society for the Prevention of Cruelty to Animals, bought Bobby a license and made him the responsibility of the town council. Bobby died in 1872 but couldn't be buried inside the cemetery because it was consecrated ground, so he was buried just inside the Greyfriars Kirkyard, the nearest he could get to his master, John Gray's grave. A year later, Lady Burdett-Coutts commemorated Greyfriars Bobby by endowing a statue atop a fountain at the southern edge of George IV Bridge. To this day tourists and locals alike honor his memory by visiting his statue. Yvonne's eye moistened. Humans could learn a lot from that dog, she thought.

PEEBLES

Later they gathered around the old-world mahogany dining table at the Douglas home, Cameron seated at one end of the table and Kendra at the other. Yvonne and Fiona sat with Cammie on their side, and across from them sat Marni, her husband Graham, and their daughter, Caitlin. Caitlin, a talkative seven-year-old, entertained everyone with lively stories about school and her birthday present, pup, Laddie.

During a lull in the conversation, Caitlin, in her sweet childish voice, asked the question her parents had purposely avoided, "Excuse me, Fiona." She took a breath. "Have ye found Cousin Duncan yet? Mommy says he's been lost for a very long time, and don't ye think it's time we found him?"

Silence around the table lasted a moment. "No, Caitlin, sweetheart, we haven't found him yet, but we are working on it." Fiona's tone held a note of regret.

"Can I help? Mommy says I'm good at finding things." The adults stifled their laughter.

Marni answered her daughter, "Sweetheart, finding yer cousin, Duncan, is for grownups, but we appreciate yer willingness to help."

"Yes we do," mumbled Fiona and several others at the table, seconding their appreciation.

In spite of the fact that Yvonne had thoroughly enjoyed the evening and getting to know Cameron and Kendra's family, she felt uncomfortable about the fact that she hadn't made much progress toward resolving Duncan's disappearance. That night as she sat in Marni's old bedroom, she reached for her journal and made a list of what they'd learned so far. This gave her an idea of whom she should interview next.

Chapter 11
MONDAY, JUNE 8TH

"If nobody minds, I'd like to strike out on my own today." Yvonne finished off the last of her coffee and rinsed out her cup, placing it in the sink.

"Where are you going?" asked Fiona.

Everyone focused their attention on Yvonne.

"I'm going to start by returning Craig MacIntyre's book, and while I'm there I'll offer condolences about his foreman, Randy's death. If I can do so without angering him, I'll ask again about Randy, the day Duncan went missing and about the chemicals investigation."

"Are you sure you'll be okay by yourself? I could wait in the car." Fiona's forehead creased.

"Don't worry, I'll be fine. One person asking questions will be less intimidating—I think. I hope to learn more being on my own. If anything comes up I'll let you know."

Cameron piped in, "How will ye get about? Would ye like to take my car?"

"No thanks. I don't want to leave you without a car. I'll call Linda at the travel agency and ask her to hire a car and driver for the day."

"Sounds like ye're all set then." Cameron nodded to Yvonne, excused himself and left to putter in the gardening shed.

Yvonne turned to Kendra. "Can I help with cleanup before I leave?"

Kendra swallowed the last of her toast and wiped the corners of her mouth on her napkin. "Don't be silly, be on yer way. I'll clean up."

Kendra directed her attention to Fiona. "Would ye like to tag along while I do some shopping today? I'd like to drive over to the Princess Mall in Edinburgh. I'm searching for a white dress for my little princess, Caitlin. We can make a day of it and have lunch. Maybe ye'll find some nice things to take back to yer grandchildren."

A wide smile spread across Fiona's face at that. It was the first real smile Yvonne had seen on Fiona since they'd arrived. Perhaps shopping for her beloved grandchildren would help lift her spirits.

When Yvonne knocked on the huge wood door at the MacIntyres it was Margaret who answered the door, again. "Please come in." Margaret ushered her into the foyer.

"Forgive me for stopping by unannounced, but I wondered if Mr. MacIntyre might have a few minutes to speak with me, and I wanted to return his book."

"I'm sure he'd love to see ye. Go on. Ye'll find him in the library."

"Thank you." As Yvonne turned to head toward the library, Margaret reached for her arm, stopping her.

"Shall I bring ye some tea?"

Yvonne hesitated, not sure if she should say yes or decline. "Please don't go to any trouble. I'll only be a few minutes."

"Nonsense, it's no trouble. No trouble at all." Margaret headed off in the opposite direction.

Yvonne smiled and went to find MacIntyre.

She found him sitting in the same chair as when they first met, head hung forward on his chest, dozing. A book lay open in his lap.

"Huh ... hmm ... Mr. MacIntyre, it's me, Yvonne Suarez. Sorry to wake you, but I'm returning your book."

He snorted and lifted his head. He focused on the stranger in front of him, then his memory kicked in. "I believe I asked ye to call me Craig. Have a seat, Ms. Suarez."

"Yvonne."

"Aye, Yvonne. Now that we have that out of the way, tell me, how did ye like the book?"

She sat on the couch across from him. "I found it fascinating, especially, the stories about people with second-sight."

"And why is that?" Craig lifted his ample body to sit up straighter in the chair.

"I wondered; is it inherited? A gift? Or, a curse, as your daughter claims? I'd love to hear your opinion. Maybe even your family's first-hand stories."

"Would ye now? Well, let me see. ... As to whether it's inherited, my mother had the second-sight, but she was also superstitious. I never put much credence in the old superstitions, but I did believe in her ability to sense in advance when something bad would happen. She was also accurate at foreseeing the good things in someone's future. Her gift wasn't only aboot death and the evil eye."

"Can you give me some examples?"

Craig sat back in his chair and chuckled. "My mother always believed if ye passed a funeral procession on the way to yer wedding ye were doomed to a bad marriage. Luckily, I never heard of it happening to anyone we knew, so never tested the superstition. But ... my mother could gaze into the eyes of the betrothed and say whether the marriage would be happy or sad. Often we were surprised to find that she was right." He raised his hand toward Yvonne in a stopping motion. "It wasn't what ye'd think, like maybe the guy was a lout and ye'd expect him to be a poor husband. Sometimes she'd predict that he'd make the best husband. And sometimes the sweetest bride would turn out to be a shrew or a cheatin wife. She always got it right."

Margaret had come in and placed the tea on the coffee table. "Our Darleen says she pays no heed to her feelings, but I'm not sure it does her much good. However, her visions, those are impossible to ignore."

"She gets visions?" Yvonne accepted a cup of tea from Margaret.

"Yes, I'll never forget the first time it happened." Margaret took the chair next to her husband and poured herself a cup of tea before responding.

Yvonne waited, hoping she'd continue, and her brief silence paid off.

"When Darleen was just a young girl, nine years old, she was out back behind the house playing with our dog, Gordy. It was a weekend, if I recall correctly. We could hear her laughing and running around. Then, all of a sudden she started screaming. We went running to see what had happened and found her just sitting on the ground screaming. When we finally got her calmed down and asked her what happened, she said she saw her best girlfriend, Elizabeth, underwater and that Elizabeth couldn't breathe. She said Elizabeth was trying to swim up to get air, but the water was moving her fast and pulling her under. Then, finally, she saw Elizabeth float up to the top with her face still under water and her eyes open. ...It was a horrid experience." Margaret shook her head in sadness.

Craig leaned forward and added, "That same afternoon, Elizabeth was found floating in the river Tweed. Apparently, being a hot summer day, she'd gone swimming with her thirteen-year-old brother in a shallow spot near their home, but they waded out too far and the river bottom suddenly dropped off deeply. The current got hold of her and dragged her under. The brother was able to struggle up and out, but he was unable to save his little sister."

"How awful—that poor girl—and her brother and family." Yvonne had a split second thought about how she'd feel if something similar happened to Christy. "And poor Darleen, to have experienced such a horrible thing—then lose a close friend at such a young age." Yvonne frowned, sympathizing with Darleen's feelings of being cursed.

Craig and Margaret, saddened by the turn of the conversation, glanced at each other then sat silently watching Yvonne.

Yvonne groped for a subtle way to steer the conversation to Duncan and the death of their retired foreman, but her expression remained serious. "On another sad note, we heard that your foreman, Randy, was murdered. I'd like to offer my condolences."

"Yes, yes, 'twas a terrible thing." Margaret's hand shook as she set down her tea cup.

Yvonne directed her question to Craig. "Do you think his son did it?"

"Who else could it be?" Craig stiffened.

"How well did you know—"

"What in bloody hell is going on here?" Darleen stormed into the room. "I thought I told ye that my father's not to be bothered with yer bloody questions."

"Now, now, Darleen, don't go upsetting yerself. We're having a nice chat with Yvonne." Craig gave his daughter a stern look. "Why are ye here so early? Lunch isn't for another hour."

"I came early to speak with Mother about the bagpipers we've booked for Beltane week. She was to help me decide which tunes they should play. And what do I find when I arrive? This ... this ... so-called, travel agent ... interrogatin ye." Darleen shot an angry look at Yvonne.

"I was merely trying to find out if your father had any theories about Randy and why he may have been murdered by his own son." Yvonne held Darleen's gaze.

"What business is it of yers?" Darleen spat back.

"Sit down, Darleen," commanded Craig.

Yvonne answered Darleen, "I find it curious that Fiona returns to find out what happened to her brother, and one of the people who may have been present the day he disappeared is murdered." Yvonne turned her focus back to Craig. "Does that strike you as odd, too?"

"No, I'm sure it's chust a coincidence."

"How can you be so sure? Maybe it had something to do with the chemical dumping that your company was being investigated for." Yvonne had let that slip sooner than planned. Well, she thought, in for a penny. "Maybe Duncan saw something incriminating, something Randy didn't want him to tell others."

"How dare ye. My father was completely cleared of those allegations. They were nothing more than rumors. Rumors spread by jealous competitors." Darleen stood up from her chair. "Father, I insist that ye ask Ms. Suarez to leave our home this instant."

"Calm down, Darleen. I have nothing to hide—*we* have nothing to hide. Let's chust answer Yvonne's questions and be done with it." He turned to Yvonne. "We will be done with it, won't we, Yvonne?"

Yvonne smiled sweetly at the elderly couple. "Thank you for putting up with me and my questions. I'm sure you can understand how worrisome this has been for Fiona. I only want to help her put the whole situation behind her once and for all."

Darleen stomped out of the house, slamming the back door as she left.

"I'm sorry, I didn't mean to upset her," said Yvonne. "I only have a few more questions."

Craig nodded for her to continue.

"I've heard that Randy had a nasty temper. I've heard that he rode the young men hard who worked for you. Is that true?"

"Yes. Keeping rowdy young boys in line can be quite a task. Randy kept control with a strong hand. And, often times...a hard heart. He showed no favoritism for his own son, in fact, I'd say he was downright cruel at times. Ye asked if I think Ullrick killed his father. Unfortunately, I think it's not only possible, but likely."

"Craig, understand, I'm not accusing you of anything, but do you think it's possible that Randy may have been dumping chemicals in the river unbeknownst to you? He might have bullied the boys into helping him."

"I can't see how that was possible. In my younger days, I was aware of everything that went on in my mill. I watched over all stations. Nothing got past me."

"Not even Duncan and Darleen's love affair?"

"Posh! Puppy love. They were too young to know what was good for them. I wasn't surprised at all that he took off. Boys are fickle that way, put the pressure on from a girl and they go running every time."

Yvonne looked from Craig to Margaret. "Apparently that didn't happen in your case. What do you think, Margaret? Did Duncan really love Darleen?"

Margaret glanced nervously at her husband. "I'm sure that Darleen thought he truly loved her. She was heartbroken when he left."

"Don't you mean, 'disappeared'?"

"Yes, sorry. At the time we just thought he left of his own accord."

"I guess that's all the questions I have for now. I can't promise you that there won't be more, but I appreciate your willingness to help." Yvonne got up from her seat.

Craig stood. "Ye've learned all there is to know about that day from us. There will be no more questions or answers. I'm glad ye enjoyed the book, Yvonne."

"Margaret, see Yvonne out, then see to lunch." Craig sat down and picked up the book he'd been reading.

Margaret walked with Yvonne to the front door. "I'm sorry we couldn't be more help."

Yvonne looked around the foyer, her eyes falling once again on the claymore that sat next to the door. "Goodbye, Margaret."

"What was Ullrick thinking? Killing his father like that. Bad timing for sure." Darleen plopped her forearms on her desk and looked at Keith in frustration. "Now do ye believe me when I say, I've had bad feelings? This is only the beginning."

"'Twas bound to happen sooner or later. Randy brow beat Ullrick his whole life. I'm surprised he didnae snap sooner."

"Yes, but why now? What did his father say that pushed him to snap now?" Darleen glared angrily at Keith.

Yvonne raised her hand to knock on the office door but pulled back when she heard the angry voices.

It sounds like Darleen and Keith don't know any more than we do about the timing of Randy's death, she thought. She knocked anyway.

Keith pulled the door open. "Wha—Oh it's ye again. What is it now?"

Yvonne looked Keith in the eye, stepping around him into the office. "Sorry to disturb you, Darleen, but I wanted to see if you knew who spread the rumors about your father dumping chemicals in the river. And, why would anyone have done that?"

"What business is it of yers? This doesn't have anything to do with Duncan."

"That may be, but since it happened around the same time, I want to rule out any connection. Please, we need your help solving this." Yvonne pushed on. "Why do you think someone spread the rumors?"

"Jealousy, of course. Father ran the most prosperous mill back then, the other mill owners eventually went out of business or moved their operations to China. But I don't know who began the rumor. The police inspector refused to tell my father."

"Why didn't your father move his operations to China like I've heard the others had?"

"He wanted it to remain a small family business—to keep to the old ways. He thought the knowledge itself would be valuable one day and feared the technology would cause the old ways to be forgotten. He was right. We make a good living giving tours and keeping the old traditions alive. And, proud to do so." Darleen looked belligerent.

Yvonne smiled at her. "I'm glad he decided to do so. I certainly enjoyed our tour. I'm thankful he took a stand to keep the history alive." Privately, she wondered if there wasn't more to his reasoning than that. Maybe, secrets from the past buried somewhere on the property.

"Thanks for speaking with me." Yvonne felt them glare at her back as she left the office. She took her time browsing the gift shop on her way out. Back in the car she instructed the driver to take her to the police station.

"Inspector Gordon, I'd like to ask a favor." Yvonne felt relief that he'd agreed to see her.

"Go ahead, Ms. Suarez?" His piercing stare never wavered.

"I'd like to speak with Ullrick Ferguson."

"Why on earth would ye want to do that?"

"Well you see, Inspector, I think it's possible that he may know something about Duncan Ross' disappearance and that may have caused the argument with his father."

"Is that so? Ach weel, we can't have people walking in off the streets, interrogating our murder suspects, now can we?"

"From what I've heard, he was treated horribly by his father and that he snapped after years of abuse."

"That's a possibility. Another is that he's a dangerous criminal, and we don't let amateur detectives talk to our prisoners. Now if ye'll excuse me, Ms. Suarez, I have a police station to run."

"Inspector Gordon, please. I think he may be willing to talk to someone who's not connected in any way to the past or the town. Don't you think it's worth a try?"

"No."

"Can I ask you one more question, then?"

"What?"

"Is it true that Ullrick Ferguson killed his father with a hammer?"

"Why do ye ask?" The inspector leaned forward and placed his elbows on the desk, giving Yvonne a serious look.

"It seems a particularly gruesome way to kill someone, especially one's own father."

"As it happens, he was not killed with the hammer, but we are keeping the details to ourselves for now. It's an ongoing investigation."

"How did it happen that the police who arrested Ullrick thought he'd beaten his father with the hammer. We were here when they brought Ullrick in, remember?" Yvonne leaned forward to meet his serious gaze.

"That will all be explained in due course."

"Have you actually arrested Ullrick? Has he admitted killing his father? Is there any evidence that he was even there?"

"Again, when our investigation is concluded ye'll know what happens and not before." He rose. "I've given ye all the time I can."

Yvonne rose. She wondered what would happen if they found no real evidence, they'd have to let him go. That could be helpful, she thought.

Yvonne felt a growling in her stomach. Stress or hunger? Late lunch or tea? Yvonne asked the driver for his recommendation of a casual lunch. He suggested she pick up a sandwich and beverage from the Tattler Cafe and take it to the park by the river for a picnic. She bought sandwiches and soda for both of them. She thanked him profusely for the idea then strolled to an empty bench placed strategically to view the flowing river and ate her pimento cheese sandwich. The driver remained in the car, enjoying his lunch. She sipped her lemon-lime soda and mulled over the morning, realizing she'd learned quite a bit but still not enough.

After awhile she pulled out her cell phone and dialed David.

He'd just gotten into his stride at the office when his cell phone rang. "My, my. Bored already?"

Yvonne laughed. "No. Just missing you."

"That's what I like to hear."

"I'm sitting here on the bank of the River Tweed enjoying a quiet, *private* lunch. Thought I'd take advantage of the alone time to say hello."

"I'm glad you did. I'm missing you too. Any idea how much longer you'll be there?"

"Not exactly." Yvonne stared at the sparkling water and took a breath. "I do feel I'm making a little progress, but there are still a lot of unanswered questions. One of our...not sure if I should call him suspect...was brutally murdered. The police think it was his son who did it. I'm not so sure."

"Why not?" David sat up straighter at his desk, a frown creasing his forehead.

"I don't know really. It's just a feeling. It goes against the popular belief that he snapped after years of abuse, but my question is; why now?"

David's voice deepened. "Yvonne, if there's one thing I've learned about you, it's that you should trust your gut feelings. Which makes me worry that you are now putting yourself in danger." His grip on the phone tightened.

Yvonne smiled at his concern. "Sorry to worry you, David. Believe me. I've seen nothing to suggest that anyone would come after me in a violent way. Actually, for the most part, everyone we've talked to has tried to help. At least it seems that they have."

"It sounds like you're not sure about what you say."

"Well, I do wonder about some people I've talked to. Whether they're telling me all they know. Craig MacIntyre, for example: He seems very helpful, yet he gives me only the kind of information I could get anyway. I get the feeling he's hiding something, but I'm not sure what. His wife, Margaret, is a dear, and their daughter, Darleen—Duncan's old girlfriend—well, she's just strange."

"Strange how?" David switched hands on his phone and held it to his other ear.

"First of all, she is the least friendly and very protective of her father, but the weird thing is, she supposedly gets visions and has what they call the second-sight, but it strikes me as odd that if that's the case, why wouldn't she have seen what happened to the young man she loved so much."

"That is odd. Have you asked her that?"

"In a round-about way. She brushed it off, said she doesn't always see things that pertain to her personally. I suppose that could be true. Her parents told me of one vision she had that happened to her as a child. I had to admit it was pretty convincing and scary. I see why she feels it's a curse."

"A curse?"

"That's for another conversation. I need to get going. I have a driver waiting in his car, and I've kept him long enough."

"When will I hear from you again?"

"I'll call as soon as I have some new information. It helps me to talk it out with you. Of course that's just an excuse to hear your sexy voice."

"Don't tease me like that, Yvonne. I may just have to jump on a plane and come get you."

"Now who's teasing who?" Yvonne grinned. "*Adiós cariño.*" She closed her phone.

"*Adiós cariña.*" David stared at the phone, hesitant to close it.

Yvonne asked her driver to make one more stop at Villeneuve Wines before heading to the Douglas home. She picked out two bottles of 2002 Domaine de Vissoux Beaujolais to present as a hospitality gift.

During dinner, Kendra and Fiona talked about their shopping day and promised Yvonne a peek at the children's clothing they bought.

Later, when they'd finished dinner and cleanup, Kendra shooed them to the living room where they continued to sip on wine while Yvonne caught them up on her day's events.

"I think we've hit a brick wall, and I'll never know what happened to my brother." Fiona sniffed, tears filling her eyes.

"Perhaps ye've had enough wine." Cameron seated next to Fiona on the sofa, gently took the half empty wine glass from her, and placed it on the coffee table, and then put his arm around her in a gentle hug. "Don't worry. We're not going to give up this time. We'll find out what happened to Duncan if it's the last thing we do."

Yvonne wondered if their efforts were futile, or would they, as Cameron said, finally learn what happened.

Kendra yawned. "I do believe this wonderful wine is making me sleepy. Think I'll turn in. Good night all." She got up and headed to bed.

Cameron followed a few minutes later.

Left alone with Fiona for the first time that day, Yvonne said, "Cameron is right. We're actually making progress. I think it's only a matter of a little more time, and we'll know what happened. We'll keep at it."

"What do you have planned for tomorrow?" Fiona stared hopefully at Yvonne.

"Sorry, nothing so far. We'll have a meeting in the morning and discuss our options. I'm sure the next course will present itself. Let's go to bed, get a good night's rest, and things will be brighter in the morning." Yvonne got up from her chair and reached out to help pull Fiona up from the couch.

Chapter 12
TUESDAY, JUNE 9TH

Yvonne arrived in the kitchen to find Cameron reading the morning news, Kendra frying eggs, and Fiona seated at the table with a cup of coffee. "Good morning," she said brightly and poured herself a cup of coffee. Yvonne sat down at the table, noticing rose petals scattered around, having fallen from the arrangement placed there two days before. She inhaled the pungent rose smell mingled with butter and eggs frying in the pan and took a sip of coffee adding yet another layer of aroma to her senses. "Hmm..." She closed her eyes and smiled, a feeling of déjà vu washed over her. She'd never experienced this exact scenario before, but it seemed so familiar. 'Perhaps in another lifetime,' she thought.

"And what's on yer schedule today?" Cameron closed and folded the paper, placing it neatly on the table. "Will it include us? We're anxious to help ye know."

Before Yvonne could answer, the phone rang. Kendra grabbed it. "Yes, he's right here." She handed it to Cameron.

Cameron listened to the caller. "Thanks for letting me know, Innes. And give my best to yer lovely daughter." He hung up the phone and turned to face Yvonne and Fiona. "Well now, what do ye know, they've gone and let Ullrick out for lack of evidence. Seems someone hired a solicitor to intervene on his behalf."

Fiona noticed Yvonne smile. "You seem pleased to hear this."

"I am," answered Yvonne. "This means we have our plan for the day—a perfect opportunity, I'd say."

"Ye have a mischievous twinkle in yer eye, if I've ever seen one. What are ye up to lassie?" Cameron sat back in his chair and waited while Kendra put plates of eggs and toast on the table for each of them.

"First, let me ask a couple questions, then I'll tell you my plan. How did Innes hear about Ullrick?"

"Rhona told him."

"Did he give any details of how Randy really died?"

"What do ye mean? Someone beat him to death with a hammer, nae?"

Yvonne broke the yolk of one of her eggs, sopping it up with the corner of her toast, and took a bite. "Inspector Gordon told me that Randy had not been beaten to death with a hammer as they had assumed. But he wouldn't tell me how he had died. ... I wonder if Innes would know?"

"He might. I'll call him back after breakfast and ask him." Cameron spread some currant jelly on his toast and took a bite.

"Did he say who hired the solicitor?" asked Yvonne.

"I don't think he knew."

"I think our next move is to talk to Ullrick—find out if he knows anything about Duncan's disappearance or the chemical investigation. It may be the reason he argued with his father. Given his reputation for violence, we should go together."

"Good," said Cameron.

"Agreed," said Fiona.

"Count me in," said Kendra.

They finished breakfast and Cameron called Innes back. He didn't have the details of Randy's death, so they made plans to stop back at the police station before heading to see Ullrick.

Fiona and Kendra stayed in the car while Yvonne and Cameron went inside the police station. Rhona sat at her desk, speaking on the phone while typing on a computer keyboard located on the other side of the counter. Wispy strands of orange hair peeked out from under her cap.

Cameron harrumphed and Rhona ended her call when she heard him. She greeted them in her brisk, efficient manner with a cautious smile.

Cameron spoke first. "We've heard that Ullrick Ferguson's been released for lack of evidence, and there's some confusion as to the murder weapon? Can ye tell us how Randy Ferguson was kilt? Do ye have any other suspects?"

"Ye should know I can't discuss an ongoing investigation with the public, Mr. Douglas."

Yvonne spoke up, "If there's a killer on the loose, we need to know who the suspects are? We don't want to step on anyone's toes during our own investigation or anger the wrong person."

"Then ye should leave the investigatin to the police. And, just because they've let Ullrick Ferguson loose doesn't mean he's not *still* the main suspect of the investigation." Rhona turned beet red at this comment, realizing she'd imparted too much information.

Yvonne touched Cameron on the forearm, indicating that they should leave.

"Thanks anyway, Rhona. Please give yer dad my best," Cameron turned toward Yvonne.

Yvonne smiled at Rhona. "Sorry, if we overstepped our bounds, asking questions. We're just trying to help solve this old case and bring peace of mind to our friend."

"I understand, but my hands are tied, and I can't help ye. Best of luck to ye though ... and ... be careful."

Back in the car, Fiona asked, "Where to now?"

"Off to see Ullrick, I suppose." Cameron steered the car out of the car park toward A72, running along High Street, Eastgate, and finally, Innerleithen Road.

Yvonne enjoyed the rural scenery. About a mile after passing the woolen mill, Cameron turned onto a side road that dead-ended in front of a grass covered yard split down the middle by a gray gravel walkway. The walkway led to the front door of a small, square stone cottage. Sitting atop the cottage like a hat was a shingled roof shaped like a triangle with the top lopped off about halfway down. From the right side of the roof rose a chimney like a feather in a cap. Rickety old window boxes, sprouting brown weeds, hung loosely from two windows, one on either side of the front door, reminding Yvonne of sad eyes on an old man's face.

All four of them got out of the car and walked up to the door. Cameron knocked. They heard rustling inside but no one answered. Cameron knocked again.

Ullrick yanked the door open, glaring at them. "What the hell do ye want?"

Yvonne hadn't expected him to be so burly. She estimated he stood at least six feet four inches. They each took a quick step back. In dire need of a haircut, Ullrick's black hair hung down covering his right eye. He reeked of whiskey.

"We're here to ask ye a few questions and to offer our condolences for yer loss," uttered Cameron.

"Who the hell are ye? And what do ye care about my feelins?"

"Ullrick, perhaps ye remember me. I'm Cameron Douglas, a friend of Keith and Duncan from the old days. Remember ... we worked at the woolen mill with yer father. Ye were just a few years behind us then." Cameron turned and pointed. "This is Fiona, Duncan's sister. She's come from the United States to find out what happened to her brother."

"I heard about ye snooping into things that are best left alone."

"Who told ye? Why best left alone?" asked Cameron.

Ullrick ignored the questions. His dark eyes squinted. "Who's this lass?" He jerked his thumb at Yvonne.

"She's my friend and travel agent," said Fiona.

"Pleased to meet you." Yvonne extended her hand for him to shake.

Ullrick looked at it, chuckled, and then turned. In a magnanimous gesture, he invited them to enter.

He wobbled over to a well-worn, stuffed chair and plopped down in it.

The place was in shambles. It reeked of sweat, blood, and booze. Yvonne caught herself holding her breath in an effort to keep from throwing up.

"Sorry about the mess. I haven't had a chance to clean up, yet," Ullrick said to no one in particular.

Yvonne stiffened her spine. "Would you mind if we looked at ... where your father was killed?"

"Sure. Guess it won't hurt nothin, now. They found his body over there." He pointed to the floor next to a chest of drawers at the far end of the living room.

Yvonne and Cameron walked over to take a closer look. Fiona and Kendra stood near the door where they'd entered.

"Have a seat." Ullrick brushed some trash off the couch and motioned for Fiona and Kendra to sit.

They obeyed his wish.

Yvonne pointed to an impression of a hammer head made with dried blood. Another larger spot of blood had pooled on the floor about two feet from the bloody, hammer-impression. "Hmm ..."

"What are ye thinkin?" whispered Cameron.

"It's odd. I would have expected blood spatter all over if he'd been beaten with the hammer."

Cameron called out, "Ullrick, did the police tell ye how yer father was kilt?"

"They said he'd been stabbed, through and through ... in the stomach." Ullrick waved his arm backward knocking over an empty beer bottle from the side table next to his chair. "Uh ... excuse me." He stumbled up from the chair to chase after the bottle.

Before he could get it, Yvonne scooped it up and sat it back on the side table. Ullrick turned and plopped back down into his chair.

"Why did they first think he'd been beaten with the hammer?" Yvonne watched his reaction. Ullrick's head wobbled. He appeared woozy from moving around so quickly.

He took a breath and steadied himself. "The hammer'd been leanin against the wall. He must o' fell an hit his head on it when he died. The police took the hammer for evidence. Didn't do them much good though." Ullrick leaned forward putting his head in his hands. After a moment he ran his hands through his hair pulling it out of his eyes and sat up. His heavy eyelids barely hid the fact that they were bloodshot and moist.

Could he be grieving for his father, wondered Yvonne. By all accounts he should be relieved. Keeping these thoughts to herself, she commented, "Ullrick, I realize this is a bad time for you, and we'll certainly understand if you decline our request. But would you mind answering a few questions about your father? Please understand, our time here is limited and the sooner we get answers, the sooner we can leave."

Ullrick looked down at his knees. "What do ye want to know?"

"Did your father ever tell you anything about the day Duncan disappeared?"

A troubling look crossed Ullrick's face. He didn't answer. Just as Yvonne gave up waiting, about to ask another question, he responded, "He didn't tell me anythin. But I suspected he knew somethin."

"Why?" asked Yvonne.

Fiona, Cameron, and Kendra sat quietly.

"The day Duncan disappeared, Da was gone from work all afternoon and didn't come home till late. Next mornin when I asked where he'd been, he shot me his scary look and told me to mind my own business. Some weeks later, when things were dying down about Duncan, I made the mistake o' askin him again. He beat me within an inch of my life and told me never to bring it up again. Mind ye, I was scared of him all those years ago, so never brought it up again ... until ... the day he died."

Yvonne held her breath in an effort to stay calm, sure they were about to learn the truth. "Is that what you argued about? Did he admit to knowing what happened?"

"We argued about that and many other things. I told him I was no longer afraid o' him. He'd grown weak while I'd grown strong. He laughed at me, called me weak-minded—said I'd never amount to anythin. He'd beat me down all these years. I knew he was right, so I stormed out and left. I didn't kill him. ... I thought if he'd admit to knowing something about Duncan it would give me power over him, but he must o' figured out why I wanted to know. He'd kept his secret all these years. Why should he tell me or anyone else, now?"

"So ... you didn't learn anything?" Yvonne's voice reflected her disappointment.

"No."

Yvonne pushed her luck with the next question. "Where did you go after you left?"

"To the pub in Old Town—chust like I told the police."

Yvonne changed the subject. "Did you know if your father or anyone else at Peebles Woolen Mill ever dumped chemical waste into the river Tweed?"

"I'm pretty sure they all did until the law got after them. I was pretty young then and Da never was one to discuss business dealings with young folk." Ullrick hung his head down. His eyelids grew heavier.

Yvonne feared he would pass out drunk any moment. "One last question, if you don't mind." She hesitated. "Who hired your solicitor to secure your release from jail?"

"That's none o' yer business?" He perked up. "Look, I'd o' helped with yer questions aboot Duncan if I could o', but now ye're takin advantage o' my good nature. I think it's best ye leave." He started to rise and fell back.

"Thank you, Ullrick. We'll leave you now." Yvonne waited while Cameron held out hands to help Fiona and Kendra from the couch. Ullrick closed his eyes and began snoring. Cameron, Fiona and Kendra whispered goodbye to Ullrick and left the house.

During the car ride back to the Douglas home, they discussed the visit. "Ullrick seems harmless enough. It's hard to believe he killed his father," said Yvonne.

"I feel the same," said Kendra. "He seems pretty cowed to me. Years of abuse have beaten the will to fight out of him."

"Don't be so quick to judge," said Cameron. "He was pretty drunk. Who knows what would happen if he were sober."

"Seems like we'd see the violent side if he were drunk. Isn't that when most people lose their inhibitions?" asked Fiona.

"I wonder why he wouldn't tell us who paid for his solicitor?" asked Kendra.

"Do you suppose it was Craig MacIntyre? After all, he grew up around there, his father worked for the mill his whole life until he retired."

Cameron said, "That's exactly what I was thinking."

"Call it women's intuition, but I get the feeling that Craig and Margaret are hiding something. They've been too cordial, too welcoming. Appearing to help but giving up nothing." Yvonne thought hard. She'd have to come up with another angle to go at them again.

Later that evening they gathered in the living room, watching television. About nine o'clock the phone rang. "It's probably Marni. I'll get it." Kendra answered the phone, listened for a moment then slammed it down, staring at it, dumbfounded.

"What happened? Who was it?" Cameron got up from his chair, concerned for Kendra.

"Are you okay?" asked Yvonne. "Here, sit down. Would you like me to get you some water?" Yvonne moved over on the couch making room for her.

Kendra took a seat and turned to face Yvonne and Fiona. "I'm fine," she said. "He ... a man ... said I should give Fiona and her friend a message. ... I should tell ye to go home before an accident befalls ye."

"Did you recognize the voice?" asked Yvonne.

"No. It was disguised, like an angry whisper."

"It was probably, Ullrick trying to scare us. Maybe we hit a nerve asking all those questions." Fiona wrung her hands.

"Why? Ullrick was just a boy when Duncan disappeared. What motive would he have to scare us away?" Yvonne took hold of Fiona's hands and squeezed them reassuringly.

"I agree with Yvonne. I can't see why Ullrick would bother with us. He's too busy keeping his own counsel—trying to stay out of jail." Cameron returned to his chair.

"I still think we need to go at Craig again. He knows something. Besides, he can afford to hire someone to scare us into leaving." Another thought occurred to Yvonne. "But, now we have leverage. Maybe ... we can scare him. We have Ullrick's word that his father kept it a secret about disappearing that same afternoon. I have Craig's word that in those days, he was very hands-on. He always knew where everyone was at any given moment at the mill. Let's see how Craig explains his foreman's whereabouts that afternoon."

"I don't know, Yvonne. We'd better think twice about this. I don't want anyone risking their life on my account." Fiona's chin quivered.

"And I won't be scared away by some coward who makes threats over the telephone." Yvonne looked Fiona in the eye. "Chances are he won't act on it, he's just trying to scare us away." Yvonne hoped she sounded more confident than she was. Lord, she thought, let me stay strong for Fiona's sake. We've come all this way to learn the truth. We can't go running home scared, now.

"Why don't we turn in early? We can make smarter decisions in the morning." Cameron finished the last drop of the single malt whiskey he'd been nursing all evening.

"I'll go to my room, but doubt I'll sleep well." Fiona pushed herself up from the couch.

"Would ye like a sleeping pill?" asked Kendra. "I keep them on hand for the occasional worry-nights when we can't sleep."

"No thanks. They make me dopey the next day. I'll read for a bit. If I'm lucky, I'll nod off." Fiona said goodnight and went to her room.

Yvonne spoke to Kendra, "I'm worried about Fiona. She's felt confused and responsible for her brother for so long, I'm afraid she's making herself sick. Perhaps tomorrow I should call on the MacIntyres, alone. Maybe you could keep Fiona occupied."

"I do have another meeting for the festival to attend, I could take her with. But I think ye should bring Cameron with ye. We're worried about yer safety, too."

"I'd be glad for his support if he's willing to risk it."

"He's losing sleep over this, too. He won't be happy unless he helps find Duncan this time around."

"Okay, it's settled then. Goodnight ... and ... Kendra ... thanks for putting up with all this."

"No need to thank me. I'd expect the same from my family and friends if one of my children went missing."

Yvonne retreated to her room. It was early. She placed a call to Christy and was told she'd gone to dinner with Yvonne's parents. Gino's tone told her he'd been reluctant to let her go but knew better than to disappoint Christy or Grandpa Eduardo. "Please tell her I called and give her my love. She can call me on my cell when she gets home if she'd like to talk."

"If it's not too close to bedtime, I'll let her call." Gino hung up on her with no goodbye.

Next she called David. "*Hola mi amor.*"

"Darling, what a pleasant surprise. I didn't expect to hear from you so soon after our last call." David clicked the mute button on his TV control. "Is everything okay?"

"Yes ... I think so. ... We're finally making some headway ... it's too soon to know for sure. ... Tell me, what's been going on with you?" Yvonne leaned back on the headboard and brought her legs up on the bed.

"Oh no you don't. You're not changing the subject that quickly. Tell me: What's happening with your investigation?" David sat up straighter in his club chair.

"David, I really don't want to talk about it, now. I just want to get my mind on other more pleasant things for awhile. Can't you just go with me on this?" Yvonne fiddled with the button on her blouse while she talked. "I have no idea what you've been up to while I've been away."

"Oh you know, saving the banking industry one machine at a time. We've got a new prototype ATM machine designed to protect the user from peepers, and we're writing and rewriting the software with deeper levels of security in the hopes it will cut down on identity theft. Boring stuff, really. Now will you tell me about you?"

"Ay Dios mio! Fine! I'll tell you. ... We're getting close. I know this because ... we've been threatened. Now are you happy?"

"No. Tell me more. Who made the threat?"

"We don't really know. We received a phone call. The voice was disguised. Kendra said it was a man. He just said we should go home, or we might become victims of an accident."

"I don't suppose you're coming home, are you?" David took a deep breath. "I'll be on the next plane to Edinburgh."

"No, David, please. I've got plenty of support. Cameron will be with me tomorrow when we question suspects, and we have become quite well known by the local police inspector, so I'm sure he'll be around if we need him."

"Somehow, that doesn't make me feel any better. I won't come on one condition?"

"And what is that?"

"That you call me at least twice a day and keep me updated on all that's happening."

"Oh please ... that's silly. I'll call if anything happens. You know I won't take any foolish chances. I've too much to lose."

"And, don't you forget it." David clenched his empty fist and banged the chair arm cushion.

"I've got another call coming in. I'll call you tomorrow. Goodnight, David."

"Good—" He'd been cut off.

"Hola cariña. Did you have a nice time with Nana and Papa?"

"Yes, Mommy. We went to a fancy, grownup restaurant, and I used good manners."

"Oh, really. Where did you go?"

"I don't remember the name, something like Capitole ..."

"The Capital Grille?"

"Yes, that's it. I had a small steak called a ... petite feelay ... and I had aw rotten potatoes, they were sooo delicious with cheese all in them."

"Did you have any vegetables?"

"Grandma shared her salad with me. And, they had the best bread. I got stuffed."

"Did you have dessert?"

"No. We didn't have any room left in our bellies for dessert. But next time, we'll save room. We already talked about it."

"That sounds wonderful, Christy. I hope next time I'll be with you to share in the deliciousness of it all."

"Me too, Mommy. I've gotta go now, Daddy's calling me. I love you Mommy. Come home soon, Mommy, I miss you."

"I miss you too. *Buenos noches, cariña.*" Yvonne reluctantly closed her phone.

Chapter 13
WEDNESDAY, JUNE 10TH

Craig MacIntyre answered the door. "This is becomin a habit. I don't know how things are done in the states, Yvonne, but here we call ahead to make an appointment." Craig acknowledged Cameron. "I see ye've brought reinforcements with ye this time."

"It's nice to see you again, Craig." Cameron stood next to Yvonne.

"Sorry for the inconvenience, Craig, but we're pressed for time. We'll be leaving for home soon and we're determined to get to the bottom of Duncan's disappearance before we leave." Yvonne waited a moment, but he still did not invite them in, so she continued, "Some things have come to light, and we'd like to get your take on it."

"What makes ye think I can help?" He stood his ground in the doorway.

"It involves your foreman, Randy," she answered.

"Well then, I guess ye better come in."

He moved away and ushered them into the house.

The house was quiet, and Yvonne wondered why Margaret hadn't answered the door.

Craig led them into the library. He indicated that they should take a seat on the couch, and he took his chair. "What is this information about Randy?"

"We've spoken to Ullrick and learned that Randy disappeared the same afternoon that Duncan did, and Randy didn't return to his home until very late at night. He'd kept his whereabouts secret from Ullrick and we'd like to know why." Yvonne looked Craig directly in the eye as she spoke.

Craig blinked once then forced himself to hold Yvonne's gaze. "Ye can't possibly expect me to remember everyone's whereabouts that afternoon, so many years ago."

"Oh, but we do. After all, you assured me that you were on top of everything regarding the woolen mill and your employees in those days. I hardly think you'd forget such an important day." Yvonne broke her staring match with Craig and glanced at Cameron.

Cameron had the faintest hint of a smile on his face. He clearly enjoyed the standoff between Yvonne, the spunky travel agent, and Craig, the laird of the manor. "Wait chust a minute," said Cameron. "Something about that day has come back to me."

"Is that so?" Craig focused on Cameron.

"I reported for work that afternoon—after school had let out and after Duncan had come and gone. I vaguely remember Margaret giving Keith and me our work orders. I don't remember seeing ye or Randy that day."

"What were yer work orders?" asked Craig.

"I was sent to muck out the sheeps' pen, and Keith was sent to the wool washin room with Darleen. Later I saw Darleen crying on Keith's shoulder. I knew Duncan had left, but I didn't know he'd disappeared. I found out later that night when his mother called me at home to ask if I'd seen him."

"How convenient—after all these years ye remember details about who was where. Of course ... it was payday, so that explains why ye'd gotten orders from Margaret and may not have seen me until later when ye picked up yer paycheck."

Craig's look of superiority only made Yvonne more suspicious. "Stop side-stepping the question and tell us where you and Randy were that day."

"As to me, I'd o' been in my office. I'll have to think on it —see if I can remember where Randy was. I'll let ye know when and if I do."

"Is Margaret here?" asked Yvonne.

"She's in bed—caught a bug and not feeling well."

"How awful. Is she up for a visitor? Maybe it would cheer her up." Yvonne's genuine concern was evident.

"No—she's not. Darleen and I are taking good care of her. Now if ye'll excuse me, it's time I checked on my wife. Please see yerselves out." Craig got up from his chair and waited for them to head to the front door. He made his way to the stairs and went slowly up to Margaret.

Something niggled at Yvonne's mind. She couldn't figure out what bothered her. "Rather than leave, let's talk to Keith, see if he remembers the afternoon the same way you do. He might shed light on where Craig and Randy went or at least whether they were around at all."

"Good idea," agreed Cameron.

They bypassed the gift shop and walked to the sheep pens. Not seeing Keith, they asked one of the laborers tending the sheep where they might find him. He pointed them toward the wool spinning cottage.

They found Keith speaking to one of the spinners.

"Will ye be ready fer a batch o' wool comin later today?"

"Yes sir," said the spinner. "I've asked my niece to come help spin later, so we'll have enough yarn ready fer the extra scarves fer Beltane week."

"Good." Keith looked up and saw Yvonne and Cameron waiting. He rolled his eyes in disgust and walked to meet them.

"Now what? Can't ye see I'm busy?"

"Then we won't waste your time," said Yvonne. "On the day Duncan disappeared, who gave you your work orders?"

"What in the devil does that have to do with anythin?"

"We're just getting the stories straight." Cameron stepped between Yvonne and Keith. "I was there that day, remember? Be careful how ye answer."

"Are ye threatnin me now?" Keith balled his fists and stepped in close to Cameron.

"Please, calm down you two. No one is threatening anyone." Yvonne tugged Cameron's arm pulling him out of Keith's space. "We're trying to establish where you were and who you may have seen—or not seen, that day. We have information that Randy was missing or scarce the afternoon Duncan went missing. Did you see Randy at all that day?"

"I don't recall."

Cameron asked him again, "Who gave ye work orders and what were they."

"Ye were there. Ye know 'twas Margaret. I was sent to wash wool."

Yvonne asked again, "Do you recall seeing Randy that afternoon?"

"No, 'twas too busy workin."

"And comfertin Darleen," added Cameron.

"She was upset. What was I supposed to do? Ye know I had a crush on her, even back then."

"You must have been happy that Duncan disappeared." Yvonne pressed on.

"No, I liked Duncan. We were friends. Besides, I dinna ken he'd gone missin yet. Darleen was upset because she thought she'd never see him again. I tellt her he'd be crazy to forget aboot her."

"One last question: Did you call Cameron's home and threaten Fiona and me with harm if we didn't leave?" Yvonne caught Keith off guard.

He sputtered, taking a little too long to answer. "I have no idea what ye're talkin aboot. Why on earth would I be makin threats?"

"Good question. There're not too many people who'd care, except those involved. ... And ... Keith, just so you know—we're not leaving without finding the truth." Yvonne gave him her sternest look.

"Ye're free to do as ye like. Now, if ye don't mind, I'll be gettin back to work. I'm warnin ye too, don't go botherin Darleen with any more o' yer questions either." He looked hard at both then walked away.

When Fiona and Kendra arrived home from their meeting, late afternoon, they found Cameron and Yvonne preparing a combo tea-luncheon. Cameron insisted it be set out in the formal dining room where he felt they'd enjoy planning their next move. They ate an assortment of watercress and cucumber, tuna fish, and pimento cheese sandwiches, then, munched on short bread for dessert.

The conversation through lunch stayed light, focusing on discussions about family and travel destinations.

Kendra opened a new discussion. "Let's take a little break from the case. Cameron and I would like to take ye on a driving tour of Glasgow tomorrow. I know Yvonne wants to see Glasgow before she leaves, and this might be the perfect opportunity. What do ye say?" Kendra looked expectantly at Yvonne.

"I think it's a terrific idea," said Yvonne. "What about you, Fiona?"

Before Fiona could respond the phone rang. Kendra signaled to Fiona to hold her answer until she'd answered the call. "Hello." Kendra listened attentively. "Thank ye. I tell ye what, let me check with everyone and I'll give ye a call back." She clicked off and replaced the phone on its base, a look of dismay on her face.

"Who was that, my love?" Cameron asked for all of them.

"It was Margaret MacIntyre. They're having a dinner party tomorrow evening, and we're all invited. ... Ye could knock me over with a feather. We've never been invited to their home before." Kendra returned to her seat.

"I wonder what prompted that?" Fiona broke a cookie and dunked a piece into her tea and took a bite.

"She said Craig and she have enjoyed getting to know ye three." Kendra laughed at that.

"It's more like 'keep yer friends close and yer enemies closer,' I imagine," said Cameron.

"It could be interesting. I wonder who will be there, besides us?" Kendra's eyes shot upward in thought.

"What do ye say? Shall we accept?" Cameron looked at Yvonne and Fiona.

"Sounds like fun. Who knows, it might be another chance to learn something further about Duncan. Of course we'd have to be subtle about it." Yvonne drummed her fingers on the table.

"I'm in," said Fiona.

"Good. I'll give her a call right back then." Kendra called Margaret giving her their acceptance of the invitation.

"Are we still on for Glasgow tomorrow then? We'll have plenty of time to tour around and get home in time to dress for dinner." Kendra looked at Fiona for her answer.

"Sure, I'd like that too. Yvonne's been so good to help me. It's the least we can do to help her learn more about Scotland." Fiona seated next to Yvonne, patted her on the shoulder.

"Thanks." Yvonne smiled at her, looking forward to a day of sightseeing.

Chapter 14
GLASGOW
THURSDAY, JUNE 11TH

*T*he drive from Cameron's to the heart of Glasgow took an hour and a half. Cameron took A72 west and north picking up other highways until he got to M8, also known as the Glasgow-Edinburgh road. He started their city tour by showing Yvonne and Fiona the City Chambers building where the council meetings for Glasgow politicians are held. "The Chambers building overlooks George Square." Kendra pointed to the large square as they drove past.

Yvonne and Fiona watched the sights from the back seat of the car. When Cameron drove them to the medieval Glasgow Cathedral he found a shady spot to park and mentioned that the Queen attends services there when she's in town. "As ye can see it's built of stone and dates back to the 1100s, but I've heard the stained glass windows have been redone over the last century."

"What's the religious denomination?" asked Yvonne.

"It's Christian, Church of Scotland."

"It certainly looks beautiful from here."

"If we had more time we'd tour inside—maybe next time." Cameron pulled away from the curb. Next he drove them through Merchant City Square, an upscale area for hotels, restaurants, shops, and art galleries. From there he drove past the space-age, dome-like building, of the Glasgow Science Center. Then he took them to the Riverside Museum and Tall Ship on Kelvin River and parked again. He suggested that they stroll along the Glasgow Harbor. They watched the tourists go in several directions, some toward powerboat rides and ferry rides, and some onto the Tall Ship or into the Riverside Museum.

"The Riverside Museum is Glasgow's museum of transport," Cameron spoke with enthusiasm. He became more animated when referring to the restoration of the tall ship, the Glenlee, built originally at the Bay Yard in Port Glasgow. "What say we take a tour of the ship? It won't take long, and I'll treat."

"Sounds like fun," agreed Yvonne.

Fiona and Kendra followed along.

Approaching the ship, Yvonne admired the long red hull sitting on the water, a band of white above the red, and shiny black railings at the top glistened in the sunlight. Three bare masts stood tall with small red, white and blue triangular flags blowing in the wind at their very tops.

Cameron paid five pounds per person to board. They entered port side onto the weather deck. A crowd of tourists, many with children, meandered at their leisure. They joined a small gathering led by a tour guide and learned that Glenlee was one of a group of ten steel sailing vessels built for a renowned shipping firm as a bulk cargo carrier. She took to water the first time in 1896. Yvonne noted in her journal Glenlee's impressive history. She had circumnavigated the globe four times and weathered the fearsome storms of Cape Horn fifteen times before being bought by the Spanish navy in 1922. The Spanish turned her into a sail training vessel, modified her and renamed her Galatea. She served in that role until 1969. She then operated as a training school until 1981 when she was laid up in Seville Harbor and mostly forgotten. In 1990 a British naval architect visiting Seville happened to see her and two years later, the Clyde Maritime Trust succeeded in buying her at auction for forty thousand Pounds, the equivalent of five million Pesetas, saving her from dereliction.

"She's one of only five Clyde-built sailing ships afloat in the world today. Her purpose now is education and entertainment. We offer year-round maritime programs to school children and adults, locally and from around the world. We also offer her for special occasion parties and events." After quoting the brief history of Glenlee, the guide led them on a tour of the ship pointing out the equipment and places such as the galley, the heads, the captains and first mate's cabins, the bell, chart room, sailmaker's room, hatch, and wheel.

Watching the children and their parents climb aboard to peer into the inner workings of the Glenlee caused Yvonne a momentary bout of homesickness. She wished Christy were here enjoying this fun experience. She reached in her bag for her small camera and took several snapshots to remind her of the tour and to share later with Christy. As they left the ship, she took a final round of pictures of the boat and the harbor with Cameron, Kendra, and Fiona in the forefront.

After leaving the port Cameron continued his tour, driving them past the University of Glasgow. His final stop brought them to the Botanic Gardens. There, he suggested that they look through the conservatory, one of ten glass houses, not counting outdoor gardens, and finish the tour enjoying a light lunch in the garden café.

The conservatory showcased seasonal floral arrangements year-round. In June the summer flowers were at their showiest. Among the hundreds of brightly colored flowers, Yvonne saw many that she recognized from gardens in Florida. They saw several varieties of late blooming lilies, snapdragons, delphiniums, highly scented freesias, marigolds, chrysanthemums, and roses of all colors and scents. The conservatory was a profusion of color and perfume, the perfect way to end the sightseeing portion of their tour. They followed up with lunch in the garden café as suggested by Cameron.

PEEBLES

They arrived back at Cameron and Kendra's home at four-thirty.

"We have enough time for a short nap and to ready ourselves for the dinner party." Kendra gave them a tired smile. "Let's meet back here at six-thirty for a drink, and we'll be on our way." She left the living room and headed to her bedroom.

Cameron followed her.

"Yvonne, come here." Fiona had pulled back the living room curtain and was pointing to a dark blue mid-size sedan parked out front of the house. "I noticed him pull up just as we closed the front door. I wonder who it is. Is he watching us?"

Yvonne looked out the window. A tight cramping grew in the pit of her stomach. The car door opened and out he stepped. *"Ay Dios mio!* Wha-What is he doing here?"

"Who?" asked Fiona.

Yvonne opened the door and rushed out to meet him. "David, I thought you said you'd not come."

"I changed my mind. I missed you and wanted to be around in case you needed me. I've taken a suite at the Hydro Hotel. ... Won't you join me there for dinner tonight?" David stood with his hands in his pockets.

Sweet, Yvonne thought, he looks as if he's resisting the urge to take me in his arms for a hug. She gave him a mischievous smile. "I'm sorry, David, we have plans. We've been invited to the MacIntyre's for a dinner party. I've told you about them. They're the owners of the Peebles Woolen Mill.

David frowned. "Aren't they suspects in your investigation?"

"Come in, David. Let me introduce you to Fiona. Cameron and Kendra have gone to take a nap, but they'll want to meet you later. I'll call the MacIntyres and see if they can stretch the invitation to include one more person."

"Are you sure? I don't want to impose. I could wait till tomorrow to spend time with you." He looked around the yard trying to hide his disappointment.

She looked him in the eye. "I should be mad, you know. Especially since I asked you not to come, but ... well ... It's nice to see you. There's so much I've wanted to share with you since I got here." She grabbed his arm and walked him indoors.

"Fiona, this is David. David, Fiona." Yvonne grinned, unable to hide her delight.

David reached his hand to shake Fiona's.

Fiona sized him up as pleasant looking and offered her hand limply. "I've heard some very nice things about you, young man. Have a seat." She nudged him over to the couch. "Not only from Yvonne. ... Janice told me how you helped her and Yvonne during their trip to Greece last year."

"Well, mainly I supported Yvonne's efforts." Uncomfortable with the compliment, he glanced at Yvonne and changed the subject. "Tell me, Ladies, how is the investigation going? Do you have any new leads?"

Yvonne brought him up to speed on their latest encounters. "Though it's strictly social tonight, we're hoping some new information might slip out of someone's mouth."

"Frankly, we're surprised at the invitation. The older MacIntyres have been somewhat helpful and welcoming, but their daughter and son-in-law have not taken kindly to our questions," added Fiona.

"It makes you wonder if they're hiding something." David picked up on her point.

"Do you have any theories about what might have happened?" he asked.

"Let's go into it all later. When did you arrive? What airport did you fly into? Glasgow or Edinburgh?" Yvonne leaned toward David.

Fiona sighed. "If you'll excuse me, Yvonne. I think I'll go to my room. ... Nice to meet you, David." Fiona got up from the couch and sauntered away, turning back for one last glance at the couple. Smiling, she thought, Yvonne deserves a little cuddle.

"Nice meeting you," said David to Fiona's back, his gaze never leaving Yvonne. "I flew into Glasgow. It had the only last-minute seats available. The flight was fine. I rented the car and here I am. Now, why did you change the subject?" He leaned over and gave her a gentle kiss on the lips.

"Mm ... *Muy bonito*." She'd closed her eyes during the kiss. When she opened them his deep blue eyes were level with her brown ones. She smiled at him. "Let's take a walk out back. There's a lovely rose garden and a bench. I'll tell you my theories. Then, I'll have to leave you while I dress for dinner."

They strolled outside and seated themselves, surrounded by a rose arbor filled with lavender-colored roses. A pungent rosy scent permeated the air. They breathed deeply. David held Yvonne's hand and turned slightly on the bench to face her.

Yvonne sighed. "Okay then, my theories. ... The first and most likely is that Duncan saw something he shouldn't have and was killed for it. His body disposed of by the foreman, Randy."

"What would he have seen?"

"I have a theory about that too." Yvonne repeated to him, her theory about illegal chemical dumping in the River Tweed.

"You said you have other theories?"

"The only other theory that makes sense—jealousy. Craig MacIntyre, the father, was hostile toward Duncan's relationship with his daughter. He felt Duncan wasn't good enough for Darleen. MacIntyre had the money and power to make him disappear. Or ... Keith, everyone knew he had a crush on Darleen. Maybe he decided to put a stop to their plans of marriage and bringing Darleen to America. He became a convenient shoulder to cry on after Duncan disappeared."

"I don't suppose there's any actual evidence? If there were the police would have arrested someone by now."

Yvonne rolled her eyes. "The police have been no help at all."

"There's another possibility," said David. "He ran away."

"I don't think so. He had no reason to run away, even if he'd had a reason, wouldn't someone have heard from him by now? No. I think we can eliminate that possibility."

David glanced at his watch. "What time is dinner?"

"Seven. We're planning to have a drink here at the house before we leave. It's only a few minutes from here."

"Perhaps I'd better go back to the hotel and change into a suit. Why not check with the MacIntyres to be sure I'm invited and give me a call if it's a go."

"Alright, now that you're here, I hate to let you go." Yvonne tugged on his shirt collar.

David stood and pulled her into his arms. "I'll be back before you know it. Ask for the Kailzie suite when you call, or reach me on my cell."

She walked him back through the house to the front door.

Instead of taking a nap, Yvonne did a simple standing yoga pose known as *Ardha Chakrasana*. Its flowing then holding motion increased circulation into her neck and shoulders reducing stress and expanding her chest, re-energizing her. Afterward she lowered herself gracefully into the cross-legged position, *Sukhasana*. In preparation for the coming dinner party, she meditated by clearing her mind of all thoughts, concentrating on stillness and keeping an open mind so that later she'd observe any minute detail about Duncan's disappearance that might be revealed.

After meditation, she rose slowly from the floor. Checking the center drawer of the desk in her room, she found a phone book and dialed the MacIntyre residence. "Margaret, this is Yvonne Suarez."

"How are ye, Yvonne? We're looking forward to yer visit this evening. I hope everythin's all right." The pitch of Margaret's voice went higher.

"I'm fine, but I may have to cancel. My good friend, David Ludlow has arrived in Peebles unexpectedly and ... I wondered if you might have room for one more dinner guest?" Yvonne took a breath and held it.

"Oh, is that all? Not to worry, we can easily add another place at the table. In fact, he will even out our guest list, nicely. Please, bring yer young man along. We'd love to meet him."

"Thank you so much, Margaret. We're looking forward to seeing you." Mission accomplished, thought Yvonne as she hung up the phone.

She gave David a quick call to let him know he'd been included in the invitation. Then she went to the closet and laid out the only dress that she'd brought with her. Recommended for travel, her little black dress could go dressy or casual, depending on accessories. Tonight, she'd wear a sparkly faux diamond necklace set in gold with matching dangle earrings. She'd wrap a black knit shawl with fringe around her shoulders to finish the look. She'd keep her hair down and simple with the left side clipped behind her ear. She caught herself smiling in anticipation of the social evening and prayed for a pleasant outcome to the party.

David returned looking sharp in a dark gray tweed suit, greeted warmly by Cameron and Kendra. He accepted a shot of whiskey from Cameron. He paused, glass half-way to his lips when Yvonne entered the room. She was stunning. He took her hand and sat next to her on the couch. They told David about their day in Glasgow, avoiding talking about the investigation, before Cameron looked at his watch and herded them out to his car. They arrived at the MacIntyre residence, fashionably, five minutes late.

Craig introduced the newcomers to their dear friends, Nigel and Glenna Sutherland. "Nigel and Glenna are the proprietors of the Sutherland Guest House in Old Town. The Sutherlands are an old and respectable name in Peebles."

"Now, now, let's not be stuffy, Craig." Nigel offered handshakes to Cameron and David. "Lucky ducks—keeping company with such bonnie lassies."

When he smiled his eyes bugged out. His puffy red cheeks and thick mustache reminded Yvonne of the Esquire Magazine mascot from days of old.

"How do ye do," said Glenna, offering a limp handshake to the men and tight-lipped smile to the ladies.

Proving opposites attract, Glenna's thin face and long nose with dark hair pulled severely back into a bun, struck Yvonne as harsh, but when Glenna spoke her voice was soft and sweet. She wore a well-cut, magenta-colored suit that complemented her complexion. A matching multi-colored scarf hid any neck wrinkles, and her ears, wrist and fingers, showed off tasteful jewels.

The maid served everyone Rob Roy cocktails made with equal parts scotch whiskey, and sweet vermouth. A dash of Angostura bitters and a maraschino cherry added the final touches.

Yvonne sipped her drink, enjoying the sweetness and the warm feeling that came over her. She watched David converse easily with the men and listened to Margaret chatter to the ladies about her attempt to nurse a sick mother sheep back to health after its having a hard labor giving birth to its twin lambs. The men sat on one side of the parlor. Yvonne strained to hear what they were talking about. She didn't like being segregated from the men.

Darleen and Keith entered the room. They were dressed for dinner. Of course, thought Yvonne; they live here, it's natural they'd be included.

Darleen smiled gaily. "Hello, everyone." Her green eyes shined mischievously.

Everyone said hello back. Keith smiled and nodded, not saying a word. He settled down with the men and Darleen took a seat by her mother. Margaret left the room, and when she returned the maid followed with drinks for Darleen and Keith.

"How are ye enjoying Peebles?" Darleen directed her question to Yvonne.

"Very much. The town is charming." Yvonne nodded her head at Kendra. "We're fortunate to have wonderful hosts and tour guides. Cameron and Kendra have done a superb job of showing us the sights."

"And ye, Fiona. Is it how ye remember it after so many years away?" Darleen took a sip of her drink.

"Some—the newer housing projects lack character. Cameron took me by March Street. It looks the same, but the houses are smaller than I remember. Whoever is living in our old house had the decency to paint it and maintain the yard. Some of the neighboring homes are run down though."

"The neighborhood where ye once lived is making a comeback. Younger families are moving in and renovating the area. It was bloody ugly for several years."

"I wonder whatever happened to my old school chum, Bonnie Stirling? Do ye know? Is she married? We lost touch after I moved," asked Fiona.

"Yes—married and moved to London—a doctor, I think." Darleen switched her focus to Kendra. "I've seen ye at the Beltane Fancy Dress committee meetings. I delivered the donated ribbons for the dresses and the maypole."

"Of course, I thought ye looked familiar. It's quite a task, but we're hoping to have all the dresses and decorations finished soon. Will ye be there for the parade?" asked Kendra.

"No. We'll be busy setting up for tours of the Mill. We have our own festivities planned to follow after the parade. We'll have a pipe band and dancers doing the Highland Fling."

Yvonne sighed. "Sounds like we're going to miss a great time. Wish we could extend our stay, but my daughter's expecting me home soon. And to be honest, I miss her terribly. Someday, I'll bring her back for a visit. She'd love the Festival, especially the Fancy Dress Parade."

"We understand, dear," said Margaret. The ladies smiled, giving Yvonne their sympathies and understanding.

Margaret received word that dinner was ready and asked everyone to follow her to the dining room.

Velvet-flocked, burgundy-colored wallpaper in a floral design covered the walls. Eggshell-colored moldings and ceiling medallions added architectural details. An enormous brass chandelier with numerous lights cast a surreal sparkle and warm glow of light on the table.

Yvonne recognized the china as Royal Albert's Old Country Roses and the stemware as the Edinburgh Thistle Crystal. The expense of these items told her the woolen mill business must be a good one. Two maids appeared and served a starter course of smoked salmon paté with crackers.

"Pardon me for asking, but I hear ye're conducting some sort of investigation. Have ye made any progress?" asked Nigel.

Everyone looked up in surprise then shifted their gaze to Yvonne. She smiled nervously while trying to think of a pat answer. "Some, I suppose." She spread a small amount of paté on a cracker and popped it into her mouth, then took a sip of water and looked to see if she still held their attention. She did. "Perhaps we should save this topic for another time." Yvonne glanced over at Darleen.

Darleen looked at her father and then down at her plate.

"Why? We're all on pins and needles to know what ye've found out." Nigel waved his cracker at Yvonne then shoved it into his mouth and chewed.

"Don't be rude, dear." Glenna gave him a stern look.

"Listen to yer wife, Nigel." Craig's tone left no room for argument.

Except for compliments to the cook, the guests remained quiet through the second course of cold squash soup. When the main course of Lamb, roasted potatoes, and asparagus had settled in front of everyone, David directed questions to Craig that he thought would steer the conversation to a safer direction, "How long have you been in the woolen mill business? Do you enjoy it?"

"The MacIntyre family has owned the Peebles Woolen Mill since 1869. I enjoyed the business while I ran it, but the ones to ask aboot it now are Darleen and Keith." He looked at his daughter.

"Of course we enjoy it, Father. Don't we Keith?" Darleen looked at Keith.

Keith nodded his agreement.

Well, so much for that conversation, thought Yvonne. She knew that David, ever the diplomat, had tried to open a safe conversation to lighten the mood. Kendra had managed to make small talk surrounding the Beltane festivities, but that had run its course quickly.

"Let's take dessert and coffee in the music room. Darleen will entertain us on the piano, and Keith will play us a tune on the bagpipes." Margaret beamed at her daughter. She waited for Craig to rise from the table and pull out her chair, then the rest of the guests followed.

A light and airy room located at the back of the house had a large picture window with a view of the meadow and hills. At nine o'clock it was still light out. Yvonne was surprised to see a Steinway grand piano centered in front of the window. A seating arrangement of Queen Anne sofa, loveseat, and chairs faced the piano. An elegant coffee table held coffee service and dessert.

Keith opened a closet and pulled out his bagpipes. "I'll go outside a bit and warm up. In the meantime, Darleen can play a tune on the piano."

Darleen sat at the piano thumbing through a book of music. She began her recital by playing *The Bonnie Banks O' Loch Lomond*. Yvonne always felt sad when she heard this hauntingly beautiful song. Next, Darleen lightened up the atmosphere by playing the *Blue Bells of Scotland* and a couple of old ditties. She ended with a reverential arrangement of *Amazing Grace*.

"Bravo!" said Nigel

"Bravo!" said everyone.

"I had no idea you were so talented," said Fiona to Darleen. "What a blessing to be able to entertain your family and friends."

"Thank ye." Darleen got up from her piano bench and took a seat near her father. She looked around in anticipation for Keith.

The sound of his piping *Bonnie Dundee* reverberated throughout the house, preceding his entry into the music room. He then took a stand next to the piano and piped the lamenting *Massacre of Glencoe* and finished up with *Scotland the Brave*. The history of Scotland played so dearly in music gave Yvonne goose-bumps. She never cared much for bagpipes but being so close to them struck a chord deep inside her, and she finally understood the beauty of the pipes. She could only imagine how it must have sounded when dozens of pipers marched in battle.

Margaret served the traditional bread pudding immersed in a rich caramel sauce for dessert. Topped with cream and taken with coffee, it was the ideal end to a delicious meal. Yvonne caught movement and watched as Darleen leaned back against the chair. Her head fell back and her lashes flitted and her eyes rolled heavenward and closed. She seemed in a trance. She shook her head back and forth and moaned, this lasted for a few moments before Margaret called out to her daughter, "Darleen, what is it? Wake up! Are ye okay?"

Darleen continued to moan and jerk her head back and forth. Margaret shook her shoulders but Darleen kept her eyes shut tightly and continued moaning. The guests watched helplessly.

"Let her be. Don't wake her. It's dangerous." Keith went to Darleen's side and squatted down by the chair. He put his arm around her shoulder and held her but did not attempt to wake her. "She's having a vision. It's best to let it play out."

If I hadn't seen it, I wouldn't believe it, thought Yvonne. After several minutes, Darleen opened her eyes abruptly. She turned and looked at Keith, a look of horror on her face. She got up from the chair and ran from the room. Keith followed her. Margaret got up to go after her daughter.

"Margaret, stay here. Keith will handle it. We have guests, after all," Craig nodded for her to sit down.

Margaret looked guiltily around the room and returned to her chair.

Cameron stood. "I think it best we take our leave." He turned to Margaret. "Thank ye for dinner. 'Twas lovely."

Kendra, Yvonne, David and Fiona rose giving their thanks and compliments.

"It was nice to meet you," said Yvonne to Nigel and Glenna.

"Lovely to meet ye too, my dear." Nigel nodded to Yvonne and the rest of the guests then rose and turned, extending his hand to Glenna. "We shall leave too. As always, Craig, it's been an interesting pleasure." He turned to Margaret. "Superb dinner, Margaret, give our regards to Darleen and Keith when ye see them."

Craig and Margaret stood and walked their guests to the door.

Cameron and his passengers held their comments until they returned to the comfort of the Douglas home. They all wondered what had gotten into Darleen—curious about what may have caused her vision.

"It must have had something to do with Duncan," said Yvonne. "We need to ask her about it."

"She'll be angry if we do." Fiona had settled down on the couch with a cup of chamomile tea.

"I know, but we have no choice. She knows something, even if it's subconscious on her part." Yvonne slipped off her shoes and tucked her feet up under her on the couch.

"Any chance she'd get violent?" David directed his question to Cameron.

"I don't think so, though I haven't seen Darleen for years until recently. I've never heard of her throwing tantrums or the like." Cameron rubbed his chin, thinking.

"What did ye think of their friends, Nigel and Glenna?" asked Kendra.

"They were a bit of an odd couple, wouldn't ye say?" answered Cameron.

"I suppose they were there to bring a balance to the evening," said Kendra.

"I thought Craig would croak when Nigel brought up the investigation," said Fiona.

"It may have been on purpose—a fishing expedition—set up by Craig to see what we know," said David.

"Interesting. I hadn't thought of that." Yvonne gave David a pat on the arm. "It's nice to have an objective point of view now and then." She smiled at him.

Watching this interaction between Yvonne and David, Cameron said, "Well, I think I'll toddle on off to bed now. Join me, won't you Kendra?" He raised his eyebrows and gave a quick glance at Yvonne and David.

"Oh ... yes. ... Sounds good." Kendra smiled knowingly and headed off with Cameron.

On her way by, Kendra gave a look to Fiona that suggested she follow suit.

Yvonne chuckled softly. "Not too subtle are they."

David put his arms around her and pulled her close for a kiss.

"Mm... that was nice." Yvonne leaned in for another one.

"Come back to the hotel with me. I'll wait while you pack a few overnight things."

"As much as I'd like to do that, I don't think it would be a good idea."

"Must you always be so proper?" David pulled away from her. "After all, I flew all the way to Scotland to see you."

David's frustrated tone of voice irked Yvonne. "I know, but, I have to think of my client, and I don't want her to think I'm abandoning her just because you showed up. You do remember why I took this trip, don't you?"

"Heaven forbid. I hardly think she'd worry you're abandoning her."

"Maybe not. But how would it look? You show up, and I run off to shack up with you."

"Well, when you put it that way," he said, sarcastically.

"Don't pout. I'm sure we can find a way to be together for awhile without upsetting anyone."

"First of all, I never pout. Second, what's your bright idea for getting together?" David nipped at her ear.

Yvonne drew back and gave him a smug smile. "I'm sure I can find some time away, tomorrow, and we can meet at your hotel suite. I am, after all, a travel agent, and I am required to familiarize myself with local hotels. I can always arrange for a hotel inspection."

"Is that right. I suppose next you'll want to set an appointment. We wouldn't want to do anything spontaneously, now would we?" He pulled her close again and gave her a forceful kiss.

She wrapped her arms around his neck and gave it right back to him.

He pulled himself out of her grip. "Oh no you don't, I'm saving my good kisses for our rendezvous tomorrow." He laughed lightly and got up from the couch. He pulled her up, and she walked him to the door, giving him a light kiss goodnight. She closed the door after he got in the car and pulled away from the curb.

Chapter 15
FRIDAY, JUNE 12TH

David picked up Yvonne and drove her to the woolen mill. When they entered the gift store, she left David to browse while she went to Darleen's office.

"I'm busy, Yvonne—no time for visitors." Darleen remained seated at her desk.

Yvonne stepped into the office. "I just wanted to make sure you're okay. Last night must have been scary for you."

"I appreciate the concern, but I assure ye, I'm fine."

"Look, Darleen. I'm not going to beat around the bush. Did your vision have anything to do with our investigation of Duncan? If it did, I think we have a right to know." Yvonne crossed her arms and waited.

Darleen rubbed the crease between her eyes. "It didn't ..."

"You're not convincing me. Please Darleen ... tell me what happened. I promise I won't tell anyone if it doesn't concern finding Fiona's brother."

"The trouble is; I don't know what it means. I only caught glimpses."

"Glimpses? Of what?" Yvonne took a seat in the desk chair, directly across from Darleen.

"Angry voices—blood—lots of blood." Darleen cringed.

"Who? ... What did you see exactly?" Yvonne leaned in closer.

"It was him ... Randy. His eyes—they were open wide—scared. When he stepped back, I saw a long blade being pulled out of his stomach. There was blood on it. He stumbled backward into the chest of drawers. He knocked something off, and when he fell, his head landed on it making a horrible popping noise. It turned my stomach."

"Did you see who stabbed him?"

"I couldn't see. I tried. ... It was like I was watching through the killer's eyes." Darleen cried, "I hate this. I have no control over it, and it doesn't do anyone any good."

"There must be a reason for your visions. I don't believe they aren't helpful in some way."

"Mostly, when I see things, it's too late."

"Maybe ... if you open yourself up to the idea, you'll see who did it, then you can help get justice for Randy."

"What if I don't want to see it? What if I don't want to know who it is?" Darleen laid her arms on the desk and placed her head down and cried.

Yvonne waited until she'd cried herself out. "I'm sorry to have upset you with all this. Should I get Keith?"

"No!"

The abrupt answer startled Yvonne. "Okay. ... Have you told anyone else about your vision? Your mother? Father?"

"No. And, I want ye to promise that ye won't tell anyone what I saw. Ye said ye wouldn't tell if it didn't help yer investigation and it doesn't have anything to do with it—so promise me." Darleen's eyes shot daggers at Yvonne.

Yvonne thought for a moment. "There's nothing new here, so I don't see any reason to tell anyone anything."

"Good. Now, I really must ask ye to leave."

"Alright, but, call me if you *see* anything else—please—I will help you any way I can."

Darleen nodded half-heartedly and turned staring at her blank computer screen. Yvonne got up and left.

They entered the Hydro hotel. David went to his suite and left Yvonne at the reception area. She noted in the brochure that the hotel offered conference facilities, so she asked to see the events manager. As expected the manager, an attractive young woman in her late twenties, happily gave her a tour of the hotel and discussed their group services and amenities. After receiving a corporate packet with pricing options and ending the tour, the manager offered her a free lunch in, Lazels, their bistro-style lunch restaurant. Yvonne mentioned that she was meeting a friend for lunch who happened to be a guest and that she'd love to take her up on the offer.

"Come. I'll take you to Lazels and have a word with the Maitre d," said the manager.

"Is there a house phone? I'd like to call up to my friend's room and ask him to join me."

The manager directed Yvonne to the lobby phone. She called and asked David to meet her in the restaurant.

During lunch she reluctantly confided in David about her conversation with Darleen. "I promised her I wouldn't tell anyone so please keep this to yourself."

"Who would I tell?" He smiled at her concern.

"I'm not sure it helps us much anyway. Of course, if she intuits who stabbed him, then it would take everything to a whole new level, and she'd be in grave danger."

"Do you suppose, she doesn't want to see who it is because she's afraid she might know the person?" David took a bite of his fried haddock and watched Yvonne's expressive face.

"I did wonder about that. But I think it's subconscious on her part, and that she'd be relieved if she could know who'd done it." Yvonne took a bite of her smoked salmon salad. "How's your fish and chips?" she asked.

"Delicious. How's your salad?"

"Yummy."

"That reminds me. I've ordered dessert in the suite for later."

"Mm.... Does it involve chocolate by chance?"

"You'll have to wait and see. It's a surprise."

"Guess we'd better finish our lunch then." Yvonne's eyes sparkled as she looked David directly in the eyes and took a slow seductive bite of salmon.

The first thing Yvonne noticed when she entered the Kailzie suite was the large picture window with decorative glass panes overlooking the Glentress Forest. Centered in front of the window sat a small round table, formally set and accompanied by two chairs. On the table were plates of fruit and petit fours covered in decadent chocolate and whipped cream.

To her right, a sitting area with a couch, coffee table and two comfortable chairs cozied up the room. A silver ice bucket holding a bottle of champagne graced the center of the coffee table.

The other side of the suite held a grand four poster bed with white linens and burgundy bedspread that matched the ornate draperies and furnishings. The bed had been turned down inviting occupancy.

Yvonne walked over to the window and gazed at the view.

David came up behind her, took hold of her shoulders, and kissed her gently on the nape of her neck. "It's been a long time since we've had time alone together. I'm having a difficult time refraining from ripping your clothes off. But the ambience of the room calls for taking it slow for maximum enjoyment." He wrapped his arms around her and gazed with her at the view.

She leaned into him.

"Wake up sleepyhead." David kissed her on the top of her head as it rested on his chest.

"Must I? I'm sooo comfortable. I could stay here, forever." She snuggled down under the covers.

"Oh no you don't. We have places to go, people to see." David lifted the covers and sighed, and said, "What nice boobs ye have lassie."

"You are so geeky, or should I say corny." She giggled.

"What's your preference? We can take a shower with those crazy jets splashing all over us? Or a bath in that deep bubbly tub?"

"The bath!"

"You stay here and I'll get it going." David scooted out of bed to fill the tub.

"You know you're not so bad yourself, laddie," she murmured to herself. She climbed out of bed and strolled over to the table. Finding a lonely, chocolate covered strawberry, she took a bite and washed it down with some flat champagne left in her glass. When she turned around David stood there close, smelling musky. He swept her up in his arms and carried her to the tub.

Later, wrapped in their terry cloth robes, they snuggled on the couch watching the local news on the hotel's television. Yvonne's mind wandered. Shutting out the news, she marveled at the way their lovemaking flowed like a well-practiced dance and like a shot out of nowhere, a twinge of guilt washed over her, turning her serene mood dark.

On the drive from the hotel to the Douglas' home, David noticed Yvonne's change in demeanor. "You're awfully quiet. Is something wrong?"

She hesitated a moment then blurted out, "Here I am across the Atlantic ocean—miles away from Christy. What if something terrible happened? How would I get to her in time?"

"This, my sweetheart, is your usual knee-jerk reaction to having a good time with me and allowing yourself to forget your responsibilities for a few hours. Christy will be fine and you'll be home before you know it." David released one hand from the steering wheel and patted her leg.

"I know you're right, but this whole thing seems to be dragging along and we're not getting anywhere ... and ... I'm not touring as much of Scotland as I would have liked." Yvonne picked his hand up from her leg and held it on the seat between them.

"Someday, we'll come back strictly for pleasure and do a tour. We'll bring Christy too."

Yvonne smiled. "How did I get so lucky to have you in my life?"

"You deserve me. Think nothing of it." He gave her a cocky grin.

Yvonne punched him lightly in the shoulder.

He pulled up to the street in front of the Douglas's home to park. He got out and walked around to open the door for Yvonne as she gathered up the packet of information she'd brought from the hotel.

She stepped out of the car, and they turned to walk inside. A gunshot shattered the peace. David shoved Yvonne to the ground and shielded her with his body.

They heard the wheels of a car spinning, driving off in the direction that they'd arrived from.

"Ow ..." Yvonne's voice croaked weakly. "I think I've been shot."

David pulled himself off of her and quickly looked around. Cameron had come running from inside. David looked for blood on Yvonne and saw that the suit-jacket of her left arm had blood on it. "Can you walk if I help you up?" he asked.

"Yes. I think so." She sat up holding her arm.

"Let's get her inside." Cameron looked around. "I've told Kendra to call the police."

Once inside they removed her jacket. The bullet had grazed her arm removing the top layer of skin. Kendra cleaned the wound and bandaged it. "After it forms a scab it will heal. I'm not sure if it will leave a scar or not. It's pretty deep."

"Thanks, Kendra. I'm okay. Really." Yvonne tried sitting up on the couch where David had insisted she lay down when they brought her in, but Kendra pushed her gently back down.

"I know ye're fine, but ye may be in shock, and I think it best ye rest for awhile."

"Are things moving too slowly for you now?" David's look of concern tore at Yvonne. "I'd say that you've made someone very nervous."

Fiona who had been silent up until now, said, "I won't blame you, Yvonne, if you want to leave. I don't want anyone hurt because of me."

"It's not because of you, Fiona. You have every right to know what happened to your brother. Maybe now the police will take this seriously and help us." Yvonne sat up again resisting Kendra's efforts to keep her down.

"I agree with Fiona. You should leave. It's not worth getting shot over. You have a child to think of." David gave her a stern look.

"Like I said, we can get the police involved now. They will keep us safe."

"You were worried about something happening to Christy, well, losing her mother would be the worst thing that could happen." David held his ground.

"Nothing's going to happen to me."

The argument was interrupted when Cameron opened the door to bring in Police Inspector Gordon. Cameron introduced him to Kendra and David.

"I'll want to take all yer statements, starting with Ms. Suarez." He sat on the couch next to her. "Tell me exactly what happened."

"Can't it wait? She needs rest," said David.

"The sooner we get this over with, the sooner we can catch who did this." Inspector Gordon turned his focus once again to Yvonne.

She held her arm protectively against her body. "We'd just returned from the Hydro hotel, and when I got out of the car—David had opened my door—we started to go into the house, and I heard a shot, and David pushed me to the ground, and I heard a car speed away. That's when I felt a burning sensation on my arm and realized I'd been shot."

"Did ye see anyone waiting when ye drove up?"

"No."

"Did ye see a car parked anywhere?"

"No. ... I'm sorry. It all happened so quickly, and it was the last thing on my mind. I wasn't paying attention. ... I should have ... paid attention."

"People don't pay attention to *things* unless something unusual occurs to catch their attention. Never mind then. Chust concentrate on getting better. If ye think of anything later that might help, give me a call." He laid his card on the coffee table.

Inspector Gordon questioned everyone and got the same story. They'd all heard the shot, but no one had seen anything. "I'll bring in our forensics team to see if they can find the bullet and any other evidence of the car. I expect ye all to stay available, but out o' our way while we investigate the shooting."

"What about the investigation of Fiona's missing brother? Can you help us with that?" asked Yvonne.

Fiona's angry words broke into the conversation. "You have not helped much in the past and now look—" She waved her arm in Yvonne's direction. "If you had been doing your job this wouldn't have happened, sir."

Inspector Gordon's jaw tightened for a moment before he answered, "Aye, we will take another look at yer brother's disappearance. Question those who were around back then. Perhaps the bullet will give us a clue."

"Good. Then we'll expect to hear from you soon about the bullet and whatever else you might learn." Fiona was visibly shaking but her eyes never left his, insuring that he understood her resolve to take up where Yvonne had left off due to her temporary injury.

Yvonne held back a laugh, amused at seeing Fiona stand up to the burly police inspector.

After the inspector left, activity continued outside as the forensic team scanned the yard for the bullet and any other evidence.

"Darling we could all use a drink, if ye please, and I'll warm up supper again, hopefully it won't have dried out too much." Kendra finished giving her directions and reminded Yvonne to stay put on the sofa before retreating to the kitchen.

"I'll help Kendra get dinner on." Fiona headed to the kitchen.

Cameron filled five rocks glasses with scotch. "It's time for a pow-wow. Wouldn't ye say?" Cameron handed Yvonne and David their scotch then picked up his own glass.

"David, how long are ye planning to stay in Peebles?"

Cameron's question surprised David. "As long as it takes to see this through and be sure Yvonne and Fiona are safely on their way home."

"Good. As we Scots say, 'there's strength in numbers.' From here on in, I suggest that none of us go out alone and that we make sure someone knows where we are at all times."

"Do either of you have even the slightest idea who might have taken the shot tonight?" David looked first at Yvonne then Cameron.

"There are only two people that make sense, Keith or Ullrick. Do ye agree, Yvonne?"

"Yes ... except ... I can't help but think that Craig MacIntyre could easily hire an outsider to do his bidding if he is somehow involved."

"What do you know about Margaret MacIntyre," asked David. "Do you think she is capable of hiring someone?"

"I can't think what her motive would be. She seems an innocent bystander in all this. Yet ... she certainly loves her daughter and may be protecting her somehow. Though I can't see a way that makes sense." Yvonne took a drink with her right hand.

"Tomorrow we should have another talk with Ullrick, don't you think?" Yvonne looked at Cameron, then David.

"Didn't you hear Inspector Gordon? We're to stay available. And what about your arm? You need rest." David gave her a stern look.

"Talking to someone's not strenuous," said Yvonne. "Besides, even if they find the bullet, it will take days for forensics to determine who might own the gun that it came from." She raised her chin in defiance.

"Cameron and I will talk to Ullrick. You will stay here with Fiona and Kendra." David banged his glass down splashing scotch on the coffee table.

Cameron handed him a napkin. "David's right. The two of us will have better luck speaking with Ullrick, alone. Man to man."

"Eso es una tontería." Yvonne's angry tone left no doubt as to her meaning.

The men weren't successful at hiding their amusement, making Yvonne even madder.

"I won't be relegated to the backseat while you two take over my job." Yvonne tried to stand but winced when she realized it took two arms to keep her balance. "Fine. I'll be much better tomorrow. You'll see." She sat quietly through dinner and the rest of the evening while everyone made small talk in an effort to appease her.

Chapter 16
SATURDAY, JUNE 13TH

Invited by Cameron, David turned up early for breakfast. "How about some coffee and scones?" offered Cameron.

David took a seat at the table. "Sounds fine to me."

Kendra poured him some coffee. "Help yerself, David." She indicated he take a scone from the basket. "There's whipped butter and strawberry jam to go with."

"I thought it best we get off early, before Yvonne comes down. Kendra gave her a sleeping pill to help her get through the night in comfort." Cameron nodded approval at his wife.

"She'll be furious when she finds out we left without her." David smeared butter and jam on his scone, a satisfied smile on his face.

"Don't worry, laddie. She'll get over it. She knows ye have her best interest at heart." Cameron sipped his coffee.

"Is Fiona not up yet either?" asked David.

"No—for the best. She won't have to lie aboot it to Yvonne."

"Ah..." David shook his head in the affirmative and took a bite of his scone. "These are delicious, Kendra. Did you make them yourself?"

"No. I get them from the local bakery." Don't care much for baking. I'd rather spend my free time in the garden."

"It shows." David's mind wandered to the afternoon before, talking with Yvonne in Kendra's rose garden.

They finished up. "Shall we go?" Cameron wiped his mouth with his paper napkin and stood up.

"The sooner the better," said David.

Cameron opened the front door and ushered David outside.

"Oh good grief." David grumbled.

Yvonne waited for them by the car, dressed and ready to go. "Good morning, gentlemen. Did you have a good night? How about breakfast? Think it will hold you okay?"

"No need to be sarcastic, Yvonne." David leaned down to kiss her on the lips but, she turned her face so that he got her on the cheek.

She stood waiting, blocking his way into the car.

"Fine." He opened the door to the back seat. "What about Fiona? Didn't she want to come too?"

"Yes, actually, she did, but I convinced her she'd be more help staying here in case we run into trouble—she'd be able to tell the police where we went." Yvonne gave him a smug smile.

"Shall we be off then?" asked Cameron. He waited while David held the car door for Yvonne and watched as she carefully climbed into the back seat. Once David was settled into his own seat, he drove off to see Ullrick.

When they arrived, David made one last attempt to get Yvonne to stay in the car, but she'd have none of it and followed them up to his front door.

Cameron knocked loudly several times before Ullrick, groggy and half asleep, opened the door.

"Not ye again." Ullrick attempted to close the door.

Cameron inserted his foot and pushed forward keeping the door open. "We have a few more questions. It's important."

Ullrick eyed them suspiciously. "Who's this guy?"

"He's Yvonne's friend, David. May we come in now?"

"If ye must." He stumbled into the living room and sprawled on the couch, leaving them to stand. His greasy black hair hung in his eyes. "What are yer questions then?"

Yvonne stepped in front of Cameron and David. "First off, Ull-rick, where were you last evening between six and seven?"

"Why?"

"Just answer the question," said David.

"Unwindin from my wark day."

"At the mill?" asked Yvonne

"Of course!"

"Can they verify what time you left?"

"I clocked out at 5:30. Gave 'em an extra half hour."

"Is that why Craig MacIntyre bailed you out of jail? Because you give him extra time—you're a loyal employee?" Yvonne pressed the issue.

"Who told ye that?"

"It doesn't take a rocket scientist to figure it out," said Cameron.

"Okay. Yeah, he bailed me out. So what? My father was a loyal employee and so am I."

"Does Craig have other loyal employees like you and your father? Ones who might do some dirty work for him?" David threw out this question.

"I don't know what ye mean?" Ullrick looked genuinely surprised.

"We want to know—does he have anyone else, loyal employees or maybe an outsider who does his bidding even if the job is distasteful."

Ullrick thought for a moment. "All his employees are loyal. He treats us fair. I suppose his *favorite* is Keith. I don't know aboot outsiders. Ye still haven't tellt me why yer askin."

"Someone took a shot at Yvonne last night." David glared at him.

Ullrick looked at Yvonne. "She looks fine to me."

"Well she's not. And if you hear of anyone wanting to harm her, you'd best let us know immediately, or there will be consequences." David's voice thundered.

"Where'd you go after work?" Yvonne softened her tone.

"Twas Friday so I stopped at the pub for a wee drop. Got home aboot ten." He turned his attention to David. "Besides, I've no reason to harm yer bonnie lassie." Ullrick swung his feet to the ground and sat up, letting David know he wasn't threatened by him.

"I suppose ye were drinkin at Port Brae?" Cameron moved in closer to Ullrick.

"That's right. Nevin, the bartender, will tell ye the same. I'm done answerin yer questions. Now let yerselves oot." Ullrick started to get up from the couch.

David and Cameron stepped in closer to Ullrick forcing him to stay put. "We'll leave then," said Cameron.

Ullrick took a breath and settled back down on the couch.

Yvonne seated herself in the back of the car. "Our next stop should be Keith, agreed?"

"Just hope we get some answers that lead somewhere this time." Cameron slapped the steering wheel in frustration.

"Cameron, what's your take on Ullrick? He seems harmless but both times I've seen him he's been hung over. Is that his natural state of being?" Yvonne watched his eyes in the rear view mirror.

"I haven't seen him often, 'cept when I've been at the pub. He drinks alone, doesn't bother anyone. When we were young he was quite the wild one. I always felt his bravado was meant to get the attention of his father, but mostly it got him the belt on his backside. Seein him now, it's like he's givin up on life. Maybe the drink has turned his brains to mush.

Yvonne thought about this. She felt sad that a young boy, starved for love, would grow up and turn to drink to dull his senses. He must have spent many years suffering hurt feelings. She'd go to any lengths to see that nothing like that ever happened to Christy.

They found Keith out back of the buildings at the edge of the meadow watching the mill shepherd training a young border collie to herd sheep. It was a humorous encounter as the young dog ignored the trainer's commands, chased the sheep in a playful manner, and split the herd so they ran in all directions. Fortunately they were enclosed in a round pen, and the trainer, using much patience and consistent firm commands, eventually brought the dog under control and in charge of the sheep.

Keith had ignored them as long as he could. "Here ye are again. Is there no end to yer intrusions?" He spat at the ground.

"We were good friends, once, Keith. I don't understand yer problem with our discovering what happened to Duncan." Cameron crossed his arms indicating he expected a reasonable response to his remark.

"Twas many years ago. Where've ye been all these years? All of a sudden ye care about what happened to Duncan? Where's Fiona. If this is so important, why isn't she here?"

"We're here because someone took a shot at Yvonne last night," interrupted David.

"Who are ye?"

"I'm a friend of Yvonne's. Where were you between six and seven last evening?" David cut right to the point.

"It's none o' yer damn business. Now off with ye, I have work to do." Keith avoided looking David in the eye as he turned to walk away.

Cameron caught up with Keith. "It'll be a shame when the police come by askin ye the same questions. Ye'd be better off to talk to us."

"I have nothin to hide. Send the police if ye like." Keith stomped away.

"He's hiding something. Did you see? He wouldn't look us in the eye?" Yvonne whispered excitedly.

"Maybe we should put a bug in Inspector Gordon's ear. Make good our threat to sic the police on Keith." Cameron stroked his chin. "Doubt the good inspector would learn anythin, but it might push Keith to talk to us."

"If he is somehow involved in Duncan's disappearance he may do something dangerous—out of desperation. We'd better be ready to handle whatever comes from our pushing his buttons." David looked seriously at Yvonne.

"Don't worry about me, David. I can take care of myself."

"Still we need a plan before setting anything in motion."

"Makes sense to me," said Cameron. "Let's go. We'll work on it at home this afternoon."

"I thought David might like a mini tour of Peebles. We can take his car, maybe stop for lunch and be back at the house around four. ... Any objections?" Yvonne watched him in the rear view mirror.

"None from me," said Cameron.

"I'm still trying to get the hang of this driving on the left side of the road. It will be good practice for me," said David.

Later, after they'd toured around Peebles, David took her to lunch at the Tontine hotel. "It's nice having you to myself." He reached across the table to take hold of her hand.

Yvonne pulled her hand into her lap. "I haven't forgiven you yet for trying to sneak out on me this morning." She gave him the hard stare that said he was in the dog house.

"We were only trying to let you recuperate from the close call last evening."

"Honestly, it's only a little friction burn. You'd think I was a baby. I've had worse scrapes when I played soccer in college."

"You played soccer in college?" David's eyes lit up with amusement.

"Yes. And I was pretty good at it, too."

"I'm sure you were. That reminds me. I've been meaning to ask you when did you start taking up yoga?"

Yvonne put her hand back on the table. "I've done yoga since I was very young. Long before it became trendy. I used to practice with my mother. She had several Indian friends in England who inspired her to take it up as a young woman."

"Well it certainly keeps you in good shape ... and very agile."

His smile told her that he'd be talking her into going back to his hotel room, so she changed the subject. "Did you and Cameron have a nice bonding time without me this morning?"

"I like him ... and, Kendra, too. They're very down to earth. Fiona's lucky to have them for family."

"Do you have any suggestions to flush out Keith or whoever is behind Duncan's disappearance?" Yvonne took a sip from her tea cup.

"I think Cameron's suggestion of talking to the police is a good one. We may learn some things. Didn't you say he was investigating, also?"

"So he says."

"The more important question is: How are we going to keep you and Fiona safe if things get ugly?" David reached for her hand again.

"I'm sure we'll think of something when we get to our brainstorming session. Speaking of which, shouldn't we get going?"

"Ah ... I was afraid you were going to say that. Maybe later we can go back to the hotel—have a quiet dinner in my room?" David's eyes widened.

"We'll see how it goes." Yvonne smiled. "Should you signal the waiter for the check?"

"Can I get anyone a cocktail? It's a little early, but I'm sure it's five o'clock somewhere." Cameron couldn't resist the famous Scottish cliché.

"I'll join you," David piped in.

"Perhaps I should remain sober to be sure we don't come up with something too risky?" Yvonne sat up straighter on the couch.

"Go on, Yvonne, relax. Pretend you're on vacation." Fiona swatted her hand at Yvonne in a friendly gesture.

"Might as well make it drinks all around." Kendra laughed lightly.

"*Ay Dios mio*. I don't want to be the only sober one in the bunch."

Cameron passed drinks around to everyone.

Yvonne sat back and relaxed. "Who knows, if we're not so wound up we might come up with a better plan."

"Way to justify your actions." David patted her on the shoulder.

Yvonne teased him with a dirty look, then laughed at him and took a drink of straight scotch. The laugh was on her when she choked and sputtered as the heat from the drink shot up her nose.

From the depth of his cushy chair, Cameron said, "Let's call this meeting to order."

The jovial group saluted Cameron who looked small and vulnerable, swallowed up by his favorite chair.

"One thing we get straight—" David looked at Yvonne. "No one goes anywhere alone. Understood?"

Yvonne nodded her agreement, and the others chimed in with their promises to honor their pact.

"First things first. Who is going with me to the police station tomorrow morning? And what exactly shall we tell Inspector Gordon that will prompt him to speak to Keith?" Yvonne waited.

"Logic would dictate that I should go and perhaps Cameron." David looked around the room at each of them. "Any more and he may feel ganged up on. Don't you agree?"

"I'm not doing enough. This is *my* brother after all." Fiona looked to Yvonne for a response to her comment.

"That's exactly why you should keep a low profile. You are so close to the situation, it will be difficult to remain objective. It will be harder for Inspector Gordon to brush us off."

"You can stay here and help me in the garden," said Kendra.

"That's settled then. Should we steer Gordon toward anyone else? What about Ullrick, or Craig?"

"I'm pretty sure he already has those two on his radar. Let's find out what he knows first. Besides, I'm not sure what we could say about them that would pique his interest. Do ye?" Cameron asked Yvonne.

"I suppose you're right, he must know that Craig paid Ullrick's bail. That, in itself, should look suspicious. I wonder if Gordon looked into the chemical, waste-dumping angle, or, he just said he would to appease us." Yvonne tried another sip of the scotch.

Chapter 17
SUNDAY, JUNE 14TH

At Kendra's request they attended the Peebles Old Parish Church of Scotland for Sunday services.

Afterward they exited using the many steps that led to High Street. "It's strange ... I feel a strong spiritual connection in this beautiful old church," Yvonne said this to Kendra and Fiona as they walked out of the church and down the steps to High Street. "We have some pretty churches in Fort Lauderdale, but they're modern and don't have the ancient vibes."

"Not as ancient as you might think. The church has been moved and rebuilt several times through the centuries. In the 1800s it was moved here on the hill where the old Peebles Castle once stood. Now we have a wonderful view of the bridge over Tweed River, and the church tower can be seen from anywhere in the city." Kendra waved her arms around in gesture to encompass the whole town.

"Never the less, the stained glass windows are beautiful, as is the architecture and furnishings in the nave. I love the organ. It's magnificent!"

"I'm glad we had a chance to show it off." Kendra smiled broadly.

"Yes, it's very pretty," agreed Fiona.

Yvonne looked past her and saw David and Cameron chatting with Craig and Margaret at the sidewalk level. "Hmm, I wonder what they're talking about."

"Let's go see, shall we." Kendra led the way.

As they approached, Yvonne noticed Margaret's glum expression and smiled sweetly at her. "Hello. It's nice to see you again."

"Hello," said Fiona and Kendra.

Margaret nodded at Yvonne, her smile not reaching her eyes.

"Nice to see ye as well." Craig took hold of Margaret's arm. "We were just saying what a lovely day it is."

"Yes ... so it is." Yvonne tried to read Margaret's expression and wondered if she'd taken ill, again. "Are you feeling okay, Margaret?"

Margaret glanced at Craig. "I'm a bit tired ... things are quite hectic coming up to Beltane. I'll be fine when things settle down."

"Come my dear, let me get ye home." Craig kept his grip on Margaret's arm and nodded to them. "Good day to ye. We'll be on our way then." They walked away toward the public parking, adjacent to the river Tweed.

David stepped next to Yvonne and put his arm around her waist. "She seemed rather up-tight, wouldn't you say?"

"Maybe she's worried about Darleen—perhaps she's had another vision."

"Could be, I suppose. What if her vision revealed the killer this time? Darleen could be scared out of her wits." David hugged Yvonne as she wrapped her arm around his waist too.

They followed arm in arm a short distance behind Cameron, Kendra, and Fiona, on their way to the car.

After a leisurely lunch, Yvonne, David, and Cameron left Fiona and Kendra waiting in the car and entered the police station to find that neither, Rhona nor Inspector Gordon, were in. "It's their day off," said a friendly young constable.

"Well that makes perfect sense. It is Sunday after all. Now what?" Yvonne looked at David and Cameron for an answer.

"We take the rest of the day off, too." Cameron said without hesitation.

"I'm with Cameron on this. We haven't had nearly enough time to enjoy being here. Why don't we go back to my hotel and take advantage of the spa facilities, my treat." David extended the invitation to Cameron too.

Cameron not wanting to infringe on David's goodwill, suspecting his desire to be alone with Yvonne, declined the invitation for himself, Kendra and Fiona. "We'll be very happy to relax at home and talk gossip about the families with Fiona. Ye and Yvonne go ahead though and enjoy yerselves." He gave David a knowing look.

Yvonne didn't miss the signals between the two men but thought she could use the break time to recoup and come up with a plan to flush out the guilty party or parties. *That is if David doesn't derail my plans.*

David treated Yvonne to a Hydro Aromatherapy massage that included a facial and scalp treatment. He booked the more vigorous Swedish massage for himself.

"Ay Dios mio. That was the most luxurious afternoon I can ever remember having. I thought I was going to melt right off the table." Yvonne let her plush robe fall to the ground and climbed under the bed covers to join David who'd been reading. She loved watching his eyes light up with delight when he saw her naked body.

She snuggled up against him, putting her head on his shoulder.

"You smell delicious." He turned into her and nibbled on her ear.

"Umm ... and, I wanted to spend time meditating on the investigation. I must be insane."

"I love your ambitious nature." He nibbled some more.

She snuggled down under the covers and kissed him in all the right places.

The afternoon turned into evening and several hours later they lay back exhausted with sleepy smiles on their faces.

Around nine, David asked, "Are you hungry?"

"Famished, but I feel like a wet noodle and I don't want to move." Yvonne sighed with pleasure.

"I'll order room service. How about a nice steak, the red meat will revive us."

"Yum."

He laughed at her one-word answer and ordered two filet mignons, baked potatoes, asparagus, a hearts of lettuce salad with the restaurant's famous Stilton bleu cheese dressing, and port for after dinner drinks.

Seated at the small table by the window wearing a bathrobe, Yvonne took a bite of her steak, savoring the tender flavor, and grinned with excitement.

"You look like the Cheshire cat from *Alice in Wonderland*—" The phone rang interrupting his comment. "I wonder who that could be?"

David moved his napkin from his lap to the table, got up, and answered the phone from beside the bed. "Hello?"

"Uh huh, okay." He looked at Yvonne and motioned for her to take the phone. "It's Margaret MacIntyre. She wants to speak to you."

Yvonne looked at David, a questioning look on her face, and shrugged. "Hello, Margaret. Are you okay?"

"Can we meet? Privately? I need to talk to ye." Margaret sounded rushed and out of breath.

"Yes, of course ... where do you want to meet?"

"Come to the mill at midnight—alone. Turn off yer headlights before you turn in, and park near the entrance. I'll be waiting and we can talk there."

"Are you sure—" Yvonne stared at the silent phone. Chills ran up her spine. She turned to see David waiting patiently to hear what had happened.

After she explained, he stated his concerns. "I'm going with you. No way am I letting you go anywhere alone at night."

"I'll be fine." Yvonne unconsciously rubbed her arm where the bullet had grazed it.

David looked at her arm and then directly into her eyes. "Need I say more?"

"Alright, but promise me that you'll stay in the back seat and keep quiet. I don't want to spook her. This could be the important lead we've been waiting for."

He nodded compliantly.

They finished their dinner in silence. The steak and vegetables had lost their appeal while the port assisted in warming and calming their nerves.

Yvonne asked David to drive. She had never driven on the left and wasn't about to try it in the dead of night in unfamiliar surroundings. They arrived about fifteen minutes early, so he could move into the back seat. About ten minutes after they'd parked, Yvonne saw Margaret approaching the car. She'd come from the rear of the manor house, glancing nervously behind her, several times. Margaret walked directly to the passenger side of the car. "Hello, Yvonne. Thank ye for meetin me." She sensed movement from the backseat. "What is he doing here? I asked ye to come alone."

"I wouldn't allow it. Not after someone took a shot at her last evening." David's voice left no room for argument.

"Don't worry. You can trust David. He's only here to help. Please … get in."

Margaret opened the car door and got in. "I … wanted to talk to ye about Darleen. I think she's in danger. Maybe … ye could help? I dinna ken ye'd been shot. Are ye okay?"

"I'm fine. The bullet just grazed my arm. … What makes you think Darleen's in danger?" asked Yvonne.

"She's evasive and jumpy. It's like she's waiting for something bad to happen."

"Have you asked her about it?"

"She denies it. She never wants to worry me. It's like there's this big secret. I'm really afraid for her." Margaret reached over and grabbed Yvonne's hand to hold. "Please, ye have to help me find out what's goin on."

"What makes you think I can be of help?"

"Ye're helping Fiona, so I thought ye might help me, too. I dinna ken who else to ask."

"What about your husband, can't he talk to Darleen? Won't she confide in him? Or what about Keith?"

"Bah! Keith. He won't tell me anything. And my husband, he's as bad as Darleen. When I try to talk about her, he always brushes it off, says I'm worrying for nothing and she's chust being overly dramatic. ... It's different this time. I can feel it, and I'm afraid."

"Do you know if Darleen's had any visions lately?"

"No. Do ye think that's what it is?"

"She seemed pretty upset the other night when she had the vision, maybe she saw something upsetting that scared her." Yvonne debated with herself about keeping Darleen's secret. Should she tell Margaret? No. It's too soon. She'd do well to hold the information until she learned more. Maybe Darleen had seen more in her vision than she'd let on. Or maybe she's had another more revealing one. Something was certainly amiss if Margaret was sensing Darleen's fears.

"She won't talk about it to anyone. I even suggested she see a counselor, but Darleen chust scoffs at all my attempts to help." Margaret's frustration led her to tear up.

"I'll figure a way to talk to her, see what I can find out. Don't worry. I'm sure it'll all be okay." She squeezed Margaret's hand, reassuring her. "Is there anything else, even something minor, that you think we might need to know?"

Margaret thought for a moment. "Well ... there was something funny ... at least I thought so at the time. Several days ago, I noticed the claymore—ye know—the one by our front door. Twas missing. I didn't think anything about it at first. I thought maybe Craig was having it cleaned; he does so periodically, but it was gone for two days and then it showed up. What I remember about it being so odd ... is ... that it showed up two days after Randy had been killed.

For some reason, I got a really bad feeling when I saw it back in the stand. Ye don't think ... no ... that can't be." Margaret verged on hysterics.

"What can't be? What do you think?" Yvonne held her breath waiting to hear what she said.

"Is it possible that someone I know might have done something ... awful? Is that why Darleen is so upset?"

"Who, Margaret? Who do you think might do something like this?" Yvonne pressed her for an answer.

"I don't know!" Margaret sat up straight. "I'd better go. Thank ye, Yvonne. This was a mistake. Nevermind. I don't need yer help after all." She got out of the car and ran back to the house.

Yvonne sat there stunned. She started when David opened the door to get out of the back seat. She scooted over to the passenger side and he resumed his spot behind the wheel.

"Let's wait a few minutes. Be sure she's settled in okay before starting the car. I wouldn't want to wake anyone at this point." After awhile he started the engine, and they drove away. "She suspects someone of something, that's for sure."

"Yes but, who, exactly?" Yvonne wondered.

Chapter 18
MONDAY, JUNE 15TH

"Inspector Gordon, have ye learned anything about Duncan's disappearance yet?" asked Cameron.

"I'll be sure to tell ye when I do." The inspector looked at each of them in turn.

Yvonne, David and Cameron had made the police station their first stop.

"Have you done any investigating at all?" asked Yvonne.

"All in good time, Ms. Suarez. We have dozens of *current* open cases that need working. I can assure ye we'll get to it. The sooner ye go on yer way, the sooner we'll get back to our cases. Don't ye worry, we'll let ye know as soon as we learn what happened."

"What about the bullet? When will you know where it came from?" David shot Inspector Gordon a belligerent look.

"The test results should be here in a day or two. We'll let ye know where it leads."

"Did you find anything else? Tire tracks? What about the neighbors, did they see anything?" David pressed on.

"I'm afraid not. The tire tracks were mixed with others. Not clear enough to distinguish." The inspector paused a moment. "If that will be all, I'll get back to wark." He picked up a file of papers on his desk, dismissing them.

"That was a waste of time," David stated the obvious.

"We're on our own to solve this now." Yvonne felt a momentary pang of homesickness for Christy and her family and parents. "I just hope we can do so soon."

On the way back to Cameron's, Yvonne flipped open her cell phone. "I'm going to call Darleen and invite her to lunch. See if she'll open up to me. I think she knows more than she's telling." A mother herself, she knew that Margaret was not overdramatizing her concern for her daughter last night. It took some convincing, but Darleen reluctantly agreed to meet with her at half past noon at the new Halcyon restaurant on Eastgate road recommended by Cameron.

Cameron pulled into the driveway. "I am goin to run in and get Kendra and Fiona. We'll drop ye off to meet Darleen, and we'll take David and Fiona to lunch nearby so ye can meet up with us when ye're done."

"Perfect!"

Yvonne walked up the stairs to the Halcyon restaurant located above the Villeneuve Wine Shop. Decorated with white linens and creamy yellow wall colors, and coupled with sunlight from the many windows, it gave off a cheery elegant atmosphere. Seated by an attractive hostess, Yvonne had arrived a few minutes early and was looking at their extensive menu when the same hostess escorted Darleen to the table.

Darleen wore a crisp navy-blue business suit, having taken the time to blow out her massive curls, her thick curls were tamed into waves. She smiled warmly at the hostess, thanking her. Her attitude cooled when she settled onto her seat across from Yvonne. "I assume ye had a good reason for inviting me to lunch."

"I've been worried about you." Yvonne took a sip from her water glass to break the tension.

"Worried ... about me?" Darleen looked nervously around the restaurant. "Why?"

"I thought you may have remembered something about the man in your vision. Or, maybe you had another vision. Anyway, I thought you might be frightened. After all, whoever murdered Randy may know about your visions. He could suspect something. If he does, he might come after you." Yvonne studied her reaction. Darleen tried valiantly to hide her fearful feelings, but the eyes never lie, and Yvonne saw nervousness in them.

Darleen looked quickly around the restaurant and back to Yvonne. "I've had another vision," she blurted out.

"Tell me about it," Yvonne spoke softly, encouraging her.

"I ... I can't tell ye or anyone." Darleen looked down at the empty space on the table where a plate of food would soon sit.

"Are ye ready to order?" asked the waitress.

Darleen looked up sharply at the interruption. She sighed, picked up her menu and glanced at it. "I'll have the crab cakes."

"I'll have the same," said Yvonne.

After the waitress left to place their order, Yvonne asked Darleen, "Why can't you tell me who you saw in your vision?"

"I just can't."

"Is it someone you know? Someone close to you?"

"I'll leave now if ye keep questioning me."

"Please, Darleen, don't leave. I'm trying to help you." Yvonne looked around to be sure no one was listening in. "We can go to the police. I'm sure they'll protect you. I'll go with you if you need me to."

"Ye don't understand. I don't want to go to the police. Once ye leave, everything will blow over and go back to the way it was before." She spoke fast and spittle flew out of her mouth hitting Yvonne's water glass.

Yvonne's cheeks grew hot. She made a failed attempt to control her flaring temper, and her words sounded harsh to her own ears. "And how was that? Everyone keeping secrets? Fiona still won't know what happened to her brother!"

"There are no secrets." Darleen's tone was half-hearted.

"I think there are." Yvonne called her bluff.

"Some secrets are nobody's business. Especially not yers." Darleen started to get up.

"Wait." Yvonne looked up. The waitress headed toward them with their lunch plates. "I'll drop the subject of going to the police, but please—" She waited while the waitress set their food on the table. "Tell me who you saw in your vision."

"He would never hurt me. I'm afraid for *him*, don't ye see? ... Now, will ye please let it drop?"

Yvonne thought about Darleen's statement while she ate. Why had Darleen accepted the lunch invitation if she was so dead set against telling her anything or accepting her help? Maybe another approach would work.

After they'd finished half their meal, Yvonne tried again. "Darleen, I understand why you wouldn't want to confide in me but I think you should talk to someone. What about your mother? She's worried about you." Yvonne prayed that bringing Darleen's mother into the conversation wouldn't backfire on her.

"My mother's always worried aboot somethin. I won't add to her worries."

"Holding everything in is unhealthy." Yvonne cut into her second crab cake and took a bite.

"Yvonne, I appreciate that ye're trying to help, but ye have to trust me on this. The safest thing for me and everyone else is to keep what I know to myself."

"At least tell me this: Does it have anything to do with Duncan's disappearance."

"I honestly don't know. I don't think so." Darlene picked at her side salad that had come with the crab cakes. She looked up from her plate. "Please, tell Fiona I'm sorry that I can't help her." She took a drink of water, pulled a twenty pound bill out of her purse and set it on the table. "This should cover lunch. Go home and take Fiona with ye. Forget ye ever met us." Darleen got up from the table and walked out leaving Yvonne to wonder if they'd ever find out what happened to Duncan.

Yvonne finished her lunch, paid the bill, and descended the stairs to the sidewalk below. Her arm had started aching a little so she fumbled with her cell phone. David answered on the first ring. "Hi. Have you finished lunch, yet? We're done here."

"Almost finished. Can you give us about ten minutes?"

"Of course. I'll be out front of the wine store." Yvonne jumped back from the curb as a van pulled up, the engine drowning out David's last words. The side door of the van opened. A man dressed in black with a ski mask jumped out and moving with surprising speed, grabbed her in a bear hug and pulled her into the van. She tried to scream, but he held her so tight she could only squeak. He continued holding her with one strong arm and pulled the door closed, blocking anyone's view of the situation. She tried kicking him, but he held her so close she could only squirm, getting no good leverage. He shoved her to the floor of the van face down, pulled her wrists behind her, clamped on handcuffs, and gagged her mouth with a cloth so she couldn't scream. Lastly, he pulled a black covering over her head leaving her scared and disoriented.

The van sped away causing her to careen into the cold metal side. She rolled around and tried sitting up. She worked herself up, leaning her back against the side of the van. She swayed with the movement but managed to keep upright. Her mind raced.

She felt around for her cell phone. It had been in her hand when he grabbed her.

Damn, she thought, I must've dropped it—my purse too. Why would someone do this? Is it the person who murdered Randy? The person Darleen's protecting? It had to be a hired hand of her father's or Keith. That's the only thing that makes sense. Unless ... could it possibly be Ullrick? No. That makes no sense. I couldn't get a feel for who it was. It all happened so fast.

Frustrated, she stomped her foot on the floor of the van. She felt around with it. Debris that felt like strands of hay accounted for the smell.

Ay Dios mio! What will David and the rest of them think when they arrive at the restaurant, and I'm not waiting out front? What have I done? Put myself in danger and maybe others. Oh, Christy, how could I do such a thoughtless thing? You'll be waiting for a call from Mommy, tonight. I have to find a way out of this. She took a shallow breath and thought, Stop. Don't panic. Take a deep breath. She did so and it calmed her. She tried to think rationally.

I must be getting close. I'm a threat to someone, that's for sure.

David left Cameron in the car with the ladies while he went upstairs to the Halcyon restaurant to see if Yvonne had returned there. Maybe she forgot her purse or something. He looked around the restaurant and waited a minute or two thinking she may have dashed to the restroom. Then he approached the hostess. "Did you see a pretty young woman with light brown hair come back in, after leaving?"

"No sir, but ..." She hesitated, reaching into the cubby in her hostess stand. "A passerby picked these up from the sidewalk out front. She thought perhaps one our guests had dropped them." She had pulled out Yvonne's purse and cell phone.

"Those belong to the young lady I'm looking for. You're sure she didn't return perhaps to use the ladies room?"

"I would have seen her, sir."

"I'll take these for safe keeping."

"Well ... I'm not sure if—"

"Look, her name is Yvonne Suarez. Check her driver's license. She's my fiancée. I promise to return them to her just as soon as I find her."

The hostess opened Yvonne's purse, found her wallet and driver's license and verified that he was telling the truth. "What is yer name, sir? Show me yer identification so that if she turns up I can tell her who picked up her belongings."

David showed the hostess his driver's license and passport. She jotted down his name and driver's license number and handed over Yvonne's purse and cell phone.

Outside the restaurant, David looked up and down both sides of the street, hoping to see her step out from a nearby store. She was nowhere to be found.

"The police station, now!" David got into the car and explained as Cameron headed in the direction of the small stationhouse.

They entered the police station amidst utter chaos brought on by the arrest of ten or so unruly teens who'd apparently been harassing old folks going in and out of the local pharmacy. Several constables were taking statements from the elderly victims while at the same time the teens were being processed and sent to one of the two interior jail cells.

"This could take hours. We need help now. Whoever has taken Yvonne could be well away from Peebles by now." David punched his open hand with a clenched fist showing his frustration.

"Follow me." Cameron led David and the ladies through the line of teens and headed for Inspector Gordon's office. The constables were too preoccupied to notice. He knocked once on the Inspector's door and entered not waiting for a response. They piled into his office.

"Yvonne's been kidnapped! You need to send your officers out to find her before she disappears for good." David placed both hands on the Inspectors desk and leaned in close to his face.

"Ye can't just barge into my office." Inspector Gordon stood up and put his hands on his hips, shoving his face up close to David's.

David straightened up and backed off. "Are you going to help or not?"

"How do ye know she's been kidnapped? That's a pretty serious accusation. What proof do ye have?"

Fiona had been holding onto Yvonne's purse and had placed her cell phone inside. She reached over and set them on the inspector's desk.

"We found these on the ground in front of the Halcyon restaurant where we were to pick her up."

"Maybe ye better start from the beginnin." The inspector sat back down in his chair and indicated with nods that they should take a seat as well.

David took a seat reluctantly, forcing himself to tamp down his impatience. He relayed the story of how Yvonne had gone to meet with Darleen for lunch, leaving out her reasons for doing so. He explained how they'd gone to another restaurant and when she called asking to be picked up, they had been cut off. He assumed it was just a bad connection but then when they found her purse and cell phone ... David bit his lip, "Good God, man, don't you see if only we'd gone right away, she might be here now."

The inspector gave a flip of his hand. "If indeed she was kidnapped. Seeing the pain in David's face he softened his tone, "Now, don't go blamin yerself. I doubt there was anything ye could have done to prevent it. From what I've seen of Ms. Suarez, she's a smart and perspicacious lassie. She'll find a way to survive, maybe even leave us a clue or two along the way."

"I hope you're right, Inspector. I have no idea who or how many people are involved, or what they could possibly want with her."

The inspector asked them to wait a moment while he called for the constable on street duty. He gave the PC Yvonne's description and instructions to check with the Halcyon restaurant to see if any of the guests coming or going had seen anything suspicious. "Check with the nearby shops too," he added.

He turned back to David. "Tell me, why was she meeting with Darleen Turner?"

"As I said, she was meeting for lunch."

"There must be more to it than that, Mr. Ludlow. I wasn't born yesterday ye know. She's still investigatin Duncan Ross' disappearance. I'm well aware that he was dating Darleen at the time he went missing."

David glanced at Cameron and Fiona. They'd be hearing this for the first time too. "Darleen confided to Yvonne that she'd had a vision and in that vision she'd seen Randy Ferguson's murder, all the bloody details, but not the murderer himself. Apparently in her vision, it was as if she was seeing things through the murderer's eyes.

"Yvonne received a call from Darleen's mother who sensed that Darleen was afraid of something or someone. She asked Yvonne to see if she could find out what it might be. Yvonne thought it possible that Darleen had had another vision revealing who the murderer was, so she agreed to talk to Darleen—let her know we'd be here if she needed help. Yvonne was worried that the murderer might know about Darleen's visions and pose a threat."

"Did Ms. Suarez tell ye what they'd talked about during her lunch with Mrs. Turner?"

"No. It was a brief call to let me know she was finished and waiting to be picked up. David ran his hands through his hair. "Look, for what it's worth, Inspector, I think you should have someone search the woolen mill grounds. We think it's likely that Darleen's father or husband may be involved in Duncan's disappearance and that Randy Ferguson was somehow involved. That may be why he was silenced—murdered—"

"I can't search without cause." He picked up the phone receiver. "Rhona, I want ye to drive over to the Peebles Woolen Mill, pick up Darleen Turner, and bring her in for questioning. Tell her it's in regards to the disappearance of Ms. Yvonne Suarez." He turned his focus back to the small assembly in the office. He opened his mouth to speak but the phone rang, and he grabbed the receiver. "Uh huh ... okay ... thank ye Andrews. That'll be all."

Inspector Gordon took a deep breath and continued, "PC Andrews has questioned the hostess and waitress who waited on the ladies at the restaurant. They witnessed Mrs. Turner leave first and a few minutes later, Ms. Suarez. They described the person who'd turned in the purse as an elderly woman who happened to be stopping into Villeneuve Wines. She'd inquired first in the wine shop to see if they might know who had dropped the purse and cell. The proprietor recalled seeing a lady exit the restaurant and speaking on her mobile phone. The proprietor had then gone into the back to unpack liquor boxes, and when he returned to the front, she was gone. His view out the window didn't allow him to see her purse or phone on the ground."

"Surely you can see that Yvonne had no reason to drop her purse in the middle of the sidewalk, Inspector. What are you going to do about it?" David looked him directly in the eyes and waited.

The inspector remained quiet for a minute, thinking. The silence in the office was palpable as they waited for his response.

Inspector Gordon startled them when he broke the silence. "It does seem unlikely that she'd up and disappear after calling ye to come pick her up," he addressed David, "and given that she's been poking around in this old cold-case ... well ... it's likely she's stirred up a hornet's nest and gotten herself in trouble. I'll call the Justice of the Peace and request a warrant to search the Woolen Mill buildings."

"What about the MacIntyre Manor?" asked Cameron. "There's plenty of room to hide a person in that old homestead."

"First things first. I'll get a warrant for all their properties, but we'll hold off on the manor for the time being. We can always search it later if nothing turns up, elsewhere. I'd rather not tread directly on the toes of one of our community leaders, unless it's absolutely necessary." The inspector frowned.

"I don't know much about police searches," said David, "but wouldn't it be better to search everything at once? Otherwise they may move her if they're forewarned that we suspect them of harboring her."

He acknowledged David with a nod. "That's a possibility." He thought a moment. "I'll post a constable to watch the house—make sure they don't do anything fishy. We must tread carefully, we don't want to enrage them, or they may harm Ms. Suarez. Of course there's a possibility they may do that anyway, but for now we must proceed with speed and caution."

Her captor drove the speed limit. Yvonne tried to calculate the time it took and the mileage. She became confused about the direction they were heading after several turns. She thought he'd made a U-turn but couldn't be sure. Once he'd left the main highway, the rural roads curved around in all directions and seemed to go on forever. After what seemed about forty minutes, he turned onto a rough road, not paved. They bumped along for about ten more minutes then he came to an abrupt stop. He opened the van door and pulled her out shoving her roughly along. She stumbled several times and brushed up against a structure. It felt wooden and hard, perhaps a post, she thought. The air smelled of hay and sunshine. She'd smelled the same hay scent in the van. The floor of the van had been scattered with debris. She'd felt around with her foot—remembered thinking it might've been loose hay. At a distance she heard sheep bleating. He shoved her through an opening and the temperature dropped a few degrees. He stopped her and stood behind her, reaching up under the black covering over her head, he untied the gag pulling it from her mouth and out from underneath the covering. She sputtered and choked a bit while he pulled the covering down to rest securely on her shoulders. Next, he grabbed her arm roughly pulling her farther inside. She yanked her arm back. "No need to be so rough," she snapped.

He didn't respond. So far she hadn't heard him make a sound. He tugged her arm a bit more gently until he'd walked her along quite a distance. They turned a corner and he brought her quickly through another doorway. He pushed her farther in and she took a step or two, barely keeping her balance on the lumpy floor. A door closed behind her and she heard a slow scraping noise. He was securing the door by moving a heavy piece of furniture in front of it. What kind of room or door has no lock, she wondered. After a moment of silence she heard him walking away. "You could've at least taken off my blind fold," she yelled.

Again, no response. She took tentative steps. The ground was covered with straw, some sort of animal bedding, she assumed. There was a peculiar metallic smell. *Dried blood? What kind of room is this anyway?* She reached a wall, moving slowly around, dragging her arm against it in the hopes that it would signal an object to her. Surprisingly, the only thing she encountered was the doorway she'd come through. The room was empty except for the straw on the floor. She worked her way back along the wall to the center, opposite the door, and slid down into a seated position. Her shoulders ached from having her hands cuffed behind her back for so long.

Think, she told herself. What should I do now? There's nothing in the room that would allow me to break off the cuffs. Maybe I can at least work the cover off my head. It would help to see. She tried pulling the back of her head downward against the wall forcing the cover to rise up. She could get it just so far, then when she moved her head out to try and bring it farther up, the cover would fall back to her shoulders. She thought a moment. *Ay Dios mio!* I'll do a modified *Uttanasana*—standing forward bend. Glad she'd worn comfortable slacks, she wriggled herself sideways against the wall to get some purchase. She struggled to her knees then used all her strength to lift herself up without the use of her hands. Standing in Mountain Pose, she breathed deeply and upon the third exhale she slowly bent forward keeping strong legs and relaxing her upper body. She lifted her arms upward bringing her torso farther forward and down. The cover fell off easily. She slowly lifted her upper body, and smiled to herself.

The room was dusky, dark. A small open window up toward the ceiling let in a little light. She'd already realized the walls were wood paneled. They'd been darkened with age, adding to the gray gloominess. It must be an old sheep barn, she thought. I'll bet this is the ewe birthing room. She'd read how they isolate the ewes, keeping them out of drafty areas while they birthed as they and their lambs were susceptible to colds and diseases. This prevented them from getting sick. If that happened the whole herd was in danger.

She sat down again and wondered if she could wriggle out of the handcuffs by pulling her arms underneath her and pulling her legs through. She tried it, but her arms weren't long enough, she couldn't get them to go beyond her bottom. After awhile she got up and walked to the door. She leaned her backside against it and pushed with her arms. It didn't budge. "Guess I'll have to wait for David to rescue me. I'm sure he's gone to the police by now. They're bound to find me soon," she said out loud. Think positive, she thought.

Yvonne played over in her mind the kidnapping, thinking about the man who'd abducted her. He'd never said a word. A good indication that she'd recognize his voice. Judging by his height and weight she guessed that it was Keith who'd grabbed her. That would explain why Darleen wouldn't reveal who she saw in her dream. How awful, she thought, to see the one you love, murder someone. She wondered if Darleen had confronted Keith about it. She might be afraid of him, though Yvonne hadn't seen any evidence of that, and Lord knows—she was an expert on the subject.

The room was close and warm. The smell of rotting hay and blood was beginning to nauseate her. The barn wouldn't be used again until the winter to shelter animals or next spring to birth the lambs. She could go undetected for months. Where exactly was she? Still in Peebles? Or, some other town? What if he left her here to starve, or worse, came back to kill her. He'd already killed at least one person. *Ay Dios mio, por favor me ayude.*

David and the others waited in the inspector's office while he questioned Darleen in another room. David paced the small office while Fiona sat quietly twisting the strap to her pocketbook. Cameron and Kendra were silent, holding hands and exchanging glances as they watched David walk back and forth. The waiting was torture for all four of them.

Within thirty minutes the door swung open and Inspector Gordon entered. "No luck, I am afraid." He walked to his chair but remained standing. "She admitted to having lunch with Yvonne but denied discussing any of her visions. She said they chatted about the weather and the area." He paused a moment, and spoke directly to David, "According to Darleen, any talk of her having visions was purely a figment of Yvonne's active imagination—she'd had no such vision seeing Randy's murder."

Gordon further explained that he'd questioned her about Duncan's disappearance and she'd been even less forthcoming, saying that it was long ago and she'd forgotten most of the day's events. She admitted that she was as baffled by his disappearance, as everyone else.

David shook his head furiously. "She's lying. Are you going to get that warrant or not? Time is running out. It'll be dark soon. Yvonne'll be scared."

"Calm down, Mr. Ludlow. I sent the request over to the Justice of the Peace as soon as Darleen left. The warrant should be here soon."

Fiona, seated, reached up and tugged on David's sleeve. "I'm so sorry. This is all my fault. If I hadn't asked her to help me none of this would have happened." She sniffled, reaching into her purse for a tissue.

David patted her on the shoulder and took a seat. He couldn't bring himself to respond to her apology. At the moment he didn't disagree with her.

When the warrant arrived, Gordon instructed Cameron to take David and the ladies home to wait for his call reporting their findings.

"I'd like to come with you." David stood up anxious to help find Yvonne.

"That won't be possible. Rules of law, Mr. Ludlow. We can't have civilians interfering with our search. If we found something, yer presence could jeopardize our case."

"I wouldn't interfere." David stood his ground.

"Nevertheless, it'd be best if ye waited with Mr. Douglas. I promise, I'll call ye as soon as we finish our search."

Reluctantly, David agreed to wait at Cameron's.

As soon as Yvonne's friends left, Gordon rounded up six constables. He briefed them about the situation and indicated he'd personally direct them through the search.

When Gordon and his PCs arrived at the Woolen Mill he sent a constable to the MacIntyre home to bring Craig and Margaret outside. He directed the other constables to set up a cordoned off area to keep the owners and employees in one spot under his surveillance during the search. After they finished, he assigned three constables per building, one to bring the employees out to the staging area and two to begin searching. "Mind ye now, don't make a mess of the shop inventory. Be respectful," commanded Gordon to his constables.

Observing a stocky man in a tight-fitting dark suit and white shirt, giving orders to the police constables, Craig approached the Inspector. "What's the meaning of this?"

Inspector Gordon turned a serious eye toward the elderly gentleman. "Mr. MacIntyre, I'm Peebles Police Inspector Gordon." He handed the warrant to Craig. "A visitor to our fair town has gone missing and foul play is suspected."

"Who might that be?" asked Craig.

"I believe ye're acquainted with Ms. Yvonne Suarez. She was kidnapped outside the Halcyon restaurant just minutes after having lunch with yer daughter, Darleen."

"What does that have to do with me? And why are ye searching our mill?"

"We know about her inquiries into the old missing persons case that happened here in the sixties." He hesitated a moment watching to see MacIntyre's reaction. None. He continued, "Since the day when Ms. Suarez arrived with Mrs. Fiona Batson, the missing boy's sister, there's been a murder—yer retired foreman, and a shooting aimed at Ms. Suarez. Fortunately, the shooter missed. It seems that someone is trying to prevent her from finding the truth of what happened to Duncan Ross all those years ago. So, searching yer mill is the logical place to start, is it not?"

MacIntyre harrumphed.

Gordon turned his attention to the police constable bringing Darleen and her manager from the gift shop. Another brought three ladies from the spinning and weaving cottage. Another constable led Keith from the rear building where the wool washing takes place, and another led two farm hands and a shepherd from the stable area. Gordon paid close attention to Darleen and Keith. Darleen refused to meet his gaze and Keith, arms folded tightly across his chest, looked angry and defensive.

The searchers found nothing relating to Yvonne's disappearance in the Gift shop, or in the spinners and weavers cottage, or the wool washing building. The stables turned up nothing either.

"We'll be searchin the manor house too," explained Gordon to MacIntyre. "Are there any secret rooms we should know about? It will go a lot easier if ye tell us about them than if we must find them for ourselves."

"There's nothin of the sort," said Margaret indignantly.

"Don't mean anythin insultin about it, but it wouldn't be the first time we'd found secret rooms in the old buildings around here." Gordon nodded to his men. "Be respectful now, but be thorough, a woman's life is at stake."

"We would never hurt Ms. Suarez." Margaret's eyes pleaded with the Inspector. "She only met with my daughter because I asked for her help."

Inspector Gordons eyes shot open wide. "What was that ye say? Ye asked for her help with yer daughter?"

Margaret flinched, realizing she'd spoken too honestly.

Her husband asked, "Why on earth would ye ask Yvonne for help?"

"Yes, do tell," said the inspector.

She glanced away from the penetrating glare of her husband. "Well, I was worried about Darleen. She's been jumpy the last few days. She turned and addressed her husband. "Haven't ye noticed?

I thought she seemed frightened. That maybe it had something to do with her visions. I thought maybe Yvonne could help her like she's helping Fiona—find out what's wrong."

"She denied having any visions when I questioned her." Gordon looked across to where Darleen stood talking with her shop manager. He caught her attention and motioned for her to join them.

Darleen took her time, stopping along the way to reassure the workers that everything was fine. "Hello Inspector. Haven't I answered all yer questions already? What more can I say?"

"Ye can start by telling me why ye lied about having visions? It seems that yer mother was just as worried about them as Yvonne." The late afternoon sun beat down on them, causing the Inspector to sweat. He pulled a handkerchief from his coat and wiped his brow.

"It was like I told you. I haven't had any visions." She glanced at her mother then back at the Inspector. "I don't know what they're talking about."

Margaret looked stricken by Darleen's words but kept quiet.

"Play it that way then. If I find out that ye had anythin to do with Ms. Suarez disappearance, I'll be charging ye with kidnapping."

Darleen's lips were drawn in a tight line as she fought back emotion. "I promise ye. I've had nothing to do with it. Why would I? I want nothing more than to find out what happened to Duncan." Tears formed in her eyes.

"That's enough, Inspector." Craig stepped between him and Darleen. "Need I call my solicitor?"

"Whatever ye think best." Gordon turned and marched off toward the manor.

On the way back to Cameron's, David asked him to swing by the Hydro Hotel so he could grab his laptop computer. When they arrived at Cameron's David set it up on their kitchen table.

He was delighted to find that they had access to broadband for their own computer and he could access it.

"What are ye looking for?" Cameron sat at the table, a whisky and soda waiting to be sipped.

"I thought I'd do some checking on my own, of the suspects. I'd like to find out what lands and buildings that Craig MacIntyre and Keith Turner have access too. There may be something the police are overlooking. It seems illogical that they'd hide Yvonne at the Woolen Mill, there's so much traffic in and out of there."

"Makes sense." Cameron took a sip of his drink.

Kendra and Fiona retired to their rooms, leaving the men alone in the kitchen.

David began his search on the internet. Recently, Google.com had become the largest world-wide-web search engine, beating out Yahoo and AOL. David's software business depended on his being technologically savvy and up on all the latest internet services. He typed in keywords for locating landowners in the Peebles area. He was prepared to hack into governmental agencies if necessary, but within a few minutes he found a land-ownership website started the year before. The site's researcher had many-years-experience and was able to give him the information he requested for a small fee that he paid with his credit card. A short time later he received, via email, several documents showing landownership of the MacIntyres, and Keith Turner. It surprised him to learn that Keith was a landowner in his own right, having inherited his parents' sheep farm. The documents described the properties, listing the acreage each held and any buildings located on the properties. He linked up to the Douglases' printer and printed off the documents for further review.

With copies of the documents in hand, David asked Cameron to look over the maps locating buildings and give his advice as to which might be the most remote and best place to hide a person.

"Look here," Cameron pointed to a sheep barn on the Turners' farm tucked at the edge of a small forested area. "Forest on one side and open pasture and hills on the other. This is an ideal location for a shelter for the animals. In the very hot weather the forest offers shade to the shelter, and in the very cold winters the hills and forests act as barriers against the wind. It's quite remote too, so there's probably a farm road accessing it." Cameron looked up at David. "If I were going to hide a body ... uh ... person, this is where I'd put them."

Inspector Gordon returned to the staging area. "Ye are free to return to yer work," he shouted so everyone could hear. "Mr. Turner, a word please."

Keith Turner stayed behind with the inspector as the farm hands and other workers went on their way. The inspector asked him to wait while they cleared the area.

"Are ye satisfied, Inspector?" asked Craig. "Ye've disrupted our business all for naught." He continued on toward home with Margaret following behind, head down, unable to look anyone in the eye.

Inspector Gordon turned his attention to Keith Turner. "Where were ye today between noon and one o'clock?"

Keith fidgeted from one foot to the other. "I was taking my lunch break."

"Answer the question. Where were ye?"

"I took my sandwich and drove to the river to relax."

"Any witnesses?"

"Nae. The point was to be by myself."

"So let me get this straight. Around the time that Ms. Suarez was kidnapped, ye were nowhere to be found, and ye have no alibi."

"Piss off, Inspector. Ye have no proof that I'd done anythin to Ms. Suarez." Keith turned and walked away.

"Don't leave the area, Mr. Turner. We'll be wantin to talk to ye again." Gordon scratched his head. The afternoon had turned up nothing. His superiors would be angry that he'd wasted the man hours searching—turning up nothing. He'd go back to the station. He had an idea where to look next, but he'd need to check out some things first. In the meantime, he should stop by to report as promised to Mr. Ludlow.

The door was answered by Kendra. "Won't ye please come in, Inspector."

He stepped inside and looked around the cozy living room. "I'd liked to speak to Mr. Ludlow."

"I'm afraid he's not here."

The inspector looked shocked. "What? I thought they were waiting to hear the results of the search."

Kendra's eyes lit up with excitement. "Did ye find her, Inspector?" She looked beyond him to the street.

"No. We found nothing."

"Oh ..." Disappointment flashed across her face.

Fiona wandered out from her room. "What is it? Has there been word about Yvonne?" she asked with hope in her voice.

Gordon ignored Fiona and asked Kendra, "Where is Mr. Ludlow then?"

"He and Cameron have gone to check on an old sheep barn on Keith Turner's family farm."

"Damn! ... Oh ... pardon me. Where is it then?" His agitated tone made it clear there'd be hell to pay when he caught up with them.

"I'm not sure, Inspector. They rushed out, and I didn't get the details. David looked it up on his computer." Kendra pointed to the kitchen.

The Inspector ran to the kitchen, sure enough the computer was up and running and the documents were still open. He scanned them quickly until he came to the Turner farm information. After studying them, he located the sheep barn Kendra spoke of. He rushed out of the kitchen, passed by the ladies with no words of goodbye, and went to his car. He radioed in asking for back up and rescue squad to the Turner farm, then raced off.

It took them about a half hour pushing the speed limit in Cameron's car. David thought it best that Cameron drive since he knew the area and the roads. They entered the farm property. The grounds were overgrown and neglected. All was quiet, not a soul or animal in sight. According to the map the barn was three-tenths of a mile from the farm house. Cameron drove slowly with his low beam lights on. It was dusk and hard to see. A minute or two later they spotted the building. It was long with many open stalls on one side and closed off on the other three sides. They pulled up in front. The place looked deserted. When they got out, David spotted tire tracks. "Look." He pointed them out to Cameron. "They look recent."

At the far end of the barn they saw a dark opening leading inside. They approached it quickly, stepping inside. Turning right they came to a wall with a large tool cabinet sitting against it. On impulse, David yelled, "Yvonne!"

"David, I'm in here!" shouted Yvonne.

"We're right here, darling. We'll have you out in no time."

As David and Cameron moved the tool cabinet, the police arrived, sirens blaring. David opened the door into the darkened room.

"Over here." Yvonne sat against the wall, hands still behind her back. "What took you so long?"

"I got here as fast as I could. How ... how did you know it would be me that found you?"

"I'd been sitting here meditating, picturing you being the first to come through the door."

David laughed at her comment then pulled her to her feet and hugged her. "Are you okay? Did he hurt you?"

Before she could answer, Inspector Gordon burst into the small room. "Is she all right?"

In an instant there were bright flashlights and police everywhere.

"Can someone please get these bloody handcuffs off me?" She turned her back toward them and lifted her arms. Police Inspector Gordon took his handcuff keys from his pocket and found one that unlocked her cuffs.

She rubbed her arms and hands to get the feeling back in them. The paramedics insisted on taking her blood pressure and listening to her heart. They pronounced her okay and released her to Inspector Gordon.

The police took a cast of the tire tracks that David pointed out to them, and began looking for fingerprints, though it was likely they'd be Keith's since he owned the property.

"We'd like to get Yvonne home now, Inspector." David had wrapped his arm protectively around Yvonne's shoulders.

"I'll need a statement. Best ye follow me to the station before her memory gets foggy." Inspector Gordon turned on his heel and headed to his car, leaving them no chance to argue.

"Don't worry, I'll be alright," she said to David. "I'd just as soon get it over with. That is if you two don't mind coming with me." She looked at David and Cameron.

"Of course not. If you're sure you're up to it?" David watched her intently.

She smiled at them. "Really, I'm fine."

Inspector Gordon recorded Yvonne's statement. "Stop by in the morning. We'll have it typed up and ready for yer signature." He got up from his seat and came around to escort them from his office. "Don't worry, Ms. Suarez. We'll bring Keith Turner in tonight for questionin. Ye should be safe if ye stay with yer friends and don't go anywhere alone until we have the kidnapper behind bars."

Yvonne was touched by his compassion. Maybe she had misjudged his indifference to their investigation.

Chapter 19
TUESDAY, JUNE 16TH

David insisted Yvonne spend the night with him at the hotel. At six in the morning, feeling well-rested, she snuck out of bed to a quiet spot near the couch and did three yoga sun-salutations. That, coupled with a shower, restored her shoulders to their normal feel-good condition.

Yvonne sat on the bed next to David and kissed him gently on the forehead. "Good morning, sleepyhead."

He reached up, grabbed her and pulled her on top of him. "Don't you smell nice. Mmm." He rolled her over next to him then rolled himself on top of her. "Yes, you smell good enough to eat, my dear." He imitated a villain and gave an evil laugh.

Yvonne wrapped her arms around him and drew him in for a long luscious kiss. "You're not so bad yourself. Now do me a favor and go get a shower. We have places to go and people to see."

"You're such a party-pooper." He rolled off her and continued to lay there thinking. "What time do we need to be at the station?"

"Eight-thirty, I think. Why?"

"Just wanted to be sure we have time for breakfast." He turned and began nibbling on her ear.

"Oh, no you don't. I couldn't eat much last night, but I feel better this morning. I'm famished and want a full Scottish Breakfast."

"Okay, if you put it that way." David play-acted disappointment and went to take his shower.

They showed up promptly at eight-thirty. "Come in, come in." Inspector Gordon led Yvonne to a seat in front of his desk and motioned for David to take the other one. "Here's the statement. Please read it and make changes or corrections as ye see fit then sign it." He slid it in front of her and handed her a pen smiling all the while.

Yvonne read through it. "It all looks correct." She signed the document and wondered about his solicitous attitude. "You sound chipper this morning, Inspector. Have you made an arrest?"

"Not yet. We have Keith locked up, but he's not talkin. Claims he knows nothin about yer kidnappin." Inspector Gordon slammed his fist on the desk causing them to flinch. "We're not takin his word for it though. Give us time. We'll break him, I assure ye."

Could this be his reason for being so chipper? Did he enjoy breaking suspects? "Any chance I could talk to him inspector?" Yvonne sat up straighter in her seat looking very self-confident.

David and Inspector Gordon stared at her with their mouths open.

"Did I hear ye right—" Inspector Gordon didn't finish his sentence.

"Are you out of your mind?" David shouted. "The guy just grabbed you in broad daylight and threw you away to rot!"

"Look, what harm could it do. We're in a police station for Pete's sake. He might be more inclined to talk to me. The fact is—I won't scare him. He may even gloat over what happened." Yvonne turned her attention back to Inspector Gordon. "What do you think, Inspector? It might be worth a try. Don't you agree?"

Gordon stayed silent for several moments. "Well, it's lopsided logic for sure, but why not, weirder things have happened."

"Great." David rolled his eyes.

"Great." Yvonne smiled. "Show me the way, Inspector."

He led them to the door of the interrogation room. David noted that, just like in the police shows, it was fixed with a two-way mirror. Inspector Gordon entered the room leaving Yvonne and David outside. He checked to make sure Keith was handcuffed to his chair. "Ms. Suarez would like to have a word with ye." Keith remained silent. Then he brought in Yvonne. He left the room and standing next to David watched through the mirror.

Keith leaned back in his chair, not saying a word.

"You may think you're going to get away with this by keeping quiet, but I know it was you." Yvonne looked him directly in the eyes.

He blinked then gained control of his facial expression. "Ye're mistaken."

"No—I'm not. Don't forget—you grabbed me. I was close enough to tell how tall you were. I smelled the wool farm on you. Just tell me why. Why did you do it? Am I getting too close to finding out what happened to Duncan?" Yvonne glared at him.

He glared back at her.

"I thought you were Duncan's friend." She saw him flinch at this statement. "Maybe, you loved Darleen more and you wanted to protect her from being hurt, so you did away with Duncan. Does Darleen know? Is that why she's so upset?"

At the mention of Darleen, Keith gave her another dirty look.

"That's it. She does know, and she's scared of *you* now." Yvonne hoped he cared enough about Darleen that this realization would break him.

"Ye think ye know it all. Well, ye don't know anythin." At that he shut his mouth and looked straight ahead with a stony look on his face.

Inspector Gordon entered the room. "That'll be all now, Ms. Suarez."

Yvonne stared at Keith and realized she'd lost his attention. She left, frustrated at his lack of cooperation.

Inspector Gordon escorted her from the room. They stood watching Keith through the mirror, noting his impassive expression. The inspector turned to Yvonne and David. "Nevermind. I'll have another go at him in an hour or so. Eventually, he'll tire o' the questions and he'll slip up. We'll get the truth out o' him yet."

Yvonne buckled her seat belt. "I need to have another run at Darleen."

David started the car, leaving his foot on the brake. "Haven't you had enough excitement? You could have been seriously hurt, yesterday."

"But I wasn't. And besides, Keith is locked up now. This is my best chance to talk to Darleen."

"I'm coming with you this time."

"But—"

"No arguments." David pulled away from the station and headed toward the woolen mill.

Upon arrival at the mill, they went straight to Darleen's office in the gift shop. Informed by the clerk that Darleen had not come to work today, they went to the manor house looking for her.

A nervous Margaret answered the door. Her eyes lit up when she saw Yvonne. "Ye're okay! ... Please ... come in," she whispered. "Quick, follow me." She led them to the music room at the back of the house, the same room where they'd witnessed Darleen zone out with her vision. She closed the door to the room, taking care to do so quietly. "Please sit." She motioned them to the formal love seat but remained standing herself. She wrung her hands nervously. "Is it my fault ye were kidnapped? Do they really think Keith did it?" She watched Yvonne closely.

"What makes you think it's your fault?" David cut off Yvonne's chance to answer.

"I don't know. I guess if I hadn't asked Yvonne to help ..."

"How do you know that had anything to do with it?" he asked.

"I've had a bad feeling that something's not right." She looked beseechingly at Yvonne.

Yvonne shifted on the couch to sit up straighter. "Tell me, Margaret, have you asked Darleen what's bothering her?"

"Yes. She won't tell me. She says she's fine."

"You must have your own suspicions of what's wrong. Tell us why you think there's a problem." Yvonne pressed her.

Margaret looked around the room as if she thought she'd be overheard. "Well it all started with the day that Randy was killed. Remember, I told ye that I noticed the claymore that normally sits by the door had gone missing. Later, after I talked to ye about it, I asked Craig if he'd had it cleaned recently. He hadn't. I let the subject drop because I didn't want to raise his suspicions. But the more I thought about it, I worried, what if ..."

"What if what? Who do you think took it?" Yvonne glanced at David then turned her full attention to Margaret's answer.

"I worried it might be Keith. Ye see he's always admired the claymore. He's had a fascination with it really. I thought ... what if he took it and killed Randy with it. Maybe Darleen knows deep down that it was him, maybe she knows more about what happened to Duncan—she's never been the same, really, since he disappeared. She was once fun-loving and happy, but ever since ... she's become, well ... she's put up a wall around her ... becoming bitter, I suppose."

"Do you think she knows what happened to Duncan?" asked Yvonne.

"No. I think she's afraid to know what happened to him."

"So—you think she suspects foul play, too?" David interrupted, "We came here today, to speak with Darleen. It's important that we get to the bottom of this. Yvonne's been put at risk twice, now. First she was shot at then kidnapped. She feels certain that it was Keith who kidnapped her. So, while he's locked up, we're hoping Darleen will feel it's safe to speak with us."

"What do ye want me to do?" Margaret looked from Yvonne to David and back to Yvonne.

"Go and get Darleen. Tell her we need to see her—now. I want you to come back with her. We want her to understand that there will be no more secrets surrounding Duncan's disappearance and Randy's murder. In fact, ask Craig to join us too." Yvonne gave her a smile of encouragement. "Don't worry, Margaret. Everything's going to be fine."

They waited several minutes.

Craig arrived first. "What's the meaning of this, Ms. Suarez?"

"What? No longer calling me by my first name?"

"Harrumph."

"We want to clarify events surrounding the day Duncan went missing and the day Randy was murdered. We're pretty sure you can help with that."

"Why the nerve ... insinuating we're involved in murder."

"Father, ye can't believe that Keith would do such a thing." Darleen came in followed by Margaret.

"Why don't we all take a seat and a minute to calm down," suggested Yvonne.

Darleen gave her a dirty look but took a seat next to her father on the longer of two couches. Margaret sat at the other end of the couch separating herself from husband and daughter.

Yvonne and David remained seated on the love seat. David took hold of Yvonne's hand for encouragement.

"Now, are we ready to have a civilized discussion of the events leading up to today?" asked Yvonne.

"Good," she said. "First, let me tell you what I think happened and then you can tell me if I'm correct." Yvonne looked at Craig, Darleen and Margaret in turn. "I think that many years ago, Darleen was in love with Duncan but very unhappy when he chose to leave her and go to America to seek his fortune with his family. I think that in her youthful exuberance, she spilled her feelings to Keith, who had a strong crush on her. Later, when Duncan thought better of it, he changed his mind and promised to send for her as soon as he was settled and to make her his bride. By now, Keith had developed stronger, protective feelings for Darleen and his anger toward his friend for toying with her emotions led him to do something drastic. Maybe they had words, maybe it got out of hand, and he accidentally, or on purpose, killed his best friend." Yvonne took a breath and continued as the three onlookers gave her skeptical looks. "Somehow in trying to hide Duncan's body, Craig and Randy got involved. After all, you were already being investigated for chemical waste dumping, so you certainly couldn't risk being involved in a death—accidental or on purpose. So you agreed to help Keith dispose of the body." Yvonne focused her attention on Craig. "By keeping Keith close to the family, in marriage, you kept control of the situation, making sure the truth never came out." Silence ensued while Yvonne paused a moment.

"What I still can't figure out completely, is why Randy was murdered, unless he'd heard about our investigation and, after all this time, decided to come clean, or maybe he thought he'd blackmail Keith, and Keith took matters into his own hand by stabbing him with your claymore, Mr. MacIntyre."

"That's a huge leap ye've made there, Ms. Suarez. What evidence do ye have that Keith killed Randy using my claymore."

"The fact is—Margaret has admitted to me that your claymore was missing for a day or two around the time of the murder."

Craig glared at his wife. Margaret lowered her gaze to her knees.

Yvonne switched her focus. "Now, Darleen, I think it's time ye told me what you really saw in your most recent vision. Was it indeed Keith who murdered Randy?"

"I'll never give him up! He's been my loyal husband all these years." Darleen glanced at her father.

Craig's face crumpled. "Ye're wrong, Ms. Suarez. It was me. I killed Duncan and Randy."

"No!" Margaret gaped at her husband. "It can't be." She got light-headed and leaned back on the sofa.

Craig looked at his wife. "Ye couldn't leave it alone."

Margaret stared at him with tears in her eyes.

"No, Father. Please, don't say another word. I'll call our solicitor. He'll know what to do."

Darleen rose from the couch directing her next comments to Yvonne. "Are ye happy now? Leave—leave our house this instant. We're entitled to our privacy while we sort out what to do next."

"We'll need to inform the police," said David.

Yvonne rose from the couch. "Why, Mr. MacIntyre? Why kill Duncan? Where is he buried? Please, Fiona's been waiting a long time to learn the truth."

"Randy disposed of the body, he didn't disclose the details to me. I'll not tell ye another thing."

"Come along, Yvonne." David led her outside. "We'll learn the details soon enough.

They returned to Cameron and Kendra's, to give Fiona the news about Craig's confession. Afterward they called Inspector Gordon with the news.

During dinner that evening Yvonne said, "Inspector Gordon sounded puzzled by the confession. He felt confident Keith would confess at any moment. Something doesn't feel right."

Everyone looked up from their meal. "What do you mean?" asked David.

"Yes, what exactly do you mean." Fiona perked up momentarily.

"It all seems too easy. The way Craig confessed out of the blue like that. You don't think he'd be protecting Keith for Darleen's sake, do you?"

"It hardly seems likely. If what you said about Duncan not being good enough for his daughter was true, he probably felt the same about Keith. I would imagine there's no man good enough for his daughter. So why protect Keith." David cut a bite-sized piece of his roast beef and speared a bit of Yorkshire pudding to go with it, popping it all into his mouth.

"Yes, but that's just it. His world revolves around his daughter and her wishes. Maybe he recognizes that she truly loves Keith now and he doesn't want to jeopardize her marriage." Yvonne took a sip of wine.

Cameron added, "That doesn't clear Keith from his part in this. Don't forget he's the most likely person to have kidnapped Yvonne. I hardly think Craig could have pulled that off at his age."

"Good point," said Yvonne.

David rolled his eyes upward, thinking. "Maybe it's a case of 'a comedy of errors.' Everyone's running around trying to protect someone else."

"Well, I for one, think there are still questions that need to be answered." Yvonne glanced over at Fiona and her heart sank. "I'm so sorry, Fiona. I know you're grieving. Is there anything I can do?"

Fiona had been pushing her food around on her plate, not joining in the discussion. "No thank you, Yvonne. I guess I knew it would end this way, but I also hoped ..." She got up from the table. "If you'll excuse me, I'm going to lie down." Tears welled in her eyes.

Kendra got up from her chair to comfort Fiona.

"Please, I need to be by myself." Fiona rushed to her room.

"Poor dear." Kendra took her seat again. "Give her time. Naturally, she's upset. But, at least now she can grieve and move on. That must be a relief." Kendra had voiced what everyone else was thinking.

"Tomorrow, I'll make the changes to our return flight home. We've overstayed our welcome, but I can't tell you how much I've enjoyed getting to know you two." Yvonne smiled at her hosts and raised her wine glass in a cheering gesture.

"It's been our pleasure, I assure ye," said Cameron. "I can't thank ye enough for helping us get to the bottom of our cousin's murder. Let's hope ye'll come again for a relaxing vacation next time."

"I'm sure we'll have all the final details of Duncan's disappearance over the next day or two. Then we'll be on our way, and you can return to your normal day's activities, just in time to enjoy the Beltane Festival."

Simultaneously, the four of them breathed a sigh of relief.

"Are we ready for coffee and dessert?" Kendra got up and began clearing the dinner plates.

"Sounds good to me." Cameron winked at Yvonne and David.

Yvonne grabbed the leftover plates of food and carted them into the kitchen for Kendra. Kendra asked her to set out the coffee cups, cream and sugar while she scooped up some plum pudding with hard sauce for everyone.

"I don't know how you stay so trim, eating such rich goodies." Yvonne carried out the creamer and sugar bowl.

Before Kendra could answer, the doorbell rang. "Cameron, see who's at the door, please."

"Look who I found on our doorstep." Cameron had invited Inspector Gordon to join them for dessert.

"To what do we owe this unexpected visit, Inspector?" Cameron moved his dessert and coffee cup in front of the inspector.

"I'm afraid that I have some rather disturbing news."

"What now?" Yvonne and David asked at the same time.

"We've picked up Craig MacIntyre and confiscated his claymore. The medical examiner has confirmed that Randy was killed with a long sword. Though, we'll need to send it off to the Forensic Science Support Department in Edinburgh to test for blood and DNA samples. In the meantime, now Keith has confessed to killing Duncan and Randy. It's darned confusing. All this time we had no leads, now we have two confessions."

"How long will it take to get the results of the testing and what are you going to do with them in the meantime?" asked Yvonne.

"I'm lettin them sit in jail tonight. We'll see tomorrow which one can convince us he's tellin the truth." Dark circles under the inspector's eyes gave away his tiredness. "The tests, I'm afraid will take weeks, possibly months. There's always a backlog of cases."

He reminded Yvonne of a dog that wouldn't let go of his bone. He wouldn't let go of the case until he had all the facts. A good quality in a police inspector, she thought.

Chapter 20
WEDNESDAY, JUNE 17TH

Yvonne had declined David's offer to spend another night with him at the hotel. She wanted to be available to Fiona if she needed her. She'd had a fitful night's sleep, awaking at four in the morning. She lay there thinking, replaying all the encounters with Darleen and her family and Ullrick. She thought about what she'd learned at the newsagents about chemical waste dumping. Was there something more to it that she needed to discover? Hadn't she asked any and all possible questions? The right answer eluded her. She felt it was within her grasp, but she couldn't quite put her finger on it. Once she did, it would solve the mystery and clear up all the confusion.

At five she decided to get up and meditate. She spread a towel on the floor facing the window, sat in the easy cross-legged position and began concentrating on her breathing. The comfortable smells of aged wood, well-worn fabrics, and dying rose buds filled her nostrils. Any thoughts racing through her mind were pushed away. It was difficult, but eventually, her breathing evened out and a serene calm came over her. She stayed like that for about fifteen minutes and gradually allowed an awareness of her surroundings to bring her back to the present. A moment of knowing that all would be revealed came over her. She offered peace to the universe by saying Namaste and rose gracefully from the floor.

After dressing, Yvonne called the airlines to schedule their return flights for Friday, June, 19th. She lucked out, seats were available at this late date, though they weren't good ones. Yvonne and Fiona would be seated in the back, in the middle section of the plane. But at least she'd be home for the weekend to recoup and spend quality time with Christy before returning to the agency. David's last minute ticket had been first class, so she'd had no trouble changing his flight to match with theirs.

She found Fiona already in the kitchen enjoying coffee and toast with Kendra and Cameron. "Good morning everyone." Yvonne studied Fiona to see how she felt.

Fiona picked up on Yvonne's stare. "No need to worry, Yvonne. I'm doing okay. Cameron's told me about Keith's confession." Fiona fidgeted with the paper napkin next to her plate.

"I'm sure Inspector Gordon will get it all straightened out today." Yvonne sounded confident but knew first-hand what hard nuts both Craig and Keith were.

"We should check on Darleen and Margaret. See how they're doing." Yvonne felt sure Darleen had more to tell them.

"Do you think that's a good idea?" David stood in the kitchen doorway, having arrived from the hotel unannounced. "Darleen was pretty angry with you. No telling what she might do."

"And, good morning to you." Yvonne, still in a serene state of mind, smiled broadly at David.

"David's right." Fiona frowned. "You've taken enough heat on my account already."

"I plan to see this through to the end." She ambled over to the coffee pot and poured a cup of coffee, leaving no room for argument. She handed the coffee to David then poured a cup for herself.

David rolled his eyes heavenward and sighed. "All right, if you insist, but you're not going alone. Fiona and I will go with you." David took a seat at the table. "After all, Fiona needs to be part of the final outcome if she wants to get her closure." He nodded at Kendra who passed him a plate of toast.

"That's right." Fiona smiled at Yvonne. Regaining her confidence, she said, "One for all and all for one." She placed her hand in the center of the table and giggled. "I've always wanted to say that, ever since I read the Three Musketeers as a young girl."

Yvonne and David gave each other a knowing look and placed their hands on top of Fiona's then Cameron and Kendra added theirs.

"Now this is what I call a worthy cause," said Cameron, having the last word on the subject.

It was eleven by the time the dishes were cleared away and they were ready to leave the house. On the way out the door, Yvonne's mobile phone rang. Gino's number came up on the caller ID. *Ay Dios mio*, she thought, it's five hours earlier in Fort Lauderdale. It must be around six. I hope Christy's all right. "Hello? Gino—"

"How dare you!" Gino screamed at her.

"Wha ... what's wrong? Is Christy okay?"

"You know damn well what's wrong. Playing games with me and keeping your daughter on edge."

"I don't know what you're talking about." Yvonne looked nervously at the others, embarrassed.

"You told me you were only going to be gone two weeks and it's now going on three. Did it ever occur to you that I might have plans? That I might have a life? One, that doesn't include taking care of the kid?"

"Gino calm down. You'll scare Christy."

"She's still in bed. Answer my question. When are you coming home?"

"I told you it would take a few days longer than anticipated. You said Christy was fine and that you'd taken off the whole month to be with her. Why are you so upset now?"

"I'm upset because I'm tired of you taking me for granted and always manipulating the situation. How am I supposed to plan my life if I don't know when you're picking up Christy?"

"If you'd told me you had plans, I could have made other arrangements."

"Other arrangements! What kind of mother are you anyway?"

This brought tears to Yvonne's eyes. She was so mad and hurt she couldn't think what to say. How could he turn so ugly with no warning? What am I thinking? This is how he manipulates me. Catches me off guard. Confuses. Intimidates. I should know better. "I have a flight scheduled to leave here day after tomorrow. I'll be home Friday afternoon. In the meantime, I'll call my mother and father and have them pick up Christy. They can keep her until I get home. Tell Christy I'll call her later today." She hung up the phone. Fiona, Cameron and Kendra had retreated back to the kitchen. David stood by her side.

"Come here." He hugged her to him. "Don't worry. It'll be alright. Let's go sit on the couch. You need to calm down."

Yvonne broke down and cried when she heard her mother's voice. She stumbled through the phone call from Gino, and her mother assured her they'd pick up Christy right away. "Mom, would you call ahead, and let her know you're coming? I'm too upset. And, Mom, please call me when you have her so I know everything went okay.

"Of course, darling." Nancy Suarez looked at her husband. "We're going to make sure this is the last time Gino pulls something like this."

"Be careful, Mom. You know how he gets when he's angry. Don't make matters worse."

"Don't worry. We'll be fine." Nancy's hand shook with anger when she hung up the phone. She told Eduardo what Yvonne had wanted and why. "I think you'd better be the one to call Gino. Tell him we'll be there in one hour to pick up Christy." She handed him the phone.

Yvonne had calmed down after hearing from her mother that they'd picked up Christy with no hassle.

"It was quite simple," her mother said soothingly, "Christy was waiting on the front porch with her suitcase and she was excited to see us. I don't think she knew how angry her father was."

Yvonne breathed a sigh of relief, now that Christy was safely with her parents she could concentrate on the issue at hand. She leaned back in her seat and looked out at the scenery. She wished to remember the beautiful parts of Peebles, Edinburgh, and Glasgow. She sincerely hoped to return one day with Christy and David, just for the pleasure of it.

David drove his rental car with Fiona seated next to him. Yvonne had insisted on taking the back seat. They arrived at the MacIntyre manor at 12:30 to find that Margaret and Darleen were gone. They assumed they'd gone to the police station in the hopes of retrieving their husbands.

"What should we do now? Wait for them here? Or head over to the police station."

David said, "I doubt the inspector would welcome a visit from us. Why don't we enjoy a leisurely lunch and come back later after they've returned. Who knows, maybe the innocent party will be with them, and we'll hear what really happened."

"Wouldn't that be nice? I think that's a super idea," agreed Fiona.

"Whatever you wish." Yvonne felt frustrated and angry at the way the day had developed so far.

"Okay. Lunch it is." Without asking, David took the ladies to Lazels, the bistro lunch restaurant at the Hydro Hotel.

"What a treat." Fiona, sensing Yvonne needed some positive reinforcement, said, "I have a feeling we might actually resolve the mystery of my brother's disappearance. I can't tell you what a weight will be lifted off my shoulders. And, I can't thank you enough, Yvonne, for coming with me and doing all you've done—putting yourself into harm's way—for me. And you, too, David. I am so grateful you came." Her eyes were moist with tears again.

Yvonne gave Fiona's hand a gentle squeeze. "Putting this behind you and having a happy future with your family will be thanks enough."

After eating lunch David left the ladies to enjoy a cup of tea while he went to his suite to make a few business calls. He returned to the restaurant to find them relaxed and eager to get back to their task.

This time Margaret, her eyes swollen and red from crying, answered the door. "I think ye'd better go. We don't need any more trouble."

Fiona spoke first, "Margaret, I want you to know how sorry I am that things have happened the way they have. I hope you'll understand that we never meant to hurt anyone. Are you and Darleen okay? Is there anything we can do?"

"There's nothing anyone can do." She started to close the door.

Yvonne took hold of the door before it closed completely. "Who do you think killed Duncan and Randy? I know you have suspicions that something's wrong—something to do with Darleen and her visions."

The door opened wider, Margaret just stared at Yvonne.

"We need to speak with her, again." Yvonne stepped a foot in the door.

Margaret backed up letting them in. "Darleen's in the music room."

They found her stretched out on the formal couch, staring out the window.

Darleen turned and saw them standing there. She sat up, looking beyond them to her mother. She looked tired, her frizzy hair smashed flat on one side. Her eyes narrowed. "What do they want? To send us to jail too?"

"No, dear, they're concerned about ye. Don't ye want to know the truth of what happened? Ye can't believe that yer father had anything to do with those murders. I know he can be hard at times, but he's a good man. He'd never do anything so heinous."

"So, I guess ye're saying—ye think Keith did it."

"No that's not what I'm saying at all, but ... Keith was young and in love and maybe he acted rashly—impulsively. ... I ... I wish it hadn't happened at all, but I want my happy loving daughter back, the beautiful young girl who always saw the best in everybody before she lost the young man she loved."

"That young girl is gone, Mother. Gone! Don't ye understand? She's seen too much darkness. And no one can bring her back." Darleen turned her back toward them and curled up like a child facing the back of the couch. "Leave me alone," she whispered hoarsely.

"What is it you're hiding?" asked Yvonne.

Darleen ignored her.

"I think ye'd better leave," said Margaret. "She'll be alright. I'll take care of her." She ushered them out of the room, closing the door behind her. Ye can show yerself out from here. She stood guard outside the music room door until they left.

It niggled at her. Something Darleen had said at their second meeting. Something about her second-sight or was it the Cailleach's curse? What was it? A quiet place to think, that's what she needed. "David, it's a beautiful day. Would you mind driving us to the park downtown by the river? Let's get out and walk awhile." Yvonne turned to Fiona. "Is that okay with you? We can drop you at home first if you wish."

"A walk in the park will do me good, too."

They parked and strolled along river-walk. The warm air and sunshine felt good to Yvonne. Fiona found a bench and took a seat, fanning herself with a hand. "You two go on, I'll just sit here for a while."

As they strolled away, David asked Yvonne, "What are you thinking?"

"About my early conversations with Darleen. There's something important. I'm sure it will come to me." She took hold of his hand and they walked in silence. She ignored the faint smell of dead fish and enjoyed the cool moisture misting up from the river. They watched several white swans glide along on the river, dipping their beaks into the rippling water. Their graceful movements like a pantomime ballet was reminiscent of a Sir Walter Scott novel. The movement of the water and the fresh air brought to mind the ancient Celts who worshiped Cailleach as an old krone and as the abundant mother-nature. Then, in that quiet moment ... "That's it! I remember."

"What?" David stopped and faced her waiting for an answer.

"Nevermind. We have to go back. I have to speak with Darleen, again and this time I won't be put off."

"Should we call the police?"

"Not yet. I want Darleen to verify that what I'm thinking is the truth. I'll know if she lies."

"You aren't going to tell me, are you?"

"No. This way, you'll be an objective witness to the conversation. You'll know if I'm on the right track or not. Let's get Fiona and head back over there."

When they arrived at the manor, Inspector Gordon's unmarked police car was parked in the driveway.

"I wonder what he's doing here," said Yvonne.

"Let's find out." David led the way to the front door.

Yvonne and Fiona followed. Before they reached the door, it opened and the inspector came out.

"What are ye doing here?" His brow scrunched making his eyebrows flow in one line across his forehead.

Yvonne glanced at David, hoping he'd back her up. Then turned to the inspector and took a shallow breath. "First tell us why you are here?"

"Ye don't beat around the bush, do ye?" Disgruntled, he answered, "We believe Keith Turner had the strongest motive to murder Duncan Ross and Randy Ferguson, so I've returned Mr. MacIntyre to his home—for now. ... So tell me, why are ye here?"

"I have a question to ask Darleen."

"What question?"

"Follow me back into the house, Inspector. I think we can clear this up to your satisfaction if she answers this one question truthfully."

Gordon rolled his eyes heavenward and sighed. "Then get to it. I don't have all day ye know." Annoyed at being side-stepped, he banged on the front door.

Craig answered, his face turned dour when he saw Yvonne, David, and Fiona standing behind the policeman. "I see ye've brought back the posse, inspector. Have ye changed yer mind aboot me?"

"Ms. Suarez has a question for Darleen, would ye mind humorin us, please?"

The older man nodded and motioned them inside. He looked tired from his night in jail. "Go along back to the library, I will fetch her." Darleen entered entered the library with Margaret and Craig close behind. Darleen took a seat in a chair. Yvonne took a seat across from her and reached across taking hold of Darleen's hands. Darleen pulled away, but Yvonne held firm to them. "Relax, Darleen." Yvonne looked her directly in the eyes. "I think you know by now, we just want to help. But to do so we need the truth."

"Help?" Her voice cracked, "I've told ye all I know." She broke her eyes away from Yvonne's gaze and looked down at her hands.

"Remember that second time in your office? When I asked you why, if you had visions you couldn't have seen what happened to Duncan, and you told me that visions don't usually come to you if they actually involve you, that they come for other people."

"Yes, I remember. What of it?" Darleen's voice sounded flat and she continued staring down at her hands clasped in Yvonne's.

"Could it be then, that it was you who killed Duncan? Could that be the reason you didn't have a vision about it? You already knew it was you. Most important ... could it be the reason your Father *and* Keith confessed—to protect you?"

"That's enough!" Craig crossed over to his daughter. "I demand ye leave, right now."

"I'd rather hear the answer to Ms. Suarez' question," said Inspector Gordon.

Darleen looked at her father then her mother and finally at Yvonne. "Yes. Twas me. I did it. But, it was an accident." She pulled her hands out of Yvonne's grasp, her shoulders slumped, and she started crying.

"Tell us what happened," said the inspector, softening his tone.

Yvonne pulled a tissue from her purse and handed it to Darleen. "Go ahead, Darleen. You'll feel better when it's all out in the open."

She choked back a sob and whimpered. "He'd come to me that afternoon in the wool-washin room to say that he'd changed his mind about marryin me. He was young and thought that with so many miles between us, we'd forget each other and move on. It was the sixties, and he said in America everyone was toutin free love. Can ye believe it? She choked back another sob and looked across the room at her mother. He said he wanted to let me down easy. He didn't want to leave me with false hopes.

"I told him, I'd run away with him that we didn't need to be separated, but he wouldn't go for it. His family needed him, and he thought I should be loyal to mine. He threw it in my face that my father didn't approve of him. He wasn't willin to fight for me. That's when I got angry and pushed him. He fell—hit his head on the tub and fell in. I didn't stay to see if he was okay. I ran to my room and ..." Darleen twisted the tissue in her hands. "I chust cried. I loved him so much, but he was dead by my hand. I didn't know what to do. That evening, Father told me he'd found him drowned in the tub. He chust looked at me and he knew what must have happened."

Margaret gave out an audible gasp and looked at her husband in horror as Darleen continued her story.

"Father told Randy to dispose of the body. No one told me anything more aboot it. We never mentioned it, and I don't know what Randy did with Duncan's body." Darleen quieted.

"How does Keith figure in all this?" Yvonne urged her on.

"He didn't know. Of course, he knew that Duncan went missing, everyone knew that. He stayed by my side and offered me comfort for days afterward. We never talked about it until recently. She blew her nose and looked at the Inspector. "Keith has always been jealous of my feelins for Duncan. He always said if Duncan ever turned up, he'd punch his lights out." She gave a half-hearted laugh and then turned to Fiona with a grimace. "And then you showed up. ... Twas right after you started askin questions. Old Randy turned up at the stables one day and told Keith he was thinkin of going to the police. He thought Keith knew all about it. Keith was furious with me. I tried to explain that I was protectin him. We'd had a peaceful life up until now." Darleen stopped talking again and just stared at Yvonne.

"So, that's when Keith took matters into his own hands and went to persuade Randy to change his mind about going to the police?"

"Yes. He didn't tell me he planned to quiet Randy for good—all to protect me."

Fiona, who had been standing quietly, trying to take it all in finally burst out, "Accident or no, you killed my brother and tried to make everyone forget him. And, you call that love?" Fiona clenched her fists by her sides and glared at Darleen.

"I'm sorry, Fiona. I never meant to hurt ye or yer family. I was young and hurt too, don't you know."

David put his hand on Fiona's shoulder. He didn't think she was capable, but the last thing he wanted was to have her take a swing at Darleen. Not that he would have blamed her if she did.

Inspector Gordon cleared his throat and asked the question that was on everyone's mind, "Mr. MacIntyre, where *did* Randy dispose of Duncan's body? We know it was at yer request."

Craig looked directly at his wife as he spoke, "Aye, I told him to take the body to the coast, Berwick-upon-Tweed. He weighted the body and threw it in the river. We thought if it ever rose or came loose it would be washed out to the North Sea. We thought if it had been discovered there, it would not have traced back to us." He shook his head in sorrow.

"I, too, am sorry, Fiona. I hope ye can understand that I was protectin Darleen."

Fiona rushed from the room. Yvonne rose and followed her.

"Darleen Turner, ye have the right to remain silent, anything ye say will be—"

Yvonne found Fiona sitting in the backseat of the car dabbing at her eyes with a tissue. She climbed in next to her and waited.

"I'm sorry, Yvonne. I know I should be over all this by now, but it seems so heartless. He was just a young boy wanting to make his way in the world. If only he'd been standing somewhere other than in front of that tub, it might have turned out differently." She sniffled. "When I think of his body at the bottom of the sea, it breaks my heart." She looked out the window. "Do you suppose there's a heaven and he's been up there watching over us all this time?"

"I'd bet on it." Yvonne gave her a hug. "Is there anything else you'd like to know before we leave on Friday?"

"I've found out what I came to learn. It's time I put this in the past and concentrated on my future. Have I told you about my grandbabies?"

Yvonne smiled. "Not really. Tell me about them."

Dinner was a quiet affair at the Douglas home. David filled in the blanks for Cameron and Kendra, including Inspector Gordon's intent to bring charges against Craig for his part in the cover up. And, murder charges against Keith. He thought it likely, Darleen's sentence would be light given that there was no proof it was anything other than an accident. She'd also be charged with obstruction of justice.

Yvonne shook her head. "Poor Margaret, she may end up alone and stuck with managing the mill by herself. I wonder if she'll be able to cope? I hope she'll find someone to help. She was an innocent by-stander in all of this."

"It's so sad. This all could have been prevented if they'd just told the truth to begin with." Kendra reached out a hand to her husband. Cameron had his own demons to deal with. "I wonder ... if only I'd tried harder to find out what happened to my cousin, would it have prevented some of this misery?"

"Probably not, you may have been another casualty if you'd got-ten in their way." David raised his wine glass to Cameron. "Here's to closure."

Everyone raised their glass to his cheer.

Chapter 21
THURSDAY, JUNE 18TH

Yvonne slept soundly in David's arms. He awoke and watched her sleep for several minutes, not wanting to disturb her. He'd need to wake her soon if he wanted everything to go smoothly for his surprise. He slipped out of bed and dressed in the bathroom, then headed downstairs to the lobby to wait. At eight-forty, the hotel double doors opened and in walked Eduardo and Nancy Suarez holding Christy's hand. They looked a bit bedraggled from the eight-hour, night-flight, but brightened when they saw him.

"Welcome to Scotland." David shook hands with Eduardo and hugged Nancy and Christy. He escorted them to check-in, then tipped the attendant who then carried their bags up to their suite.

Christy looked around. "Where's mommy?"

"She'll be getting dressed for breakfast about now. I'll go up and get her. I've arranged for us to have a corner table in the dining room. If you'll give the hostess my name, she'll seat you and I'll bring Yvonne down for the surprise." David's eyes twinkled with delight.

"Hurry up, David. I can't wait to surprise Mommy." Christy jumped up and down, excited.

David headed back to the room and heard Eduardo comment, "He's a vast improvement over that Diablo, Gino."

"Now, Eduardo, watch your tongue." She gave him a look and rolled her eyes toward Christy.

"Let's go wait in the dining room, shall we?" Eduardo took hold of his wife's arm and his granddaughter's hand.

When David returned to his suite, Yvonne had just finished dressing. "You let me sleep late. We'd better hurry or we'll miss our flight. Don't forget we need to pick up Fiona on the way."

"Don't worry, we have plenty of time. I've arranged for us to have breakfast in the dining room."

"Is that where you went? Are you sure? I don't want to miss this flight. I've been away too long already."

"We're going to have one last restful moment before we leave. You've earned it. Trust me, we won't miss our flight." David had difficulty restraining a grin.

Yvonne shrugged her shoulders, secretly anxious to leave now that it was time to fly home. "Okay, let's go have breakfast."

The second she set foot in the dining room a familiar voice rang out.

"There she is! There's Mommy." Christy bounced up and down on her seat, pointing at Yvonne.

"Sh, darling," said Nancy. "So much for the surprise." She laughed, just as excited to see Yvonne as her granddaughter.

Yvonne could hardly believe her eyes. "Wha—What are you doing here?"

Eduardo stood. "A certain someone told us you needed an extra week's vacation. There's a Beltane Festival, I believe it's called." Eduardo looked like the proud father and grandfather that he was. He gave a conspiratorial look at David.

Yvonne followed his look. "You did this? For me?"

"For you and Christy. She missed her mommy." David looked pleased but humble.

Yvonne wrapped her arms around his neck and kissed him. "Thank you!"

Then she hugged Christy, her mother and father.

Settled at the table with her family, Yvonne remembered to ask about Fiona.

"She decided to fly home, today. She needed to be with her family and wanted to put the past behind her for now. She says she'll come back to visit Cameron and Kendra when she can bring her family along.

"In the meantime, Cameron and Kendra expect us to spend some time with them during this week's festivities, so we'll be able to see everything up close and they will act as tour guides to explain everything."

"Who's the travel agent now?" Her eyes shined with happiness.

"What about Debra? She's expecting me back at my desk on Monday."

"All handled. You have vacation time coming, and she was glad to see you take a week now."

"Well, it looks like we're having a vacation." Yvonne looked around the table at her family and her eyes welled with tears.

"What is it? What's wrong?" Nancy was on alert to her daughter's distress.

"Nothing. Nothing at all. I'm just so happy." Yvonne smiled at her mother and father and reached under the table to hold David's hand on one side and Christy's on the other.

ACKNOWLEDGEMENTS

My continued thanks go to High Country Writers and to my small critique group, Fellowship of the Rose, for their encouragement, objective critiques, professional author programs, and crafting exercises to improve my writing.

A special thanks to Leigh Dingwall for her advice and insights about the culture and personalities of the Scots.

Thanks to critical readers, Jenny Bennett, Jessie Cook, Ree Strawser, and Suzanne Thompson who were willing to give me their honest opinions and editing advice regarding this, my second travel mystery.

Thanks to my husband, Walter, for his love and encouragement of my writing and his patience in answering questions about his Scottish ancestry.

Thanks to my mother, Margery, for her help in critiquing Celtic Curse and for her unconditional love and support of all my endeavors.

Thanks to my sister, Tracy, for her incredible help and support in my publishing business and the design of my novels.

Thanks to my son and web-tech guru, Greg, and my daughters, Kelly and Christine, for just being great kids and actually reading my books.

In memory of my loving sister, Patricia, who, passed out of our lives too soon.

HΣRA'S RΣVΣNGΣ

An Yvonne Suarez Travel Mystery

By Wendy Dingwall
ISBN: 978-098290542-5
Trade Paperback, $14.95
5.5 x 8.5, pp 216
April 2011

Hera's Revenge is the first in the Yvonne Suarez travel mysteries. From Metropolitan Fort Lauderdale, Florida where the Pinkerton Travel Agency is located across from the famous Galt Ocean Mile, to exotic destinations around the world, this series is sure to carry readers along on an exciting adventure.

In Hera's Revenge, when an airport employee turns up dead in baggage claim upon their arrival in Athens, the Pinkerton Travel Group gets off to a rocky start.

David Ludlow needs a vacation from his stressful job, and this itinerary to the land of mythology, Greek philosophers and early democrats is just the ticket to a leisurely escape, until grumpy passengers, missing museum art, and deadly accidents plague their journey.

ABOUT THE AUTHOR

WENDY DINGWALL

Former travel agency owner, and former sales and operations manager for a regional publishing house, Dingwall opened her own publishing company, Canterbury House Publishing, in July 2009. She is a past president and active member of the High Country Writers of NW North Carolina since 2002. Her first travel mystery, Hera's Revenge, released in April 2011, was touted as "a series to watch" by Library Journal. Celtic Curse is her second novel in the Yvonne Suarez travel mystery series. Dingwall resides on a fifty acre farm in the mountains of Northwestern North Carolina with her husband, two dogs and a cat.